To Barbara

Thank yo

Random Acts
of Malice

Hope you
enjoyed the read
as much as I did
writing this. Thanks
for your support

Sincerely
George R Holt

Random Acts of Malice

George R. Hopkins

Rev. date: 11/06/2014

To order additional copies of this book, contact:
Xlibris
1-888-795-4274
www.Xlibris.com
Orders@Xlibris.com
686365

CONTENTS

To Charles A. Kuffner Jr.

Without you, Charlie, this book would not be possible. Thank you for your inspiration, your assistance, your input, and your friendship. Your experiences and your willingness to share them freely in the writing of this book were typical of the reputation you have so justly earned as judge, lawyer, father, husband, brother, son, and one of the finest human beings anyone would be privileged to know. Thank you.

"*Random Acts of Malice* is an exciting and compelling twist-filled ride!"
—Julia Hopkinson for Readers' Favorite

"*Random Acts of Malice* reads like a perfect detective novel with multiple characters whose stories all intersect somehow, but not in the ways we initially think . . . . Nearly every page is action packed in a way that contributes to the storytelling and I was hooked from beginning to end."
—Natasha Jackson for Readers' Favorite

"No one is who they seem to be and even the least likely of characters has a hidden secret. There's no end to the surprises in *Random Acts of Malice* by George R. Hopkins and no end to the adventures of each of its characters . . . ."
—Samantha Rivera for Readers' Favorite

"George R. Hopkins' mystery novel, *Random Acts of Malice*, is a well-plotted and entertaining police procedural . . . . *Random Acts of Malice* is fast-paced and exciting, and the New York City and Staten Island venues ramp up the tension and add to the reader's enjoyment. It's highly recommended."
—Jack Magnus for Readers' Favorite

"I found *Random Acts of Malice* by George R. Hopkins to be a very well-written mystery-detective adventure. The author has put together a good, diverse cast of characters, particularly a former Special Operations soldier, now a Jesuit priest, and his long-time homicide detective brother. The plotting was good and moved rapidly along. The dialogue was spot on and a perfect fit for each character. I enjoyed it very much."
—Paul Johnson for Readers' Favorite

AUTHOR'S NOTES

Random Acts of Malice is the fourth adventure in the lives of Detective Thomas Cavanaugh and his brother, Jack Bennis, a Jesuit priest and former covert operative. In this mystery/thriller adventure, the brothers seek to track down the person or persons responsible for death threats to those responsible for the conviction of a prisoner for the manslaughter of a ten-month-old child.

The journey began, however, with *Blood Brothers*, a mystery/thriller about brotherhood and the lengths some people will go to fulfill obligations. *Blood Brothers* is the story of the ties that connect people in many different ways and the pain and consequences that occur when bonds are broken. It is also a story of love, pain, fidelity, greed, revenge, and reconciliation as the hunt to apprehend a mysterious assassin who targets mob bosses follows the detective and the priest through the streets of Brooklyn, New York.

The second book in the series, *Collateral Consequences*, finds Cavanaugh himself the key suspect in the "Maple Syrup Murders." When he abruptly leaves New York to find his brother, Father Bennis, in Havana, Cuba, both brothers become the targets of Cain Holland, a professional assassin. *Collateral Consequences* won a 2009 Premier Book Award for Mystery/Thriller/Suspense.

Letters from the Dead, the third book in the series, won second place in the 2013–2014 Reader Views Literary Contest in the Mystery/Fiction/Suspense/Horror category and was one of six finalists in the 2013 International Readers' Favorite Awards in the Mystery/Fiction/Thriller category. In *Letters from the Dead*, the brothers are in the hunt for a serial killer who calls himself "Lex Talionis" and vows revenge on all who were associated with his daughter's cyberbullying suicide. In the course of their adventures, Cavanaugh and Bennis discover things about themselves they never knew before.

If you have a moment to spare, I would appreciate it if you could give a short review of *Random Acts of Malice*. Your help in spreading the word is gratefully appreciated. All my books are available at Amazon.com and barnesandnoble.com and in paperback, Kindle, Nook, and e-book versions. Each mystery/thriller is self-contained and does not require having read a previous one. Please visit my website, *www.george-hopkins.com,* and feel free to e-mail me any questions or comments you may have at *hopkins109@aol.com.*

I especially need to thank certain people whose help and guidance made this book possible, including Judge Charles A. Kuffner Jr., Judge Emilio Mulero, Mary von Doussa, Dr. Eileen Hopkins, the Noblests, Robert Boyd, and my wife, Diane. Thank you all.

BOOK I

Cindy Waters never expected to meet her death as she rushed home from the 6:30 a.m. Mass at Our Lady Help of Christians to gather her books and papers for her students at intermediate school 7. It was Lent, the season of repentance and prayer in preparation for Easter. During Lent, she forsook her usual run through Bloomingdale Park or Wolfe's Pond to walk to and from church to attend daily Mass. She liked the new priest, who really wasn't that new. The streaks of gray in his hair and the lines etched into his face left one wondering about his age. But he was a handsome tall Jesuit whose devotion and sincerity were infectious. His homilies were short and to the point. They gave her something to think about during the day and to try to practice. After the anguish and mental ordeals she endured for almost two years, he gave her hope and confidence that she had done the right thing.

Turning onto her street, she considered the best ways to bring the priest's message to her eighth-grade students. Then she heard tires screeching and the roar of an engine. She turned in the middle of the street to see a black Ford F-150 XLT barreling toward her. She froze momentarily and then felt the impact of the truck crashing into her and sending her flying thirty feet into the air. Pain soared through her like an electric shock. Her legs, her arms, her back, her head cried out in burning anguish. Lying on the pavement, she felt blood running down her face.

Cindy heard the car stop and a door open. Where was her pocketbook? She tried to move. Strong arms reached down and pulled her further down the deserted street. What was happening? She sobbed uncontrollably. Then a hand reached down and covered her mouth. She looked up and locked eyes with the driver. That was the last thing she saw as the driver thrust an ice pick deep into her left ear.

The driver calmly walked back to his truck, backed up, and drove forward —stopping abruptly before the body, leaving skid marks. Then the driver backed up again and, this time, sped forward, carefully aligning her head with the tires of the car. The car jerked as if hitting a speed bump when it crushed the twenty-eight-year-old teacher beneath its wheels.

* * * *

"Daddy, do you have to go to court today?" six-year-old Ella asked, clinging to Judge Carlo Abbruzza's legs. "It's father-daughter day at school today. Can't you come? Emily and Madelyn's fathers are coming."

Judge Abbruzza looked down at Ella. "I wish I could, Ella-bella, but Daddy's got work to do."

Abbruzza's wife, Marybeth, appeared at the kitchen door flanked by her three sons, John, Michael, and Eugene. "Let Daddy go, Ella. He has to go to work."

"I don't want him to go! Why can't he come to school with me? It's not fair!"

"Like Dad always says, 'Life isn't fair.' And besides, he's got to send a lot of people to jail today," her brother Eugene said.

Ella started crying. Marybeth's eyes snapped at Gene, and he stepped back.

Abbruzza lifted his little daughter into his arms as their cocker spaniel jumped up on him, nearly knocking him over. "Ella," he said, "tell your teacher I will make arrangements for her to take your whole class to the courthouse to show you what we do there."

"You will, Daddy? You will?"

"Definitely, but I really have to go now, or I'll be late for court."

"Be careful, Ella, that he doesn't lock your whole class up in jail!" Gene warned.

"Back off, Gene. We all had that class trip, and it was fun. You'll love it, Ella," Michael said.

"I'm telling you, Ella, they are going to lock you and your teacher up!"

"Don't believe him, Ella," John said. "He's just jealous!"

"Jealous? My ass, jealous!"

"That's it, young man," Marybeth said. "You keep this up, and I'm going to wash your mouth out with soap. I don't care how big you are!"

Carlo Abbruzza stopped at the door. "I'll be back tonight. I want to hear about how all of you did in school today. Make sure your homework is done, and help Mom with the chores. Love you all. Remember, there is nothing we can't accomplish if we work together. Now get ready for school, and no more bickering!"

* * * *

Detective Tom Cavanaugh rubbed his eyes as he drove to the 123 Precinct. It had been another sleepless night. Why did little Stephen Michael cry so much? He seemed to have a seventh sense that as soon as Cavanaugh got him to sleep and put him down in his crib, he waited until Cavanaugh's head hit the pillow before starting to wail again. It wasn't fair. Fran could sleep through a Baghdad bombing or a nuclear attack. How could she sleep when the baby was crying? She insisted he didn't have to pick little Stephen up every time he cried, but Cavanaugh didn't see it that way.

He yawned at a red light on Hylan Boulevard and thought how easy it was for him to watch a junkie or an alcoholic go through withdrawal. He had no sympathy for them. He could sit back and watch them sweat, gasp for air, shake, throw up, and even defecate in their pants. He would fire questions at them in the midst of their seizures and hallucinations. But hearing his little son start to cry was another thing.

The doctors said little Stephen had colic. A lot of babies have colic. They said as many as 25 percent of infants have some kind of colic, and it isn't symptomatic of any disease or illness. Eventually, they told him, Stephen would grow out it. But they didn't hear Stephen crying in the night.

In the precinct parking lot, he slammed the car door and spilled his coffee. "Shit!" he muttered. "I don't care if I do spoil him! I'm going to hold him each night until he goes to sleep!"

"Is there something we should know?" a voice behind him asked.

Cavanaugh turned to see his old friend Patrolman Michael Shanley smiling. "Who are you going to hold each night until he goes to sleep? I hope, for your sake, he's gentle and has a lot of money . . . ."

"Shut up, Shanley," he said. "It's been another rough night. The little guy won't go to sleep unless I hold him . . . ."

Walking up the precinct stairs together, Shanley warned, "You're going to spoil him, Tom, if you keep doing that. Let him cry. He'll get tired and fall asleep."

"He's so tiny, Shanley. We almost lost him when he was born. He cries so much he is covered in mucus. I'm afraid he'll die. That he won't be able to catch his breath. That he'll get sudden infant death syndrome . . . ." That . . . that . . . Oh shit! I'm just too old to be a father!"

Shanley poured a cup of coffee from the lobby machine and gave it to Cavanaugh. "What does Fran say?" he asked.

"She says what you said and what the doctors said — I'm going to spoil him if I keep picking him up and rocking him to sleep."

"Did you ever think they might be right?"

Cavanaugh scratched his chin. He had forgotten to shave. "Shit!" he mumbled again. He looked up at the desk sergeant and asked, "Anything going last night?"

"Usual couple of drunks, one domestic abuse call, a couple of teenagers in a car crash on Arthur Kill, and a hit-and-run we just got a call about a few minutes ago . . . ."

Cavanaugh stared up at the desk sergeant. His name was Paul Mason. In the short time Cavanaugh had been in the precinct, he never recalled Sergeant Mason not having something to eat in his hand. This morning, he was munching on a bacon-wrapped meat loaf hero with pepper, cheese, and onion. It was hard to see how he could fit the sandwich into his mouth, let alone eat it at eight in the morning. Mason looked to weigh well over three hundred pounds, and Cavanaugh wondered how many uniforms he had grown out of.

"Are you married, Mason?" Cavanaugh asked.

Mason took another bite out of his sandwich and a piece of onion slithered down his blue uniform. "Yeah. What's it to you?"

"I was just wondering. Do you have any kids?"

"Yeah. I got six kids."

Cavanaugh's mind conjured up a picture. It wasn't a pretty picture. "Any of them have colic?"

"They all did," Mason replied.

Cavanaugh looked up at him. Six kids with colic. He shook his head. "How did you deal with that?"

"Simple, Cavanaugh. I went to work."

* * * *

As Fr. Jack Bennis removed his violet chasuble in the sacristy after Mass, his mind was jumping like an Ivorine ball on a roulette table, planning his activities for the day. He had been up since 4:00 a.m., reading his daily prayers and doing his daily exercises. His plans for the day included visiting the kindergarten and first-grade classes in Our Lady Help of Christians, visiting some of the sick in the parish and in the hospital, and then dropping by the Von Doussa Nursing Home to see his aunt. If there was time, he hoped to be able to visit his sister-in-law and give her a hand with his only nephew.

He had been temporarily assigned to Our Lady Help of Christians by the archdiocese. "Temporarily" had turned into three months and counting. During his time here, he had grown to be accepted by most people, except his pastor, Angelo Rosito, who could have been a poster child for Grumpy from the Seven Dwarfs. If Father Bennis would greet him at breakfast with a cordial "Good morning, Monsignor," the diminutive Rosito's response might be, "What's good about it?" or "What makes you think you're an expert?"

As he folded the long white linen alb, Frank Laurie, the sacristan, a man in his sixties with a congenital frown, hunched shoulders, a dancing eye, and the movements of a mouse on steroids, barged in and said, "There's a call for you, Father Bennis."

Bennis checked his watch. "Who is it, Mr. Laurie?"

Laurie grabbed the vestments from the priest's hands and started to put them away. He spoke rapidly in tune with his movements. "There's been an accident. A woman was run down. They want a priest."

"Where is she?"

"Barnard Avenue, off Craig."

Bennis looked around. "Where do they keep the oils for anointing the sick?"

"No need," Laurie said. "She's dead."

Bennis stared at Laurie's sloping back as the sacristan meticulously and rapidly folded and put away the vestments. "Where does the pastor keep the oils?" he repeated.

"Third cabinet on the left, but I'm telling you, you won't need them. She's dead as a doornail."

"Thank you, Mr. Laurie," Bennis said, removing a small black leather case from the cabinet. "I appreciate your concern."

As he rushed out the door, Bennis recalled his mother saying how life and death are what happen to us when we are busy making other plans.

* * * *

As Cavanaugh walked up the wooden stairs to the detectives' office at the 123, his right knee cracked on every other step. But he wasn't listening to his knees. He was listening to the memory of his three-month-old son crying through the night. He hoped Stephen Michael had stopped crying by now.

Opening the door, he suddenly became aware of a strange sound — silence. The only noise echoed from a tone-deaf drunk down the hall in a holding cell warbling, "Have some madeira, m' dear. It's really much nicer than beer . . . ."

He looked around the office. There was no one there. *Where the hell were they?* he thought. There was no Sebastian reading the sports pages of the newspaper and no Newhouser munching on his usual tuna sub.

The *New York Post*'s daily racing schedule covered Sebastian's desk. A crumpled wrapping and a half-eaten tuna Subway hero that looked more like eviscerated cat bore mute witness to Newhouser's sudden departure. But where the hell was everyone?

The fluorescent lights above flickered. On the far wall a five-by-four map of Staten Island hung with the confines of the Tottenville Precinct delineated by red magic marker. Various yellowed unread notices and procedures dotted the walls.

His first thought was they were abducted by aliens. But then he figured even aliens would have a hard time finding Tottenville.

Had he forgotten a meeting? He checked his desk calendar. No meeting, no message, just pictures of his wife and newborn baby.

The door behind him abruptly opened, and a head appeared. "Hold the fort, Cavanaugh," Lieutenant Parker said.

"Where is everyone?" Cavanaugh asked.

"There's been a hit-and-run a few blocks away. CIU is investigating. Sebastian and Newhouser are there. I'm headed over there now myself."

"Wait a second and I'll go with you," Cavanaugh said.

"No. Somebody's got to stay here. As you know we're short on staff, thanks to Mayor Tightwad's cutbacks. Pretty soon, he'll want us supplying our own toilet paper. If there wasn't a fatality, I wouldn't go myself."

"What happened?"

"Looks like a typical hit-and-run. Probably some teenager in his father's car rushing home from a party. But there are some irregularities, and we have to check it out."

"Maybe I can help, sir," Cavanaugh offered.

The lieutenant opened the door a little wider and stared at him. "No offense, Cavanaugh, but wherever you go you seem to generate more problems than we need. Stay here and stay out of trouble. That's an order."

Cavanaugh shrugged. "Yes, sir," he muttered and sat down, tossing a book he had taken from his car on his desk. When the lieutenant closed the door, Cavanaugh waited an appropriate fifteen seconds and then called his wife.

"Fran," he began, "how's the baby?"

"Thanks, Tom," she began. "I guess the honeymoon is over. No, 'How are you feeling, Fran?' Now it's, 'How's the baby?' What am I? Chopped liver?"

"Aw, Fran, you know I love you, and I don't like chopped liver!" He hesitated a moment and then added, "But seriously, how is Stephen? Has he stopped crying? Do you think we need to take him to the doctor?"

"He's fine. In fact, he's sleeping now."

"How come he didn't sleep last night? I had to walk him all night."

"Relax, Tom. He'll be fine. I plan to take him over to see my mother in Brooklyn later today. She hasn't seen him yet."

"Why doesn't she make the trip over the bridge to see us? You shouldn't be taking Stephen out. It looks like it might rain later. Ask her to come here if she wants to see him . . . ."

"I'm a little worried about her, to be honest, Tom. My sister, Susan, called and said Mom has been acting a little strange lately."

"Even more reason why you shouldn't go to see her. She might have some virus or something."

"Will you relax, Tom? We'll be fine. I just want her to see Stephen and let her hold her grandson."

"No, Fran. Don't let her hold him! She'll probably give him some disease. Keep him away from her!"

"I'm going, Tom. My sister will be there to help. If you need me, give me a call. We'll be fine. Don't worry."

"Sometimes I think you're more inflexible than congress. Remember what Emerson said? 'A foolish stubbornness is the hobgoblin of petty minds.'"

"Emerson never said that, Thomas Cavanaugh. And you shouldn't be the one talking about being stubborn!"

"Okay! I give up. I hope you're right. But just be careful. We had a hit-and-run around here this morning, and there might be some drunk driving around."

"I'll be careful. Don't worry." She added, "You better take care of yourself!"

"No sweat, Fran. I'm stuck here in the office, while everyone else is out in the street doing real police work. What could possibly happen in the Tottenville Precinct? Nobody even knows where we are!"

* * * *

Father Bennis arrived at the hit-and-run scene as the girl's body was about to be removed. The sacristan, Frank Laurie, was right. There was no question about it. The young woman was dead. Her face was unrecognizable and looked more like a smashed Halloween pumpkin with auburn hair. Sebastian and Newhouser allowed him to give a last blessing to the corpse before it was removed.

It was impossible to identify any facial features on the girl, but yet there was something familiar with the girl's clothing. Her running shoe and her matching pink and white running jacket told Bennis she was athletic, in good shape, and had an eye for dressing well. He thought for a moment he might have seen her at church that morning.

"What happened?" he asked Sebastian.

"She got run over."

"Who did this?"

"We don't know," Newhouser answered. "We are going to try to track down the car from tire marks, glass fragments, and possible paint chippings. We'll know more after the lab gets through."

"What's her name?" the priest asked.

A few reporters pushed against the police barriers asking questions of the police and the bystanders. "You know we can't tell you that, Father," Sebastian said, elbowing Newhouser aside.

"Come on, guys. My brother works with you. You can trust me. I thought I might be able to help her family with grief counseling."

"You can do all the grief counseling you want after we finish here and notify her family," Sebastian stated. "Now please, Father, step back and let us do our job."

Bennis moved back and stood behind the police barriers among the bystanders.

"What's her name, Father?" a reporter suddenly asked him.

"I don't know," Bennis answered.

A little woman who looked to be in her eighties, with white hair in a bun, a wrinkled white apron with red roses, and a wooden rolling pin covered with flour, interjected, "Her name is Cindy Waters. She's a teacher. She lives down the block."

The reporter pushed in front of Bennis. "What kind of person was she?"

"She was quiet," the woman said. "She seemed dedicated. A good neighbor. Not like that old drunk across the street."

The reporter wrote quickly in his notepad. "What can you tell us about her? Was she married?"

The woman looked up at the man and said in a shaky voice, "Like I said, she was a good neighbor. Never caused any trouble. A good citizen too. She served on the community council and on a jury some time ago and never breathed a word of what was going on. I think she had a dog. A little thing. It think it was one of those frankfurter dogs."

"A dachshund?"

"I don't know much about dogs, but she walked it every day and cleaned up after it too. Not like some of the slobs in the neighborhood. There's a man down the street, Mr. Gaffney, who's got this ugly bulldog that looks like Winston Churchill. His dog barks at anyone who walks past his house and poops all over my lawn. Someday I'm going to scrape the poop up and put it on his doorstep. To be honest, I don't really like dogs. I have two cats, a calico and a tabby . . . ."

Father Bennis moved away and looked around. He had the feeling someone was watching him. Behind three women down the block, he saw a tall man with a gray crew cut in an olive-drab army field jacket staring at him. They locked eyes for a moment, and then the man turned and disappeared behind some overgrown privet hedges. There was something about the way the man looked at Bennis that bothered him. He couldn't put his finger on it, but he thought he recognized him from a long time ago, and he didn't have a good feeling about it.

* * * *

Frank Stevenson leaned against the window frame in his dark-russet plaid boxer shorts, peering out at the scene in front of his house. Police swarmed all over Barnard Avenue. The Accident Investigation Squad meticulously measured skid marks, collected debris, and took pictures. He saw a priest or minister hover over the body, and then an ambulance removed it. All that remained were a puddle of blood, the chalked outline of the victim's body, a Coach leather handbag, broken glass, and one pink and white Nike running shoe.

He gulped the last of the drink in his hand, turned, and looked into the mirror. His hair was grayer and thinner, the lines and broken capillaries in his face more numerous, his stomach larger, and his ass flatter. He knew what the police were doing and would have to do. How many times had he been called to the scene of a crash to investigate a fatal accident? They used to call it the Accident Investigation Squad. Now they called it the Collision Investigation Squad. Back when he was a member, they only went to fatal crashes or those where the victim might die.

There was no question in Stevenson's mind. The woman was dead. He thought her name was Janet or Jean and that she might have been a teacher because she was always around in the summer, but he didn't know for sure. He kept to himself more and more these days.

He had seen the vehicle back up and deliberately run over her head. He wanted to get his Smith and Wesson revolver and fire at it, but he didn't have time to get it from the locked box in his closet. He wanted to get the license plate, but he couldn't find his glasses. In the early morning light, he couldn't even be sure of the make of the vehicle or if it was red, maroon, or even blue or black.

The block had been taped off. He looked at his watch. The commissioner himself had presented it to him at his retirement from the New York City Police Department. He imagined the squad calculating the friction coefficient of the skid marks.

Soon they would be questioning neighbors. A few of the nosy ones were already gawking and gossiping behind the police barriers.

He had liked being a cop. He devoted his life to it—to the detriment of two marriages and frequent but unsuccessful AA meetings.

Turning back to the window, he saw a police officer squatting down to bag shards of glass. He had trouble these days tying his shoes. It was definitely a job for younger men and women.

Images of past accidents raced through his mind. The eight-year-old girl's body thrown by the 1978 two-tone Delta 88 Royal Oldsmobile and impaled on a picket fence, the husband and his pregnant wife killed in New Brighton by a 1977 black Chevrolet Monte Carlo and their premature baby son who died the following day, the car full of foolish teenagers who looked more like spaghetti and meatballs after the driver's father's 1962 silver MGB convertible sports car crashed into the side of a delicatessen while drag racing along Hylan Boulevard. Funny, he thought, how he remembered the names of the cars but not those of the victims.

He limped into the kitchen and poured himself another glass of Four Roses whiskey. *Shit*. He smiled. *It must be five somewhere in the world!*

Somewhere in the distance, he heard a muffled sound. He paused, glass in hand. It was the door. Someone was knocking. He hoped it wasn't one of those nosy reporters. They were modern-day ghouls, vampires who sucked information only to turn it into blood for an insatiable, voyeuristic public.

"What do you want?" he shouted as he opened the door.

But it wasn't a reporter. It was a woman—a black policewoman. Her name tag read "Morris." She was petite with the brown unblemished skin of an African nun. Her black hair was tucked under her cap. Her brown eyes sparkled innocence. *She's pretty*, he thought, *but too young for this job. It will kill her.*

"Good morning, sir," she began. "We are investigating the accident that occurred outside your residence."

"It was no accident, sister," he responded. "It was frecking murder."

"Did you see the accident?"

"I already told you. It was no accident. It was premeditated murder."

"What makes you think it was murder, sir?" She started writing quickly in her notepad.

"He ran over her head, for Christ's sake!"

Stevenson held up his gold Omega watch. "See this, sister? I got it when I retired from the force. I used to do what you do. I know a few things about fatal car crashes. I used to do your job with a tape measure and a clipboard. Now you use those goddamn computers."

He held his watch up to her face. "See this watch! The commissioner himself gave it to me when I retired."

Officer Morris admired the watch. "It's cool. What kind is it?" she asked.

He checked his watch and answered, "It's ten seven."

She smiled and repeated in a louder voice, "No, sir, I meant what *kind of watch* did they give you?"

Stevenson frowned. Officer Morris stopped writing. Why would they believe a seventy-eight-year-old disgruntled ex-cop who can't see, can't hear, is drinking at ten o'clock in the morning, and is talking at his front door in his underwear? If he were her, he'd write him off as a demented, crotchety old drunk. He lifted the glass of whiskey to his lips. *Shit*, he thought, *growing old sucks.*

* * * *

In the second story of an office building in Tompkinsville above an abandoned theatre on the other side of Staten Island, a large man sat at an even-larger mahogany desk chewing on a yellow pencil. The plan was scheduled to start today. He didn't like it. It wasn't his plan. There were too many variables. He would have done it a different way. He had never seen the man he hired. His only dealings with him were by phone. They told him he was a professional, and he didn't have to worry. He was to be the intermediary, the bag man.

Suddenly, his disposable phone vibrated, and he dropped the pencil. He checked the number. It was him. *Why is he calling me now? Has something gone wrong?*

"Hello," he answered cautiously.

"Number 1 accomplished."

"Anyone see you?" he whispered.

"No. Made it look like an accident."

"Good."

"When do you want the next one?"

"Anytime you're ready."

"Next one is going to get more complicated."

"So?"

"So I need more bread."

The large man held the phone in his hand and stared at it. Beads of sweat began to form on his forehead.

"What do you mean? We agreed . . . ."

"You gave me names. You didn't tell me who they were."

"You never asked . . . ."

"Don't give me that horseshit! I did some research."

"But we agreed to a price . . . ."

"The cost just doubled and will double with each new assignment."

There was a knock on his door.

"Mr. Arbuckle, would you like your room cleaned now?"

"Not now!" he shouted at the door. "I'm busy right now!"

"You better not be talking to me!" the voice on the other end of the phone cautioned.

"No, no! Somebody was just at the door."

"I hope so. Yours could be the next name on the list," he warned.

The large man's hands were shaking as he opened a metal box in his side desk drawer and withdrew a number of hundred-dollar bills. He had more than enough money. They had given him the cash. But he tried to play the game he always played. He learned it as a child. Lowball the bid; play competitors against each other. Why give it all up? He was a middleman. Shouldn't he get a cut of the action?

He was given a name, and he went with it. He didn't want to get into a competitive war with killers. He lowballed the price for the "hits." *Someone like this needs the money,* he reasoned. *They'll be happy to get it.*

But things weren't working out that way. He counted out five $100 bills.

"How much do you want now?"

"What we agreed to. I'm a professional. Five will do for now. Like I told you before, I function on a COD level. The next one, however, will be double . . . ."

"How do I know you took care of the first one?"

"Check the news tonight for a hit-and-run in Tottenville. When you see it, leave the bread in an unmarked envelope in a copy of James Joyce's *Finnegan's Wake* in the St. George Library tomorrow."

"What if someone takes it?"

"Leave that to me." The voice chuckled. "Besides, nobody reads *Finnegan's Wake*," he added.

And then the phone went dead. The large man counted out five $100 bills again and placed them in a plain white envelope. Then he sealed the envelope and picked up the pencil again. Why did he agree to this? But he knew why, and he shuddered at the thought and started chewing on the pencil again.

* * * *

It turned into another hectic day for Judge Carlo Abbruzza. He spent most of the morning in jury selection for the rape-murder trial of a father accused of raping and then killing his eight-year-old daughter. He usually liked jury selection because he got a chance to know a little about the people in the community, and he appreciated their willingness to give their time and common sense to the justice system. But the facts in this case were so horrific they made his stomach turn.

In addition to his trial duties, however, he had been assigned the calendar judge's responsibilities. This meant his duty was to arraign the defendant, appoint counsel, supervise voluntary disclosure of evidence supplied by the DA, read the grand jury minutes, and set dates for preliminary hearings among other things. The atmosphere in the courthouse was tense after a newspaper article accused some of the judges of dozing off, doing crossword puzzles, and texting during trials. His offhanded comment to someone that he was not one of those judges was true, but when it was published in the *Staten Island Advance*, it alienated some of the other judges.

There had been more than a few attempts to remove him by vindictive, jealous, power-broking judges who accused him of "undercutting" their authority. In one case, he firmly believed he was set up when one of the judges aborted a preliminary hearing, expunged the transcript, and then sent the case to him. After studying the papers, Judge Abbruzza dismissed the indictment on the valid grounds that the DA violated the statute providing for a speedy trial for the defendant. What he did not realize at the time, however, was that the defendant, Carlos Diego Santiago, was a member of the Almighty Latin Kings and was involved in the shooting of a three-year-old girl in the Mariner's Harbor Houses. CBS, NBC, ABC, the *New York Post*, the *Daily News*, and the *New York Times* had a field day with his decision. Even Rush Limbaugh, Sean Hannity, and Fox News carried the story and fanned the fires of public outcries for his removal from the bench. Although the Court of Appeals ultimately ruled the DA violated the speedy trial rule and affirmed Abbruzza's dismissal of the case, it emphasized to him that he was a lone sheep in a den of hungry wolves.

He removed his robe and glasses and rubbed his eyes. They were burning. He was hungry and tired. All he wanted to do was go home, hug his wife and children, take off his shoes, and relax. Maybe a glass of Johnny Walker Black on the rocks would help too.

He plopped down into his former Fordham Law School chair. He spun around and gazed out his window at the Staten Island Ferry coming into dock. The sky looked calm, but it was growing darker, and he noted white caps in the harbor. Behind the ferry, the Statue of Liberty stood proudly in the distance.

Abbruzza looked back at his desk and eyed a pile of opened mail his secretary had left. Being a criminal judge was the job he had always wanted, but it came with a price. He scanned the oak-paneled room. He had made the office his own. There was an old bookcase he had brought from home filled with law books. Paintings and sketches of the New York Harbor, the Kill Van Kull, and various Staten Island scenes and pictures of his family encircled the walls and usually kept him focused. He stared at his grandfather's old American flag of the forty-eight states mounted in the corner. He smiled. His grandfather would be proud to see him now. He, like his grandfather and his father and all the members of his family, had worked hard and honestly to get ahead. It was a struggle, but here he was.

"Good evening, Judge Abbruzza," a voice called from his door. "Anything I can do for you before I head on home?" It was Court Officer Wesley Walker. Walker was a tall muscular African American who seemed to be always hanging around his office. Abbruzza had the feeling he might be spying on him and reporting what he was doing to the other judges.

"No, thanks, Officer Walker. Have a nice night."

When Walker left, Judge Abbruzza looked at the pile of letters on his desk and yawned as he flipped through them. *They could wait until tomorrow,* he thought. But then his eyes spotted a plain white legal-sized handwritten envelope from the Bedford Hills Correctional Facility.

He opened the letter and began to read.

> Horonor I writing with great concern regarding your livelihood & safety, I'am an inmate in Bedford Hills Correctional Facility and incarcerated here with me is a inmate by the name of Tamika Washington, DOB. September 15, 1977. She has been making vicious Threats Sir, about killing you and everyone associated to her case….

Who was this person sending the letter? He checked the envelope. It had come from a prisoner named Latitia Jones at the Bedford Hills Correctional Facility for Women, and the USPS time stamp indicated it was sent two weeks before. Bedford Hills was New York State's only women's maximum security prison. It housed over seven hundred prisoners serving sentences of five years to life for crimes from fraud to murder.

He continued to read.

> She's discussed with me confidentially that her only thoughts of how shes going to go about shooting you in the head. She speaks to me about how she was convicted of a crime that you supposedly had not enough evidence to convict her on. Over the 4 months I've known Tamika she's spoken Of her hatred for you several times and first I ignored then thinking that they were idol threats But its become very apparent to me that shes not only making threats, she definitely intends to carry them out….
>
> Tamika is a very Cool & Calculating dangerous individual and I'am, asking you not to take her lightly.

Fear gripped Judge Abbruzza, and a chill swept through his body. He looked at the picture on his desk of his family smiling at a baseball game in the old Yankee Stadium. He had never had a death threat before. His hands were cold and clammy. He became aware of his heart pounding in his chest. What would he tell his wife and children? How would he tell them? He didn't even have an alarm system. He checked the envelope again, hoping it was a sick joke. But it wasn't. It had come from the prison and was postmarked two weeks before. Why had it taken the postal service so long to get to his desk?

He picked up his phone and hesitated. Whom should he call? Whom could he trust? The petty politics around the courthouse were malignant, and he had learned early, to his dismay, he couldn't completely rely on the loyalty of most of the court officers. He dialed an old friend he had known a long time ago in elementary school. Judge Abbruzza hadn't seen him in years, but he read about him and knew he was now on Staten Island. He remembered him as a tenacious, stubborn, hardworking, street-smart guy who had always been a little rough around the edges but someone who was reliable and whom he could trust. He dialed the 123 Precinct and asked for Detective Thomas Cavanaugh.

* * * *

Tamika Washington stood in front of Latitia Jones's cell in the Psychiatric Section of Bedford Hills Correctional Facility. She rubbed her stomach as she spoke, "I got to get out of this shit hole!" she moaned. "I got something wrong with me, and the racist pigs don't want to fix it. They trying to kill me. It's all his fault—that fuckin' Abbruzza! He had no right to send me here. There wasn't enough evidence. He sent me here, and he gonna pay!"

Latitia stared from her cell across the way, her fingers tapping the memories of a distant blues song on the bars of her cell. "Why are you always talking trash, Tammy? Just do your time and get out of here. I've been in other places, and this ain't that bad, considering—"

"You think I'm bullshitting, Sunflower? Well, I'm not. I know people. I got a sister in South Carolina who works in the governor's office. She seen the records and know where Abbruzza live. He went down to Myrtle Beach last summer with his family. I know where he stayed."

"Come on, Tammy, how do you expect me to believe that? You ain't got no sister in South Carolina."

Tamika rubbed her stomach and grimaced. "I sure as shit do!" she stated. "Her name be Shereece Campbell, and she live in a tight little house in South Congaree, just outside of Columbia."

Latitia stood and walked to the sink of her cell running her hands through her curly black hair. "You lying again, Tammy. What's your sister gonna get mixed up in your shit when she's got a good job and house? You bullshitting me again, Tammy!"

"I ain't, Sunflower. She told me where the judge live. She don't know nothing about how I'm gonna kill him . . . ."

Latitia squatted down and asked, "And how in God's big world is you gonna do that sitting on your big black ass here in Bedford?"

"Don't sass me, almost to the bone . . . ." hesitated a moment and then spoke in a low voice, "Before they set me up on this bogus manslaughter charge, I used to carry drugs."

"What you saying, girl?"

"I ain't never told you, but the reason I got a longer sentence was 'cause I wouldn't give them my passport. If I did, they'd see I traveled to Africa and London a lot. I carried China white for a dealer I knew in South Carolina. His name be Abbas Waqas. He gonna take care of me. I be his best carrier."

"Tammy, you talking smack! You in here 'cause you killed a ten-month-old baby!"

"That be a misunderstandin'. The kid wasn't mine, and he kept cryin'. I may have slapped him around a bit to quiet him down, but I didn't kill him."

"They said his arm was broken, and the fingers on his hand were burnt almost to the bone . . . ."

"I had to roll out to deliver some serious product fast. It be business. He kept movin' around and cryin', so I maybe smacked him across the head a couple of times. I tied him to the radiator so he couldn't crawl away. I didn't mean to kill him. He wasn't mines anyway."

Latitia stood and sighed. "So how is this Abbu Wanda going to help you?"

"I told you his name be Abbas Waqas. It mean 'lion warrior' or some shit like that." She continued to rub her stomach. Then she stopped suddenly and looked up at Latitia. "I already paid him money to kill the judge. Judge Abbruzza be a dead man walking."

* * * *

Cavanaugh read from a tattered, frayed edition of Dr. Spock's *Baby and Child Care* book his brother, Fr. Jack Bennis, left in his car. His initial reaction when he saw the book was to curse and throw it out the window. He didn't want to read it. He remembered the accusations in the late 1960s that Spock's doctrine of "permissiveness" was the 'cause of anti-Vietnam War demonstrations, high crime rates, and a lack of respect for authority. Somehow he equated Dr. Spock with Jane Fonda and Benedict Arnold.

As he sat alone in the office leafing through the pages, Cavanaugh began to see Spock's advice supported some of his own beliefs. He read how Spock and he agreed it was all right to pick your baby up and hold it. It wasn't a pachysandra that just needed light and watering or a puppy that could be trained to jump through hoops and give you his paw. It was a living, breathing individual human being that needed love and affection. Babies needed to be kissed and hugged. Maybe Dr. Spock wasn't all that bad after all. And maybe that fat desk sergeant Mason was an idiot.

The section on colicky babies, however, was a different story. The suggestion that if mothers simply avoided certain foods, such as broccoli, cabbage, onions, dairy milk, citrus fruits, tomatoes, and spices, during the first four months of breast-feeding it would solve the colicky problem didn't help. Fran wasn't breast-feeding.

Cavanaugh smiled when he read the editor's comment that Dr. Spock's initial support for circumcision of males had been revised and that he came to believe "circumcision of males is traumatic, painful, and of questionable value." Thinking about it, Cavanaugh got a pain in his throat. Little Stephen Michael had been circumcised in the hospital. It wasn't something Cavanaugh had ever really thought about seriously. But now he thought maybe they should have left his little penis alone. He started thinking about his own penis when the phone rang.

"Detective Cavanaugh, Tottenville Precinct. How can I help you?"

"Is this Tom Cavanaugh from Carroll Street in Brooklyn?"

"Yeah. Who is this?"

"This is Judge Abbruzza."

"Carlo Abbruzza from Sterling Place?"

"Same one."

"I heard you became a judge. Congratulations!"

"Thanks. Do you have a few minutes?"

"Does a monkey climb trees? Is a frog's butt watertight? This place is dead. Everyone is out working a hit-and-run we had this morning. What can I do for you, Judge Abbruzza?"

"It's Carlo to you, Tom, and I need your help."

"What's up?"

"I received a death threat this afternoon in the mail. It came from an inmate in Bedford Hills Correctional Facility."

Cavanaugh put aside Dr. Spock and took out his little notebook. "That's up in Westchester, isn't it? It's a jail for women."

"Right. One of the inmates wrote me a letter about another inmate threatening to kill me."

"Judge Abbruzza, I mean, Carlo, that's a matter for the police in your precinct. Notify them immediately. They have to check this out."

"I'd like you to check this out, Tom."

"Why?"

"It's complicated, but I don't know who to trust here. I trust you."

"Hey, Carlo, I'd like to help, but I'm assigned here. I can't just go invading other guys' territory. There are procedures to follow . . . ."

Just then, Cavanaugh heard voices in the hall, and the door swung open. Sebastian, Newhouser, three patrolmen, and one patrolwoman blew into the room with the force of a small hurricane. They nodded at Cavanaugh, pulled up chairs, and gathered around Sebastian's desk as Newhouser picked up his open tuna sub and quietly resumed eating it.

"I'm going to make a few calls, Tom. I'll be in my office until you get here. Don't worry. I'll handle the bureaucracy."

"But Carlo . . . "

"No buts, Tom. See you in an hour. Please. This is my life we're talking about."

Cavanaugh heard the click as the petite black patrol officer left. He looked over at the others. They were busy giving reports. "Hey, guys," he called, "I have to go over to criminal court now. Can you handle things?"

Newhouser kept munching on his stale tuna sub, while the other police officers kept writing. Only Sebastian looked up. "Don't let the door kick you in the ass on the way out, Dickhead," he said.

Cavanaugh tucked Dr. Spock under his arm and headed out of the office. He wondered if Sebastian's mother ever read *Baby and Child Care* or Emily Post's book on etiquette. Maybe, he thought, walking past Desk Sergeant Mason, Sebastian's crudeness was merely an outward sign of insecurity or maybe deep-seated hostility or maybe a warped sense of adolescent humor. Or could it be the direct result of a traumatic, painful circumcision at birth? That was something he didn't want to think about. "Here's something to read, Mason," he said, tossing the Dr. Spock book up to him and knocking what looked like a chocolate frosted donut out of his hand.

* * * *

When Lloyd Arbuckle left his office to go for lunch, three yellow number 2 pencils lay chewed on his desk as if a beaver had feasted on them. He closed the door and locked it. He didn't like the plan. His stomach growled in agreement. It didn't make sense to him. It was too elaborate. Too much could go wrong. But he would follow the plan. He knew those who didn't didn't survive long.

He wondered who the ultimate big boss was as he lumbered down the stairs. He had never seen him or even heard his voice. For all he knew, he could be a she. Arbuckle did know that he was well-compensated for distributing information and implementing Mr. X's decisions.

He wondered how large Mr. X's realm of authority reached. He wondered how many people Mr. X employed. He wondered why he had ever gotten himself into this position, but he knew. He did it for the money.

He received the relayed messages on his computer with detailed instructions. He followed the instructions and contacted a given source who suggested hiring an ex-army ranger to implement the actions required. Mr. or Ms. X was always a few layers away.

When Arbuckle reached his car in the parking lot, he was breathing heavily. He definitely had to lose weight. Sitting in his black 2005 Cadillac, he scanned the list of names he withdrew from his pocket:

Cindy Waters – jury foreman
Claudia Buenaventura – witness
Kevin Reilly – arresting officer
Uriah Applebaum – the defense attorney
Rob Ananis – prosecuting attorney
Leonard Ketch – the district attorney
Carlo Abbruzza – criminal judge

The instructions indicated to deal with the names with "extreme prejudice."

He wiped his brow. This was the part of his job he hated.

* * * *

Driving over the Verrazano Bridge, Fran Cavanaugh checked little Stephen Michael sleeping in the infant seat in the rear of her metallic-blue Chevrolet Cruze. She hadn't seen her mother in some time. Had she deliberately avoided her, or was it just that so much had taken place in the last two years? Her father was assassinated, her godfather murdered at her father's wake, her husband killed, her older brother arrested. Fran had been driven off the road by a killer. She traveled illegally to Havana, Cuba. She killed someone. She was almost raped. She bought a home. She survived an ectopic pregnancy, and then there was Cavanaugh!

Turning onto Shore Road in Brooklyn, she glanced at a cruise ship sailing toward the Statue of Liberty. She adjusted her rear view mirror to check on Stephen Michael again. He looked like a sleeping angel.

Fran passed Fontbonne Hall Academy, where she had gone to school. She never really liked high school. Was it because it was an all-girls' school, a parochial school, or the fact her mother insisted she go there? Why was she always at odds with her mother?

The closer she came to the home of her youth, the more anxious she became. Her palms were sweating. Her eyes watered at the site of the playground swings where her father used to push her "to the sky." The days he spent with her and her brothers and sister were, however, preciously few. There were always meetings, secret meetings, rumors of his involvement in everything from money laundering and prostitution to drugs and murder. Strange she never believed the rumors. Instead, she transferred her anger and hostility to her mother who tried to hold the family fort together while savoring the lifestyle of the mob wife of an infamous celebrity.

When her sister, Susan, called to tell her she was worried about their mother, Fran hesitated. She didn't want to go home. What was it Thomas Wolfe had said about not being able to go home again? She wanted to avoid her mother and the memories of the past. But as she talked to Susan on the phone, she glanced at her baby dribbling in her arms, and a shower of guilt flowed over her like a bucket of Gatorade on the Super Bowl's winning coach—only she didn't feel like a winner.

How could she deprive her mother of seeing her grandson? Whatever had been done was done in the past. Fran looked forward to the future. Maybe there would be time for them to talk, to reconcile, to share, to accept each other.

Dreams of a future reconciliation with her mother, however, shattered like a broken glass when she saw Elizabeth Muscatelli.

Fran cradled Stephen in her arms when Susan opened the large oak-paneled door. Straight ahead in the rocking chair her mother told her came over from Sicily with her great-grandmother sat Elizabeth Muscatelli.

Fran hugged her child tighter. Her mother sat staring off into an uninhabited void. She looked thinner. Her eyes were sunken, and her once-chubby cheeks now seemed to sink into her skull. The smooth olive skin Fran remembered was now pale and sickly, and broken capillaries crisscrossed lines and wrinkles she had never seen before, giving Fran the impression of a desiccated map of a remote mountain area in the Appalachias.

Susan spoke first, "Mom had a stroke."

"When?"

"A couple of months ago."

"Why didn't you tell me?"

Susan moved behind her mother and held her shoulders. "You are not the easiest person to track down."

Fran moved closer to her mother and knelt down. "Mom," she said, "it's me, Francesca. How are you doing? I wanted to show you your grandson . . . ."

"She can't hear you, Fran. She's been unresponsive since the stroke."

"Mommy!" Fran persisted touching Elizabeth's knee. "It's me, Francesca, your daughter. I've brought your grandson here to see you . . . ."

Elizabeth Muscatelli stared into an invisible, uncharted world to all around her. Fran stood up and spoke to Susan. "Why didn't you tell me on the phone? Mom needs help."

Susan furrowed her brow, and her voice pierced Fran like a dagger of ice. "Why didn't I call you? Why didn't you care enough to even call Mother to tell her you moved, you got married, and you had a child? You haven't changed a bit! You are still the selfish bitch you always were!"

* * * *

Driving to Judge Carlo Abbruzza's chambers, Cavanaugh listened to 1010 News on his car radio. In the financial news, William George Fuller, the wealthy manager of hotels, building offices, recreational resorts, and real estate enterprises around the world was rumored to be acquiring a small biopharmaceutical company called Emisphere Technologies, which focused on unique and improved delivery of therapeutic molecules or nutritional supplements. News of the mere whispers of his planned buyout had jumped the price from 11¢ a share to $7.56. Cavanaugh smiled at the reports. He had no stocks and would rather risk his $25 on a spin of the roulette wheel than invest it in a stock-market-sure thing.

In local news, he heard thousands of rabbis from around the world were gathering at the World Lubavitch Center in Brooklyn for their annual convention. He pictured the conglomeration of black-suited men in big black hats, beards, and glasses speaking a language he didn't understand. He thanked his lucky stars that Judge Abbruzza didn't live in Brooklyn.

There was a brief piece about a Staten Island teacher killed by a hit-and-run driver and a number to call if anyone had any information.

When he reached the judge's chambers, Judge Abbruzza stood and welcomed him in with open arms. The Carlo Abbruzza Cavanaugh remembered from grammar school and high school had changed substantially. His once-curly-brown hair had been replaced by a shiny bald head. His former black horn-rimmed glasses were gone too, probably replaced by contact lens or the latest in LASIK surgery. A full gray moustache stood out on his tan face. His broad shoulders and firm handshake told Cavanaugh that his old friend worked out regularly and was no longer the skinny little smart kid whom the bullies at school used to pull his underwear up from behind to give him wedgies. Judge Abbruzza had changed physically, but Cavanaugh recognized the look of fright in his eyes. He had seen it too often.

"It's been a long time, Judge Abbruzza."

"Please, Tom. It's still Carlo to you."

Cavanaugh extricated himself from the judge's grasp and plopped down in the first chair he saw. "So what can I do for you?"

"I need your help, Tom. I received a letter from an inmate in Bedford Hills Prison that someone is planning to kill me."

"It's pretty tough to kill somebody when you are in prison. If I had a dime for everyone who wanted to kill me, I'd be a rich man right now."

"I'd like you to check it out for me."

"Why me?"

"I don't know who to trust."

"Come on, Carlo. You're a friggin' judge. There are cops all over the place. It's not that I won't like to help, but I've stepped on so many feet around here I feel I could be a shoemaker or a podiatrist. These guys around here get pretty territorial. Your precinct is right down the block. I'm stuck on the other end of this island. It took me over forty-five minutes to get here. They can walk here in less than five minutes . . . ."

Judge Abbruzza moved slowly behind his desk and stared out the window for a moment. He turned, sat, bit the knuckle on his thumb, looked at the picture of his family on the desk, and then said, "I'm scared, Tom. I don't know who to trust around here. Just between the two of us, there are people around here who would love to see me removed from the bench."

"You got to be kidding me. You have a great reputation as a fair and honest judge. There aren't many like you around here these days."

"Maybe that's the point. I don't know. This letter may be bogus. I don't know, but I don't want find out the hard way, and I don't want to give my enemies any ammunition to use against me. Can you help me? Or more important, will you help me?"

Cavanaugh stared out the window behind Abbruzza. The dichotomy of oil refineries gazing at Lady Liberty's backside did nothing to diminish the beauty of the view. He looked at Abbruzza slumped in his chair, and he recalled the words from Emma Lazarus's sonnet engraved on the pedestal of the Mother of Exiles, "Give me your tired, your poor, your huddled masses yearning to breathe free . . . ." Abbruzza wasn't poor, but he was troubled. Cavanaugh shook his head and looked down at his scuffed black shoes. Why was he such a sucker for helping people? He had held a pedophile over the rooftop of his precinct in Brooklyn to get a confession. He had planted drugs on people he knew were selling drugs but always eluded arrest. Why couldn't he just turn away?

"How do you plan to get me assigned to you?" he asked.

"I know some people. I'll make a few calls."

"Is it that easy?"

"Pretty much."

"I'm going to need help."

"What do you need?"

"I had a good partner when I worked homicide in Brooklyn. His name is Morty Goldberg. He's a pretty orthodox Jew."

"So?"

"So can you get him assigned to help me?"

Judge Abbruzza fumbled with some papers on his desk. "Why would you need him?"

"He's the best. You want me to check this out, Carlo, we have to do it right. Morty's a detail man. I trust him with my life and my family's lives."

Abbruzza started nibbling the knuckle on his thumb again.

"You're a big man now, Carlo, a regular class A VIP. If you can get me, you should be able to get Morty, at least temporarily, assigned to this case. It shouldn't take us long."

Judge Abbruzza rubbed his chin. "I'll do what I can."

"Good," Cavanaugh said, rising and heading toward the door. "Now if you don't have one already, call an alarm company right away and have them install the top-of-the-line model. I'll pull a few strings myself and see if I can get a couple of guys to watch your house. It may cost you a few bucks . . . ."

Abbruzza nodded. "Make the arrangements. I'll handle the fees."

"If we need more backup, I'll let you know."

Judge Abbruzza stood. "Thanks, Tom."

Cavanaugh waved. "I haven't done anything yet. My gut tells me this is a lot of prison BS. We'll check it out, though. If it sounds legit, we'll have to go public. Until then, against my advice, I'll keep it quiet. Just make sure you get your alarm system checked out ASAP and keep your head down . . . ."

* * * *

Father Bennis didn't wait for the police to release the dead woman's name and address. He waited for the reporter to move on to another spectator and then spoke to the white-haired woman with the wrinkled white apron and wooden rolling pin. The name she gave the reporter was Mable Sweeney.

"You knew Ms. Waters?" he asked.

She turned and looked up at him. "You're a priest, ain't you?"

"I guess the Roman collar gave it away." He smiled. "Yes, I am a priest. I'm new here."

"You from that Lady of Something or other they are working on?"

"Our Lady Help of Christians. Yes. That's where I'm from."

"I'm not Catholic. Never have been, never will be. I've been married twice and divorced twice. I never went for all that hocus-pocus stuff and all your pedophile priests. They make me sick."

"I'm not a fan of them myself." He held out his hand. "My name is Jack Bennis."

She looked at his hand as if it were a rattlesnake. "My hands are full of flour," she said, backing away.

"Did you know if Ms. Waters was Catholic?"

"Why do you want to know?"

"She may have been in church this morning. I think I recognize her clothes."

"You another of those pervert priests?"

"No. I just wanted to help if I could. Did she live alone?"

"She lived up the block. Little white house with the red shutters. Think it was her mother's."

Bennis looked up the street. He saw the house behind a tall oak tree.

"She was a good kid. Taught school and took care of her mother. Other than walk her dog, I don't think she had much of a life. Her mother has a touch of Alzheimer's. I don't know what she's going to do now . . . ."

"Who took care of her mother when Ms. Waters was in school?"

"You sure are the nosy one, ain't you? She hired one of those foreign health aides when she wasn't home. To tell you the truth, I don't like the looks of those people. You have to be careful. Some of them will steal your teeth if you don't watch out."

"How long has she been hiring help for her mother?"

"Almost a year. Cindy had jury duty, and her mother started wandering the neighborhood when she wasn't there. The first one came on a Tuesday. I marked it on my calendar. She was a big black woman. Didn't fit into the neighborhood. Looked like she was from the West Indies. That's where most of them are from, you know. I'm too old for jury duty. I'd probably throw the book at them all. Our country's going to hell in a handbag, if you ask me. I don't get out much anymore myself. I keep to myself and my cats and mind my own business."

Bennis nodded. The pieces were fitting together. He was more convinced now that he did know Cindy Waters. He thought they had spoken together. "Thank you, Mrs. Sweeney. You have been a great help. I'll see if I can help in any way."

Mrs. Sweeney's right eyebrow rose. "I'll believe that when I see it!" she said, clutching her rolling pin like a weapon in her arms.

* * * *

William George Fuller sat in his meticulous penthouse on Eighth Avenue looking out at a Circle Line ship cruising tourists up the Hudson River. He owned multiple businesses—from hotels, apartment houses, and real estate to casinos, race tracks, and bordellos. They said he had the Midas touch, but it was never enough for him. He enjoyed the rush of skiing, surfing, and mountain climbing. They were challenges. Man against nature.

He had a black belt in karate and participated in Worldwide Ultimate Fighting Contests testing his boxing, wrestling, Brazilian Jiu-Ji, judo, and Krav Maga skills with limited success against Ken Shamrock, Mark Coleman, and Chuck "The Iceman" Liddell. He even squared off once with Vladimir Putin. It was man against man.

William George Fuller was a gambler. He knew it was a "sucker bet" to bet against a baseball player fouling off the next pitch in a 3 and 2 count. He knew it was against the odds to bet any two people in a group of forty or more would not have the same birthday. He knew there was a better chance of losing than winning in parlay betting or using the martingale betting system. They were all sucker bets. But if the feeling moved him, he would make the bet. He might wager on the coin toss at the Super Bowl or how long it took to sing the Canadian National Anthem at a hockey game or how long a baseball game would last. He did it for the fun, the thrill, the excitement, and, more often than not, he won.

Perhaps it was the element of the challenge and the exhilaration that led him into crime. There, there was always the challenge. Man against himself. The more complicated the crime, the more interest he had in it. He loved power and the ability to control money, people, life, and death.

He learned early the value of people. He treasured information—and used it. He used a multilayered approach, the more elaborate, the better.

Mustafos Montega was a relatively small drug dealer in the Northeastern States but an integral part of Fuller's network. Trust, confidence, and experience bred fidelity and loyalty. He needed to defend Montega, who had been apprehended in an NYC drug sting and was scheduled to appear before Judge Abbruzza. Abbruzza's reputation was well-known. He could not be reached. His decisions and sentences were solid. Depending on the crime and the circumstances, his sentences could be severe.

Fuller never met Montega, but he knew the most intimate details about his life. He knew Montega's mother had been killed in Tijuana during a bloody war with the Gulf Cartel. He knew Montega had fathered five children from five different women. He knew the tattoos Montega wore and where he had gotten them. He knew Montega had been born with three testicles. He even knew Montega's father, whom Montega never knew, was a migrant worker in Salinas, California. Fuller also knew Montega was the first cousin of Luis "El Caudillo" Sanchez, the new leader of the Sinaloa Cartel.

Montega, on the other hand, knew nothing about Fuller. He knew he was part of a big organization, but he had no idea how big or how widespread it was.

Fuller's sources informed him that one of the prisoners in Bedford Hills voiced threats against the judge. And so he drew up his elaborate plan to use this fact to remove the judge—dead or alive.

He could have easily contracted out to kill the judge, but that would be like stealing candy from an infant, and there were other reasons. He preferred playing chess against a formidable opponent. With human beings there was always the element of surprise, chance, and challenge. He relished the challenge that to him was better than sex. The adrenaline surges were longer, the need for quick thinking critical, and the accomplishment more satisfying. He was in complete control. One way or another, he vowed Judge Carlo Abbruzza would not preside over Mustafos Montega's trial.

* * * *

Marybeth Abbruzza picked up the phone on the second ring. "Carlo, where have you been? We've been waiting for you for dinner."

"We had a few problems here today. Do you remember Tommy Cavanaugh? I called him today."

"Carlo, that's a name from the distant past. How is he doing?"

"He's a detective in the Tottenville Precinct."

There were a few seconds of silence before Marybeth spoke again, "Why did you call him?"

This time Abbruzza was silent.

"Why did you call him, Carlo? You haven't seen or spoken to him in years!"

"I trust him, Marybeth."

"What's going on?"

"Maybe nothing. I asked him to check it out."

"Check what out?"

"It's probably nothing, but I want to be sure. He's already checking it out."

"Checking what out?"

"I got a letter today from the Bedford Hills Prison from a prisoner up there. It's probably nothing. Tom thinks it's just a lot of prison bull."

"What did the letter say?"

He hesitated and blurted out, "An inmate up there claims another inmate wants to kill me."

"What? You're kidding me! How is someone in jail going to kill you?"

"I don't know. I just wanted to tell you. I don't think there's anything to worry about. I just wanted you to know."

"Why? So now I can be worried?"

"No. I'm sorry I told you. I thought you should know—just in case."

"Sometimes I think I've married a ninny. Are you still the same guy they used to play tricks on in school? You're a judge, for god's sake! Nobody in their right mind is going to kill a judge—let alone someone in jail!"

"Thanks, Marybeth. I think you're right. It's probably just one prisoner trying to get another one in trouble. I feel better already. Did I ever tell you how happy I am being married to the voice of reason?"

"Oh shut up, you silly fool and get home soon so we can have a few laughs over this with a glass of your favorite Barolo wine!"

* * * *

That night, Jack Bennis returned to Fran and Cavanaugh's new home. They thought his staying with them during the renovation of the old church they bought was neat. Gradually, what used to be an abandoned church began to morph into a modern home.

The choir loft became a den. The large nave area was now a spacious living room and dining room. The sacristy was a modern kitchen. The master bedroom and nursery were on one side of the old church and three guest rooms on the other side. Each room had a large colorful stained-glass window.

Bennis went to his room. He felt like a man without a country. Intruding on his brother and his family was not Bennis's idea. The rectory he was temporarily assigned to, however, was also undergoing renovations as the result of a recent fire. Staying with his brother was the best of a difficult situation.

He sat at a folding table he purchased at Costco and opened his prayer book. The hit-and-run victim troubled him. He was pretty sure he recognized the dead girl from her clothes, Mrs. Sweeney's comments, and a brief visit to her house. He also thought he recognized the man in the army jacket at the scene, and that troubled him even more.

"Jack?" a voice called from the door.

He turned to see Francesca. Her smudged mascara and slightly disheveled hair alarmed him.

"Fran, how are you?"

She walked in wringing a dish towel in her hands. "We're having meat loaf for dinner. Would you like to join us?"

"No. That's okay. You two need a little alone time together. I'll pick something up later."

She hesitated and looked down. "Do you have a few minutes, Jack?"

"Does a fish swim? Of course, I do for you, Fran. What's up?"

"It's my mom."

"How is she? I haven't seen her in some time."

His heart pounded against his shirt. He remembered Elizabeth Muscatelli. One of the last times he saw her, she told him she loved him. "How is she?" he repeated. "That's just it, Jack. She's had a stroke, and she doesn't seem to recognize anyone."

"I'm sorry to hear that. Your mother was a wonderful person."

"I know she thought the best about you, Jack. When you were teaching at Bishop Bergin High School and saying Mass at St. Agnes . . . ."

Bennis swallowed hard. He remembered Elizabeth's late husband, Ralph Muscatelli, mob boss, drug czar, murderer, all-around bad guy. Muscatelli dealt in prostitution and planned to introduce drugs to elementary school children before he was shot and killed exiting a Brooklyn restaurant a few years before. He remembered it clearly. It was a tough time for Elizabeth Muscatelli. Her husband was a career criminal whom the police were unable to stop. Muscatelli's killer did in one shot what the police and federal authorities could not do.

Elizabeth Muscatelli, unfortunately, was collateral damage. Bennis regretted the difficulties her husband's death caused her more than the fact he was the one who assassinated Muscatelli.

Fran's voice came to him like a voice on a descending plane. "Do you think you could visit her, Jack? You might be able to help her."

Bennis scratched his head. "I don't know about that. If she had a stroke, time, prayer, and physical therapy might be her best medicine."

"Please, Jack, come with me to visit her. I'm sure just seeing you will make her feel better. I feel guilty I haven't seen her in so long. I never even told her Tom and I were married or that we had a son."

It was happening again. Why was he always a sucker for helping people? Why hadn't he learned to say no? How many times had this scenario played out? He should have learned by now. But he hadn't. How many times had he overheard his mother saying to herself, "No good deed goes unpunished"?

"Please, Jack . . . ."

He heard his voice as if from a distant FM station say, "I'll try to see her tomorrow."

* * * *

Cavanaugh came straight back to the Tottenville Precinct. There were calls and preparations he needed to make.

"What's this shit you're trying to pull now, Cavanaugh?"

"Sebastian, you have such a loving way of saying things." Cavanaugh smiled. "But I'm not a mind reader. What are you babbling about now?"

"Where are you going?" Newhouser asked. "The captain said you have been reassigned."

Cavanaugh looked at him. There was something different about him, but he couldn't place it. "I've got another assignment."

"Sure he does," Sebastian snapped. "We're not good enough for him. A hit-and-run homicide is beneath him."

"It's not like that . . . ."

"Then what are you doing?"

"I can't tell you right now. But this shouldn't take too long."

"Newhouser, it's like I told you. He doesn't trust us. Mr. Big Shot uses his pull to get the special assignments. I used to think he was a pain in the neck, but now I see I thought too highly of him. He is just a royal pain in the ass."

It was futile to argue with Sebastian. Cavanaugh resisted the urge to have a battle of wits with an unarmed person. As his mother had often told him, "A sharp tongue does not mean a person has a keen mind." He went to his desk and printed out the police arrest records or rap sheets for both Latitia Jones and Tamika Washington.

Then he called his former partner, Morty Goldberg. The detective answering his call told him Goldberg was not in. He had been assigned as part of a special security detail to the World Lubavitch Center in Crown Heights, Brooklyn, for their annual convention. When he hung up, Cavanaugh realized he would probably be driving to Bedford Hills alone. He made two more calls to people who owed him and who needed some extra money to arrange for coverage of the judge's house. Then it was time to go. He looked around the office.

Sebastian was still muttering to himself. "Some people want the front of the bus, some the back of the church, but Mr. Big Shot Cavanaugh always needs to be the center of attention."

Newhouser said nothing. His droopy eyes and furrowed brow reminded him of a tired bloodhound.

Cavanaugh resisted the temptation to tell Sebastian to make somebody happy by minding his own business. Instead he headed for the door. "See you guys in a couple of days. Stay safe."

Sebastian called after him, "I'll give you a call if your proctologist calls and tells us he found your head."

Cavanaugh smiled. He realized why Newhouser looked different. He was hungry. He wasn't eating his usual tuna sub sandwich and looked like his belly was going to sue his teeth for nonsupport.

* * * *

Lloyd Arbuckle sat in his office chewing another number 2 yellow pencil. A steady rain pelted the window behind him. Water leaked from a crack in the ceiling. Should he ask Mr. X for more money? As the targets increased in stature and importance, the killer's demands might continue to escalate.

Soon there would be no profit for him. He should have offered him a larger sum for all the murders. By trying to squeeze out a bigger profit, he had left himself vulnerable.

He hesitated at his computer. Then he started typing. "EMPLOYEE WANTS MORE MONEY FOR ASSIGNMENT." No. This wouldn't do. Maintain deniability.

He started again. "SUBJECT REQUESTS ADDITIONAL REMUNERATION." He hit the backspace and deleted the message.

"CLIENT DEMANDS ADDITIONAL PAYMENT FOR SERVICES RENDERED." Again, he chewed on his pencil and then deleted the message.

He wrote, "CLIENT REQUIRES ADDITIONAL WORKMAN'S COMPENSATION," and hit send.

Within seconds, the response came: "APPROVED."

He sat back and smiled. That was easier than he thought. He wiped his forehead. Was it hot in the office, or was he sweating? Another beep on his computer and a note that a deposit of $20,000 had been wired into his bank account from A&R Used Tire and Junk Yard in the ironbound section of Newark for services rendered. Lloyd Arbuckle never heard of the company before. He figured it must have been a shell company of Mr. X. He didn't care. Like Ben Franklin said, "A penny saved is a penny earned." He had his money, and now he could relax. Or at least he thought he could.

* * * *

Fr. Jack Bennis decided to stay for dinner. The death of Cindy Waters, the hit-and-run victim, distressed him.

His visit to the dead girl's home was disturbing. Mrs. Sweeney was right about the small dog. Only it wasn't a dachshund. It was a cockapoo, a cross between a cocker spaniel and a poodle. It was an affectionate little thing that had cuddled up to Bennis immediately and seemed overjoyed to see him. Both he and the health aide wondered what would happen to the little thing now that its owner was gone?

The more he thought about it, the more upset he became that he knew Cindy Waters. His visit to her home, his brief conversation with her mother's aide, and a look around the house at family pictures hanging on the walls convinced him. He had seen Cindy Waters at church. He recalled hearing her confession and the fears she had voiced. His advice was to follow her conscience and to do what she thought was right. The more he thought about it, however, the more a feeling of guilt began to overwhelm him. Had his advice led to her death?

It was the brief image of the man in the army fatigue jacket, which convinced him the hit-and-run accident was not an accident.

He recognized Earle Nelson. They had served together when Bennis led a special forces clandestine unit known as Crowned Eagle. Their objective was to assassinate people. Some were political leaders, some news reporters, some activists, some arms dealers, some crime bosses, some seemingly ordinary people. They were never told the reason for the missions or even the countries they were sent to. They were a death squad of covert assassins sanctioned by their government to kill people. As the missions grew, Bennis came to see they were a team of official killers, murderers. At first, he had followed the tenet "theirs was not to reason why." But as the killings mounted, they weighed on his conscience, and he had doubts.

Nelson was older now, but so was he. The half-moon scar on Nelson's face was a marker Bennis couldn't forget. He had given it to him. On a mission to assassinate a German banker, Bennis's team infiltrated the victim's home at night and administered a close shot to his head to make it appear a suicide. But Nelson compromised the mission by garroting the banker's wife and then attempting to decapitate the victim's sleeping five-year-old daughter with a machete. When Bennis heard what Nelson had done and saw what he was about to do, he wrestled with him and, in the process, slashed Nelson's face. In their struggle, the young girl awoke and started screaming. The team narrowly escaped as police responded to neighbors' calls.

Although their mission was technically a success because they achieved their objective, Bennis reprimanded Nelson for compromising the team. Nelson responded by cursing at Bennis and threatening to kill him. The two men had to be restrained by the other members of the team. Upon their return to the States, Bennis filed an official report with his immediate supervisor, Howard Stevens, delineating how Nelson's actions jeopardized their mission and their lives.

Stevens read the report and then proceeded to rip it up in front of Bennis. "Men like Nelson are hard to find," Stevens said. "He has a stellar record of successes in Turkey, Egypt, Morocco, Bangladesh, Bulgaria, and many other places. We can't let this one isolated incident disrupt our missions."

"You didn't see his eyes when he strangled the wife and when he attempted to kill the sleeping child. He is a menace."

"He may, I admit, have a penchant for violence and may actually enjoy killing, but he is a valuable asset." Stevens placed his fingertips againstone another, moving them back and forth like they were doing pushups. "He was responsible for turning Maximiliano Gomez's lover and convincing her to poison El Moreno, who was the leader of the Maoist Movement in the Dominican Republic."

"Yes, but look what he did to the girlfriend. He killed, eviscerated her, and dismembered her body. He is a dangerous, pathological killer. You have to remove him from this team."

Stevens stood and placed the torn letter Bennis had given him in an ashtray and lit the paper. "The bottom line is, Lieutenant Bennis," he said as the flames devoured the note, "the bottom line is-he stays. Live with him. You're the officer in charge. Make it work."

Their next mission was to assassinate a former Nicaraguan leader living in Colombia. Their mission, however, was compromised, and the military was waiting for them. The screams of a little village girl alerted the military, and in the ensuing battle two of Bennis's men were wounded. He led his men through dense jungles to a waiting evacuation helicopter. Stevens was on the helicopter and ordered Bennis to climb aboard and leave his wounded men behind. When Bennis refused and went back to get the men, Stevens ordered the men onboard to shoot Bennis. Only Earle Nelson responded. They watched Bennis get hit and tumble to the edge of the jungle.

As the helicopter rose into the air, Stevens left Bennis and the other two soldiers believing they were dead or soon would be. Although his wounds were serious, Bennis managed to escape into the jungle, and he and one of the wounded soldiers survived.

Bennis had not seen Earle Nelson in over thirty years. He had tried to put that life behind him. Becoming a priest was part of his effort to make amends. But when he saw Nelson at the scene of the hit-and-run, he knew from what Cindy Waters told him in confession, Nelson had something to do with her death.

Bennis sat down at the dinner table, which had been built from the existing pews of the former church. He wrestled with the dilemma of what he knew from Cindy's confession and the presence at the scene of someone he considered a pathological killer. It could have been a coincidence, but he didn't believe in coincidences. It was like Charlie Chan said, "Coincidence like ancient egg-leave unpleasant odor."

"I was at the scene of the hit-and-run this morning, Thomas," he began. "I didn't see you there . . . ."

Cavanaugh dug into his mashed potatoes like a pile driver and shoved an enormous amount into his mouth.

"Tom!" Fran called. "That's too much! You'll choke."

Cavanaugh mumbled, "It's good. And I'm hungry. It's been a busy day."

"What's the story on the hit-and-run? Did they catch the guy?"

Cavanaugh glared at his brother. "You're not getting involved again, are you?"

"I was just wondering if you had any news. The girl was from my parish."

Cavanaugh dug into his potatoes again. "That's nice, Jack, but to tell you the truth, I have no idea. Sebastian and Newhouser are handling it."

"Why aren't you investigating it too?"

"And why are you suddenly so interested in my investigations? Like I said, I don't know. I've been assigned to another case."

Fran reached for the carrots and the salad bowl. She asked, "What's the new case about?"

"I can't tell you right now. It's probably a wild-goose chase, but I've got to travel upstate tomorrow to check something out."

"Be careful."

"No worries. I'm just going up to interview a prisoner about something."

"If you get a chance, Thomas, could you do me a favor?"

"Do you want me to visit a prisoner for you, Jack?"

Bennis smiled and poured himself another glass of water. "No. I was wondering if you could check out a name for me."

"Oh no, Jack! You're starting this again, aren't you? What now? Would you please leave the investigating to the authorities?"

"No. It's not like that. It's just that I thought I saw an old member of my army team at the scene of the hit-and-run today, and I'd like to get in touch with him again."

"If this has anything to do with the hit-and-run, talk to Sebastian and Newhouser. It's not my case!"

"They didn't seem too friendly this morning and basically told me to butt out."

"Guess what, Big Bro? I'm telling you the same thing!"

"Can't you use your computer and just check out the name for me? I'd like to talk to him again. It's been a long time . . . ." Bennis cut a piece of the meat loaf and said, "Fran, this is delicious. You've done a great job with this meal. I love your recipe. Our mother used to make meat loaf, but she never put peppers in it, and it never had the moist flavor this has."

"Okay," Cavanaugh said, "I'll look up this guy for you!"

"Thanks, Thomas."

"But promise me one thing. You are not going to get involved in this hit-and-run investigation."

Bennis shoved a mouthful of potatoes into his mouth, nodded, and mumbled something that could have been, "You can count I won't" or "You can count I will."

* * * *

BOOK II

If anything can go wrong, it probably will.
—*Murphy's Law*

Cavanaugh left in a steady rain early the next morning for the Bedford Hills Correctional Facility. It had been another rough night. Little Stephen spent most of the night crying. Fran's eyes were red and swollen, and she spent most of the night tossing and turning. Her visit to her mother had not gone well. Tom's brother, Father Bennis, seemed distracted. He kept asking questions about the hit-and-run, but Cavanaugh didn't know anything about it.

He figured it would take two hours to get to Bedford Hills in good weather. The rain, however, made things worse. Along the way he needed to stop to get new windshield wiper blades. Murphy's Law was happening again-if things could go wrong, they probably would.

He hated going into a gas station to ask to have his windshield wiper blades replaced. There was something "unmanly" about it. It was like admitting he couldn't change the blades himself-which he couldn't. So he drove around for a while looking for an open Jiffy Lube so he could have the oil changed and casually ask to have the wipers changed too.

There was an overturned truck on the Goethals Bridge, construction on the New Jersey Turnpike, and a two-lane closure on the George Washington Bridge. Minor flooding on the Saw Mill River Parkway made it an almost perfect horrible day. Patience may be a very lovely virtue that could lead to knowledge, but he was almost out of it when he exited the Saw Mill River Parkway.

At first, he thought he was lost. The road did not resemble the stereotypical prison environment he envisioned. Tree-lined streets with modest single-family homes and large multimillion-dollar estates reminded him more of a cozy suburban village from a Hollywood movie. Driving along Harris Avenue, he drove into an area of dense trees and vegetation.

The rain had stopped, and the sun struggled to shine through the trees. He rolled his window down and listened to the sound of birds. Suddenly, a deer jumped across the road in front of him, and he slammed on the brakes. He cursed the fact that he was lost and that he had agreed to come up here.

But then, ahead on his right, he saw nestled in the woods the Bedford Hills Correctional Facility. It looked more like a college campus than a prison. There were no menacing huge concrete walls like Folsom Prison. Instead, he saw a complex of many red brick and stone buildings surrounded by razor-wire fences. Aside from a guard tower, it could have been a college campus. *Maybe*, he thought, *in view of recent events, guard towers might not be a bad idea on college and school campuses.*

He went through the usual entering procedures at the prison and was escorted to the warden's office by a burly redheaded prison guard named Quinn. To say Warden Hartman was a small man would be an understatement. Cavanaugh estimated Warden Hartman, without his platform shoes, could have played a hobbit in *The Lord of the Rings* or a munchkin in *The Wizard of Oz*. He had a comb-over and one of those Ben Bernanke beards that looked more like he hadn't shaved in a few days than a real beard. He wore a three-piece sharkskin charcoal suit that looked like a blue-light Kmart special. Hartman extended his right hand to greet Cavanaugh and kept his left tucked between his jacket and vest like a miniature Napoleon.

"Good morning, Detective," Warden Hartman said, motioning for him to sit down. "We have been expecting you. Judge Abbruzza called to alert us to your visit. What can we do for you?"

"I would like to interview one of your inmates, possibly two, and some of your staff about a letter the judge received."

Warden Hartman hopped up on the edge of his desk and looked down at Cavanaugh. "Yes. I am aware of a letter inmate Jones sent. We are aware of it, and the psychiatrist and counselor have spoken to her. We believe it is just prison talk, and there is nothing to worry about. There is a lot of rumor and gossip in a women's house of detention."

"I'm not worried about it at all, but the judge is, and I traveled up here to check it out."

"I really don't think there is any need for you to . . . ."

"I went over the RAP sheets for both Latitia Jones and Tamika Washington before I got here. What else can you tell me about them?"

Warden Hartman slammed his little fist down on the desk. "I run this facility, Detective! There are 783 women locked up in here. There are murderers, drug traffickers, thieves, you name it!" The warden's legs were banging against the desk like a five-year-old in a tantrum.

"It's a freakin' full moon in case you didn't notice, and female hormones are raging. We had a food fight this morning, four lovers' quarrels, an allegation about an 'over-friendly' prison guard, a drug overdose, and an attempted suicide. I'm sick of it all! We actually found one of the inmates having sex with a service dog!"

"So, Warden, what can you tell me about Latitia Jones and Tamika Washington?"

"Are you deaf or just plain stupid? There are 783 prisoners here. I don't know the particular story on each and every one of them. And, I might add, I honestly don't give a shit!"

"Tell me, Warden, what is it? Ignorance or apathy?"

"I don't know, and I don't care. My job is to keep this place running with the limited budget the state allows. It's not an easy job!"

"I see you're a busy man, Warden," Cavanaugh said. "Can you direct me to who could give me more background on these women? Apparently, a threat has allegedly been made against a judge's life. This is serious stuff!"

"Try the prison psychiatrist. Officer Quinn will escort you to her office."

"Thank you, Warden. I'd also like to check the prison records of Latitia Jones and Tamika Washington. And I'll need a copy of their phone logs, the psychiatrist's and counselor's reports, and a copy of the commissary and financial accounts for each of them."

"I will have my secretary prepare the phone logs for you, but you will need a subpoena for the commissary accounts . . . ."

"What? You've got to be kidding me!"

"Detective Cavanaugh," Warden Hartman said, hopping off the desk and staring straight into Cavanaugh's eyes, "it's the law. Prisoners, unfortunately, have certain rights too."

Cavanaugh stood and looked down at the warden. His day wasn't getting any easier. He took a deep breath and asked, "May I use your phone to make arrangements?"

"Most certainly." The little man smiled. "It is always a pleasure to assist another officer of the law. After all, we are here to serve, aren't we?"

* * * *

The rain had stopped when Father Bennis and Fran drove together to visit Fran's mother in Brooklyn. In the backseat, little Stephen slept. Bennis turned the radio very low to check the traffic on the Verrazano-Narrows Bridge. An ad from some doctor with a strange accent announced a new radiological procedure promising to cure everything from prostate cancer to breast cancer.

Fran commented, "The next claim will be that it cures blindness, baldness, acne, and the flu . . . ."

Bennis looked over at her. Her knuckles were white as she clutched the wheel. "Improvements are being made every day. Who knows what the future will bring?"

A man's voice from the car radio promised, "You give us twenty-two minutes, we'll give you the world" and followed with an item about an unnamed woman who was gunned down outside the Arlington Apartments in the Mariner's Harbor section of Staten Island. "Police," the voice announced, "are questioning members of the Gorilla Bloods gang, but no arrests have been made. Anyone with information is urged to call . . . ."

"What's happening to the world?" Fran asked. "Why is there so much violence? It's not safe anymore to walk the streets, to go to school, even to go to the mall. Staten Island used to be a peaceful place."

Bennis nodded as they headed over the Verrazano-Narrows Bridge. "Some people blame it on this bridge, but it's more than that. People seem to have lost their direction and their sense of morality," he said. "It's become a 'me generation,' Fran, where immediate gratification is the norm. The dollar has replaced God in many people's lives, and the rich have gotten richer, and the poor poorer. It's not a good situation."

"I worry about Stephen. He's only an infant now, but what kind of a world are we bringing him into? I saw a news story last night about a missing doctor. It was followed by a story about a missing dog. The missing doctor got thirty seconds airtime while the missing dog's story was over two and a half minutes! It's crazy! We have lost perspective . . . ."

"You and Tom give little Stephen all the love and care you can. Give him rules to follow. Teach him right from wrong. Be consistent. Teach him by example. Give him something to believe in. The foundation for the future is the family."

They drove in silence into Bay Ridge. At a traffic light on Fourth Avenue, Fran turned to the priest. "I don't know if I can do it, Jack. It's too much. He cries so much. We must be doing something wrong. Tom and I are exhausted. And now my mother . . . ."

Bennis leaned over and patted her hand. "You're going through a tough time. No doubt about it. But you are not alone." He looked ahead as the light changed. "We don't always get what we want in this life, but sometimes I believe there's a reason for it, and it can make us stronger."

"I don't know, Jack, maybe I'm just not fit to be a mother."

"Sometimes I think there should be a manual for the right way to be a parent, but there isn't one. It's like Thomas going into an auto supply store to purchase shock absorbers. Then when he gets home and opens the package, there are no instructions. Parenting is more important than shock absorbers, but it's been going on for a long time. Others have done it, and you can do it. If more people bring love, rules, consistency, and communication into their relationships, I feel the world will be a better place."

"Do you really think so?"

"The way I look at it, the Roman Empire collapsed from within. If our society is to survive, it needs to build from within. That means strong families are fundamentally essential."

"I don't know. There is so much in today's world fighting against us-movies, TV, video games, divorce, abortion, drugs . . . ."

"Have faith, Fran. Rome wasn't built in a day, and as someone once said, 'It ain't over till it's over.'"

As Fran pulled over to the curb and parked, she said, "I'm scared, Jack."

"With you and Thomas as his parents, I think little Stephen may give you a run for your money, but with the grace of God, love, rules, consistency, and communication, he'll be fine."

"No," Fran said, looking at her old house. "I'm scared of seeing my mother again."

Bennis looked at the once-familiar house and admitted, "You're not alone, Fran. I am too."

* * * *

Lloyd Arbuckle looked at a puddle by the window of his office and sighed. He would have to call the superintendent to have the leaky roof fixed. He picked up a pencil and started drafting a stern letter to the owner of the building threatening to sue for failure to maintain the building. He liked to write letter drafts in longhand first. He scribbled in the left-hand column, "Toxic mold, health hazard, asbestosis, immune-compromised, dangerous, detrimental, harmful, injurious, negligent, criminal . . . ."

He paused and started chewing his pencil again as he stared at the word "criminal."

How did he get involved in this business? He knew the answer. He needed the money. He had no clients. He had large gambling debts. His divorce cost him his house and his family. And for what? A blonde Atlantic City hooker who left him in a cocaine heartbeat when his money ran out for a horny younger Wall Street broker?

It was a skinny, acne-faced drug dealer named Emanuel who started it all. If Arbuckle defended him and got him off, Emanuel promised to hook him up with people who would take care of him. Arbuckle bit at the bait. He needed the money.

Arbuckle did his homework. He scoured the law books and the evidence. He interviewed prospective witnesses. He carefully chose jurors who might be sympathetic to his client. He prepared for the trial as if preparing for a brief before the Supreme Court.

But there was one credible, steadfast eyewitness to the alleged drug deals who was key to the government's case. Arbuckle told his client no matter how hard he prepared for the trial because of this witness it would be difficult to guarantee an acquittal. He advised taking the plea bargain the D.A. offered. Emanuel sat back and smiled. "Let's go for broke, Counselor!

I ain't afraid. I've got God on my side!" Arbuckle remembered how Emanuel pounded his chest and his gold tooth glistened when he laughed. "Tell the D.A. to shove his deal up where the sun don't shine!" Recalling his laugh sent shivers down his spine. Somehow, Lloyd Arbuckle knew then that he had already gone too far.

The next day the government's star witness disappeared, and Arbuckle realized he had made a deal with the devil.

Suddenly, the door to his office flew open. Lloyd Arbuckle stared at a large man in an army field jacket.

"The office is closed," Arbuckle stated. "Make an appointment with my secretary in the morning."

"You ain't got no secretary, fat boy. And I'm not here to make an appointment. I want my pay!"

"What? What are you talking about? You have the wrong office. Leave now before I call the police!"

"Spare me the drama, shithead. You owe me $1,000 for knocking off the Buenaventura chick last night."

Arbuckle jumped up and pointed. "Close the door . . . please." He felt dizzy. "Who are you?"

"You know damn well who I am. You hired me to kill six people." The big man moved quickly to Arbuckle's desk, grabbed him by the tie, and whispered in his ear, "The name's Nelson, Earle Nelson. You remember me, don't you?"

"You're not supposed to be here. I didn't want to see you . . . ."

"So you could deny culpability? It's too late for that, asshole. Pay up!"

Arbuckle stammered, "The news said a street gang shot her."

"That's 'cause I made it look like they did. Now shut up and pay me."

Lloyd Arbuckle stared at the long jagged scar that ran from Nelson's right eye to his lip. It seemed to grow darker as the veins in his neck pulsated.

"I don't like this," Arbuckle said. "You weren't supposed to come here."

"Oh, I'm sorry. Is there some law that says I can't be here? Does it apply to the six people you hired me to kill?"

"Shhh!" Arbuckle's eyes darted around the room. "I didn't hire you to kill anyone. I'm just the intermediary, the go-between, if you will. I don't know why someone wants you to do this. I was given your name. That's all."

"Maybe I should knock you off and deal with your boss!"

"I don't know who that is. I was just given your name and instructed to give you the names and pay you for your services. I didn't know you were killing these people . . . ."

"Right! I almost believe you, but I don't! You are so full of shit your eyes are brown. You're just like most lawyers. Scum like you are lower than whale shit." Nelson stood back, placed his hands on his hips, and said, "Pay me. Now!"

Arbuckle's hands shook. He felt a tightening in his chest. He reached down and opened his desk drawer. Next to the green metal cash box was his .38 caliber police Bulldog revolver. He hesitated. Nobody pushes Lloyd Arbuckle around like Nelson did. Arbuckle wasn't going to be intimidated by a gruff, gray-haired man with a wrinkled neck, an ugly scar, and an old army jacket. He reached for the box with his left hand and grabbed the gun with his right.

Maybe Arbuckle was too slow, or maybe Nelson was too fast. Something hard hit Arbuckle's hand sending the gun across the room. And then he felt himself flying across his desk. The metal box crashed to the floor. Hundred-dollar bills blew around the office.

Lloyd Arbuckle woke up naked, his mouth and eye swollen, his hands tied behind his back and six firecrackers taped around his scrotum. On his large stomach a message had been written in Magic Marker:

IT'S BEEN A PLEASURE.
THANKS FOR THE BONUS.
SEE YOU SOON FOR MORE!

His head ached. He looked around the room. The money, the box, and the gun were gone. There was a strange, unfamiliar salty taste in his mouth like a cross between Ajax cleaner and Brie cheese. When he realized what it was, he threw up.

* * * *

Prison Guard Quinn escorted Cavanaugh through the halls of the Bedford Hills Correctional Facility to the prison psychiatrist, Dr. Yelanda Garland.

"So what's this place like?" Cavanaugh asked.

"I'm just a prison guard, Detective. I don't get involved."

"Do you know either Latitia Jones or Tamika Washington?"

"Seen them both."

"What can you tell me about them?"

"Nothing."

Cavanaugh stopped in the hallway across from the laundry room. Inside, three women stared at them.

"Come on, Quinn, I'm just trying to do my job. What you tell me stays here. I'm not involving you."

Quinn looked around. "Jones is a snitch. Her nickname is Sunflower. She tries to curry favor by ratting people out. If she sees an officer talking to an inmate, she reports them. If she learns someone has obtained anything from razors to glass, floor tiles, screws, even foil packets of skin cream, she'll run to the warden."

"Why? Do they use them like a shiv and go after one another?"

"Sometimes, but not that often. I've been here for a long time. Around here, as you probably know, we get some nuts. I don't know whether they were nuts before they got here, or this place drove them nuts, but we have some seriously disturbed inmates. For some reason, self-mutilation is a fairly frequent occurrence."

"And this Latitia Jones is a squealer."

"Yep. She'd blow the whistle on her own mother if she thought it would help her."

"How does it help her?"

"She gets special privileges. She doesn't have to work with the general population."

"Is she credible?"

"Hard to say. She's intelligent, street-smart, manipulative. Figure it out for yourself. She's been in six prisons in five different states basically for the same thing — forgery. I wouldn't trust her with my wallet if I were you, Detective."

As they continued down the hall, Cavanaugh became aware of a strong smell of ammonia or disinfectants. "What's the other one like, Quinn?"

"Washington has been in and out of sick bay a lot. She claims there's something wrong with her and we are trying to kill her. She hates white people. I heard she was hoping for parole, but she threw a concoction of ammonia and Clorox in the face of another inmate she says dissed her. She doesn't come across as violent, but she's got a temper. I doubt she's going to get her parole."

"Is there a lot of violence here?"

"Are you serious? Almost 65 percent of the women here are here because of violent crimes. Over 70 percent of them are mothers. Your inmate Washington killed a little baby. I wouldn't put anything past her."

Quinn stopped and looked at Cavanaugh. "You know, before you got here this morning, I had to take an inmate to the hospital. She was a swallower. She swallowed a lightbulb! Don't ask me why. I've seen them swallow safety pins, uniform name tags, even bedsprings. It's their way of hurting themselves." He shook his head. "They may come in here sane, but it's rare they come out sane. Your inmate Jones has been in and out of prisons for so long, I think it's gone to her head. She actually told one of the guards that when she was in federal prison, they inserted some kind of computer chip in her."

Prison Guard Quinn pointed to the door in front of them. "That's Dr. Garland's office. Good luck. I'll be here waiting for you unless we have a riot, or I have to take a piss."

* * * *

Cavanaugh knocked on Dr. Garland's office door and entered. The scent of winter forest and lemongrass ginger candles hit him immediately. Green leafy plants sprouted from every corner of the room. Boston ferns, grape, and English ivy hung from the ceiling, and rubber trees, philodendrons, snake and spider plants mingled with a jungle of other plants against mint-green walls. The soft Buddhist meditation music playing in the background reminded him of elevator music. Compared to the halls he left, he felt like he had entered another world.

Sitting on a black leather couch against the wall sat a woman in a tight blue dress. Her long legs were crossed, revealing a lot more skin than he expected.

"You must be Detective Cavanaugh," she said, patting the seat beside her. "Come. Sit down."

Cavanaugh froze. He felt nervous. "Are you Dr. Garland?" he asked.

She giggled and fluttered her eyes. She had tattoos on her legs, arms, hands, and neck. She seemed to exude an almost jungle essence. For the moment, he forgot why he was there.

"Come. Sit," she repeated. "The warden told me you would be coming. What can I do for you?"

Cavanaugh suppressed his initial response and then moved with caution toward her like a mongoose approaching a cobra. "I'm here to investigate a death threat on a judge."

"And how can I help you?"

"I'd like to learn more about two inmates, Latitia Jones and Tamika Washington."

Dr. Garland stood. She was taller than he expected. A silver star dangled from one ear and a gold half-moon from the other. She reached out and gently touched Cavanaugh's arms, motioning him to sit on the couch.

"May I get you a drink, Detective?"

Cavanaugh sank into the leather. His mouth was suddenly dry. "If you have a glass of water that would be great."

Dr. Garland walked across the room to a black cabinet next to a large wax plant. Cavanaugh forced his eyes away from her tight ass and long legs. He wondered how many people said behind her back, "Nice ass." Looking around the room, he saw pictures of the Isle of Arran, a Buddhist Retreat in South Africa, Muir Woods, and Sedona, Arizona. Photos of a number of women, including Lorraine Hansberry, Audre Lorde, Ma Rainey, and Billie Jean King were meticulously arranged around the office.

"Would you like something stronger in your water, Detective Cavanaugh?"

"It's Tom, and no, thanks. I just wanted to ask a few questions."

"Would you like ice?"

"No, thanks. What can you tell me about inmates Jones and Washington?"

She brought the water back and sat next to Cavanaugh, casually rubbing her leg against his. "I don't usually get visits from tall, handsome detectives," she cooed seductively.

He took a sip of water. "Thanks. To tell you the truth, I didn't expect this."

She placed her hand on his leg. He looked at it. Gold rings on all her fingers covered indistinguishable small tattoos. She leaned closer. He pulled back at the overwhelming scent of Opium, Fran's favorite perfume.

"So, Dr. Garland, what can you tell me about Latitia Jones."

"You can call me Yelanda, Tom," she said, brushing back her long black hair.

Cavanaugh thought he detected a slight Eastern European accent, possibly Russian. "Okay, Yelanda, what can you tell me about Latitia?"

"Maybe we could discuss this better at a restaurant I know in the village. They have wonderful beef Stroganoff . . . ."

"Okay, Yelanda," he said, standing abruptly, "let's get this straight. I'm here to investigate a death threat made on a judge. I don't have time for lunch, flirting, or anything else you might have in mind. What's the story on Jones and Washington?"

Dr. Garland stood. She folded her arms. "I'm sorry, Detective Cavanaugh. I had hoped we could discuss this matter in a more civilized manner."

"Let me save you and me some time, Doctor. If you will let me read your notes, I will be on my way."

She shook her head. "I'm sorry, Detective Cavanaugh. That will not be possible."

"What?"

"If you want to see my notes, you will need a court order."

Cavanaugh raised his arms. "I don't believe this! What do you people have to hide?"

"It's the law, Detective. Prisoners have rights. What they tell me is confidential."

Cavanaugh stepped back and took another deep breath. He scanned Dr. Garland from head to toe like an MRI machine. He turned and headed for the door. "Thanks for your help, Doc. This has really been a trip, a trip I won't forget easily — unfortunately."

* * * *

Susan Muscatelli greeted Fran and Father Bennis at the door. She ignored her sister, who was cradling her baby, and smiled at the priest. "Well, look what the wind blew in," she said. "I haven't seen you in ages. How have you been?"

"As well as can be expected, Susan. You look good. I understand your mother, however, is not doing so well. How is she?"

"Did my darling sister drag you along as a support blanket? I wouldn't put it past her."

Bennis smiled. "Maybe something like that. But how is your mom? Fran tells me she had a stroke."

"Not that she's concerned about anyone but herself, but the doctor did say Mom had some kind of stroke. Actually, she probably had a series of ministrokes we were unaware of."

They walked into the kitchen as Susan continued to talk. "After Dad's murder and Ralphie's arrest, Mom became more and more depressed and anxious. She stayed inside most of the time and started drinking — more than usual. Every once in a while she would complain of severe migraine headaches, but they seemed to go away. I realize now that her headaches might have been symptoms. The doctor called them TIAs.

"One night Mom knocked over a vase Grandma had given her on their tenth wedding anniversary, and Mom started laughing hysterically and then suddenly changed into uncontrollable sobbing and crying. Another time she tripped over the carpet in the living room and bruised her knee, but she laughed it off as just being clumsy. Another night we were watching *Two and a Half Men* and she started crying for no reason. I never knew what mood she would be in when I came over."

"When did you take her to the doctor?"

"I came home one day, and fire engines were in front of the house. Mom put a pot of chicken noodle soup on the stove and forgot about it. The water evaporated, the pot burnt, smoke filled the house, and the smoke alarms went off. When I asked her what happened, she called me Francesca. She didn't know who I was!"

Fran reached over and touched Susan's arm. "I'm so sorry, Susan. I didn't know . . . ."

"At first the doctor wasn't sure what it was. He put her through a number of tests and told me to give her things to do and watch her closely. He thought it was probably something called vascular dementia. That's when I moved back in."

Susan turned to Fran. "You know how Mom always loved to do crossword puzzles and Sudoku?"

"Yes. I remember giving her a Sudoku book of puzzles on her birthday one year."

"Well, she can't do them anymore. She can't concentrate. I found a book of them in the toilet upstairs."

"Does she still cook?"

"Everyone loved her potato salads and the lemon cake she used to make . . . ."

Bennis added, "And don't forget the chocolate chip cookies! We all looked forward to it when she brought them over to the rectory."

"Well, she doesn't remember her recipes anymore. She tried to cook a turkey and left the packaging and the bag of giblets inside. In fact, she has more and more trouble remembering anything."

A tear leaked out of Susan's eye. "It's been hard, Father, watching her slip away more and more each day. She doesn't talk much anymore. She just sits and stares."

"Where is she now, Susan?" Bennis asked.

"She's in the family room watching TV."

"Would you mind if I visited her?"

"I'd love it, but don't expect much. She may not even recognize you."

Susan led the way as Fran, Stephen, and Father Bennis followed her slowly into the family room. Fran held her baby close as if to protect him from her mother's vascular dementia.

Elizabeth Muscatelli sat like a Duane Hanson hyperrealistic sculpture staring at *The Price is Right.*

Bennis crouched between Elizabeth and the television. "Hi, Elizabeth. It's been a long time. I came to see you . . . ."

Susan and Fran sighed together when they saw their mother smile.

"How have you been?" Bennis asked.

She reached out and touched his cheeks. Susan and Fran's eyes lit up, and they smiled at each other. Then Elizabeth suddenly slapped the priest across the face and screamed, "Ralph, you dirty son-of-a-bitch, where the fuck have you been?"

* * * *

Cavanaugh returned to Staten Island frustrated. He read the prison logs for both Jones and Washington. Latitia seemed to have made a history of currying favors in prisons by being an informer. She knew all the angles to play. Prison Guard Quinn was right when he said she was street-smart. She had been in a number of different prisons for basically the same thing — fraud. She made only two outside calls in the three years she had been at Bedford Hills, and they were to a former FBI agent who had used her as a criminal informant.

Tamika Washington, however, made a number of calls. Most of them were to family. She had a sister who lived in South Carolina and worked in the governor's office, a brother in the Bronx worked for the NY Department of Corrections as a correction guard at Riker's Island, another brother, Samson Williams, who worked as a janitor at the Staten Island Court House, and a brother-in-law who was a New York City sanitation inspector. She was up for parole in less than a year, but her recent throwing caustic liquids in another inmate's eyes and her verbal threats against Judge Abbruzza diminished her chances. She was never married, but had six children by five different men. Five of the children were in foster care, and the other was out of the country.

The district attorney had offered her a plea bargain, but she refused, and a jury found her guilty of the manslaughter of a ten-month-old baby. A next-door neighbor found the child tied to the radiator and called police. Tamika claimed at first the baby was hers and then that she was babysitting it for another woman who had abandoned the child with her two months before. The prosecutor pointed out that Tamika filed a false claim for benefits, claiming initially that the child was hers and never informed Child Services about the child being abandoned. The bruises on the child, his broken bones, his burnt fingers, traces of duct tape found across his mouth, and the neighbor's testimony left no doubt in the jury's mind.

On the long ride back to Staten Island, Cavanaugh wondered if Latitia were telling the truth or just trying to gain more privileges and if Tamika had the resources and the motivation to order a hit on Judge Abbruzza.

He drove straight to Staten Island Criminal Court to obtain subpoenas duces tecum for both the commissary accounts and the psychiatrist's and counselor's notes on both inmates. The court summonses would require the recipients to produce the documents he requested.

He told Judge Abbruzza that he would head back to Bedford Hills the next day to review the reports and to interview the women. The judge's fingers tapped incessantly as Cavanaugh spoke. His eyes darted from Cavanaugh to his desk.

"What's up, Carlo? You look anxious. I'll have this thing wrapped up for you tomorrow. It looks to me like a case of prison BS and a letter writer looking for prison favors."

The judge picked up a handwritten letter on his desk. "I got this today," he said. "It was dated almost two weeks ago." His hands shook. "It's from Latitia Jones again. She's more urgent now. She says Washington has hired someone to kill me and a number of others involved in her sentencing . . . ."

"That's crazy talk, Carlo. How is she supposed to pay for a killer?"

"She claims she's already put a $200 deposit down. Her mother hired a guy named Aloysius Booth up in Harlem."

Cavanaugh quickly reviewed the names on Washington's phone log. There were no phone calls to her mother. But there were a number of calls to relatives who may have had contact with her mother.

"Tell you what," he began. "I'm going back to the precinct now. I'll make a few calls and try to check out this Aloysius Booth character and try to locate the mother. I still don't think the threat is plausible, but I think the best bet would be to notify the police and the press."

"Not yet. They'll all think I'm grandstanding or panicking if you're right. I'd lose credibility and be forced to resign. I had an alarm system installed at home. Don't worry. We'll be all right."

As Cavanaugh turned to leave, he warned, "No offense meant, Carlo, but I think those were exactly Custer's last words."

* * * *

The visit to Elizabeth Muscatelli's left Jack Bennis with an empty pit in his stomach. The image of Cindy Waters's body lying in the street fought with the heartbreaking scene he had experienced at Elizabeth's house. Dementia, he realized, is a difficult illness to deal with. It affects patients, families, and friends. Yet more and more people seem to have to deal with it. Cindy had to adjust her life to take care of her mother, just as Susan had. But Cindy, he believed, was murdered. Now who would take care of her mother?

As terrible as it is, dementia is a natural disease. Murder, on the other hand, is a deliberate crime. To take his mind off Fran's mother, Bennis decided to check on Cindy's mother.

When he reached the Waters's house, it was dark and silent. He knocked and heard something scraping against the door. He turned the knob, and the door opened. Cindy's cockapoo suddenly jumped up on him, wagging its tail like a metronome on amphetamines. He knelt, and the dog slobbered all over his face and hands. He picked it up, and it whimpered and snuggled into his arms.

He looked around. There was no other sound in the house. The house was dark. Where was the nurse's aide? Where was Cindy's mother?

Holding the dog in his arms, he walked through the house. "Hello?" he shouted. "Is anyone home?" No answer.

He flicked lights on and off in each room as he made his way from room to room. "Hello. This is Father Bennis from Our Lady Help of Christians. I came here to see if I could help. Is there anyone here?" No answer.

He was about to leave when he heard the unmistakable sound of cocking a pump-action shotgun behind him. "Make a move, and you're a dead man," a voice said.

Bennis raised one hand. "Don't shoot," he said. "I'm a priest. I came here to check on Mrs. Waters."

"As far as I'm concerned, you're an intruder, a burglar. What are you holding in your other hand? Raise your other hand slowly. Any sudden moves and you're dead!"

Bennis calculated the distance from the gun and the voice. They were too far away to make a move to grab the gun and too close for the gunman to miss. Gently, he gripped the cockapoo firmly under its chest and lifted it overhead.

"Turn around slowly."

As he turned, he looked into the barrel of a shotgun aimed at his head. Then he looked at the shooter.

"Mrs. Sweeney!" he said, lowering the dog and hugging it against his chest. "What are you doing here?"

"I'm the one with the gun, Padre. I'll ask the questions. What are *you* doing here?"

"I came to see if I could help Mrs. Waters . . . ."

"She's gone. Ambulance took her away this morning. Probably to the emergency room or a nursing home. Don't know."

"Did you see Cindy Waters get hit?"

"No. I was in the kitchen making a Spanish omelet for myself. I heard a bump. Thought it was a branch falling and then a little while later the screech of tires. I ran to the window and saw the girl lying in the street. That's when I called 911."

"Did anyone else see the accident?"

"Don't know. Saw the old coot across the street looking out his window. But he's usually so drunk he couldn't tell a heating pad from a bomb."

"May I ask what are you doing here with a gun?"

"Saw someone in the house. Got suspicious. We don't like burglars in our neighborhood. Figured it might be one of those West Indian aides coming back to steal something. Instead, I find you trying to steal the dog."

"Please put the gun down. I'm not trying to steal the dog. The door was unlocked, and the dog jumped up on me. It's probably hungry and hasn't been out of the house all day."

"Not my problem. You can explain it to the cops when they get here."

"What? You called the police?"

"Damn right I did, Padre. I'm the street watcher for this block. I see trouble, I call it in."

He started to move toward her. "You can put the gun down, Mrs. Sweeney. I'm not a thief."

"Freeze!" she shouted. "Take another step and you and the mutt are Swiss cheese!"

In the distance, Bennis heard police sirens. His mother once told him it was foolish to argue with a woman. It would be really stupid to argue with a woman with a loaded shotgun aimed at you.

He looked at the little curly white dog in his arms and imagined what his brother would say when he found out what had happened. There are good days, and there are bad days, he thought, and this was definitely one of the bad ones. All he could say as he heard the squad car doors open was, "Shit!"

* * * *

When Cavanaugh returned to the detectives' office at the 123, Sebastian greeted him with, "Well, if it isn't Mr. Popularity returning to grace us with his presence."

"Did you solve the hit-and-run yet?"

Newhouser answered. "Not much to go on. The only one who saw anything was a drunk ex-cop across the street. He can't be sure of the make or even the color of the car. Seems he has a bit of an alcohol problem. We're waiting for an analysis of the glass and tire marks. They should be able to give us the make and year of the vehicle."

"By the way," Sebastian interjected, "your buddy with the beanie has been calling you all day. Do you two have a thing going?"

"Goldberg?"

"Goldberg, Greenberg, Iceberg, Schwartzberg, Bloomberg, whatever."

"You know, Sebastian, sometimes you come across as a real *ignoranus*. That, in case you didn't know, is a person who is both stupid and an asshole."

Sebastian leaned back and smiled. "Sarcasm, I see," he said, "is just one more service you offer."

"What did he want?"

"How should I know? I didn't want to get in between your 'special' relationship."

Newhouser spoke up. "He said it was important and that you should call him back ASAP."

Cavanaugh reached for the phone and started dialing.

"Ask him if it's true that, according to Jewish dietary laws, pork and shellfish are only permitted to be eaten in Chinese restaurants!" Sebastian shouted.

Cavanaugh ignored the comment and was patched through to Goldberg. "What's up, Morty?' he asked. "I thought you were assigned to guard a couple of rabbis."

"Why do I even talk to you? There were almost four thousand rabbis, leaders, and scholars from all over the world at the

International Conference of Chabad-Lubavitch! The annual convention is a really big thing."

"One of the guys in the office here heard one of the topics discussed was the Jewish controversy about when life begins. Some of your people seem to believe the fetus is not considered viable until after it graduates from medical school . . . ."

"You're pathetic, Cavanaugh."

"Yeah, you're probably right. It's been a rough day. I apologize. I haven't been getting much sleep lately, and I traveled up to Bedford Hills today only to get jerked around like a yoyo. I have to go back tomorrow with some subpoenas."

"For what it's worth, if you want company, I'm available. The conference is over."

"That's great news. I could use your help."

"Well, I have some bad news for you too. I did a little research of my own. There was a woman murdered in Mariners Harbor last night . . . ."

"Yeah. I heard it on the radio."

"The woman's name was Claudia Buenaventura."

"So?"

"She was the main witness in Tamika Washington's trial."

"Shit!"

"It gets worse. Cindy Waters, the hit-and-run victim in your precinct yesterday, was the jury foreman at Ms. Washington's trial."

"Shit and double shit!"

"Could be a coincidence, Tom, but neither of us believe in coincidences. I think your judge may have a real problem."

Cavanaugh hung up and made a quick call to Judge Abbruzza. "Carlo," he said, "we have a possibly very big problem. It's time to call in the cavalry."

* * * *

William George Fuller rubbed his eyes. On his desk lay a copy of Schopenhauer's *The World as Will and Idea* and

Kierkegaard's *Attack upon Christendom*. He reveled in the unpredictable, blind, nonrational will of things. True genius, he believed, cannot be created by anyone who strictly follows the rules. Yet he was not willing to expose himself to unnecessary risks. Instead of family pictures on his desk, Fuller had a thirteenth-century Chinese bronze statue of Genghis Khan and a solid gold statue of Attila the Hun on horseback.

His sources told him Judge Abbruzza was worried but hadn't resigned. Instead, Abbruzza asked an old schoolmate, homicide detective Thomas Cavanaugh, to investigate the letters quietly. Fuller had tried to honor a request not to kill the judge, but that might now not be possible.

The connection had been made between the jury foreman and the witness, and instead of backing down, Judge Abbruzza notified the police and the press. If the publicity would not force him to resign, the killings would continue with all the evidence pointing to Tamika Washington.

A new twist, however, had been added to the equation. The killer Lloyd Arbuckle hired had attacked him. Arbuckle was scared. He was weak. He was vulnerable. He became a liability that needed to be erased.

Fuller pressed the intercom button. "Hold all calls," he said. "I'm going out for a cup of tea."

The streets of New York were crowded. People were rushing, jaywalking, talking on cell phones, texting. Taxi cabs blew by honking their horns and weaving in and out of traffic. Fuller loved the city. It was alive, vibrant, stimulating. Here he could get lost in a crowd and hide in plain sight.

He walked at a brisk pace for a few blocks, passing a Dunkin' Donuts, two Starbucks, a McDonald's, and a number of restaurants and pubs. He stopped at a new small bistro called Tranquility on Fifty-seventh Street. It looked neat and dark. Soft piano music greeted him as he entered the dimly lit restaurant.

The tall handsome, white-haired maître d' greeted him, "Good evening, Mr. Fuller."

"Good evening, Paul. My usual seat, please."

"Of course, Mr. Fuller."

There were a few tourists scattered around the room. The music carried a subduing effect, and the atmosphere resembled a church more than a New York restaurant in the heart of Manhattan.

"Is that Jonny playing?"

"Yes, Mr. Fuller. Shall I tell him you're here?"

"Please, Paul, and have the waitress bring me a cup of chamomile tea."

Fuller walked to a solitary table in the back corner and sat against the wall. From there he could see the main door, the bar, and the piano player. He watched Paul go to the piano and whisper in the player's ear. The musician glanced at Fuller, smiled, and nodded.

Fuller liked Paul. He was affable, congenial, efficient, and discrete. Jonny recommended him, and he trusted Jonny.

Jonny "Sweet Fingers" Fiore finished playing "Fly Me to the Moon" and glided over to Fuller's table. With his muscular six-foot-seven frame, he could have been mistaken for a football player. He bowed slightly before sitting down at the table. His brown shaved head glistened in the shadows. Wearing a classic tailor-made black tuxedo and red bow tie, he looked like he stepped out of the pages of *GQ*.

"How do you like the new Hamburg Steinway?"

Jonny smiled. "It is a joy to touch the keys and hear the melodies. Thank you."

"I always believe in quality. It's a special limited edition grand piano flown directly in from Hamburg, Germany." Hidden beneath a ream of shell companies, Tranquility was another of William George Fuller's secret enterprises.

Jonny nodded and folded his long fingers. "What can I do for you?"

"You are a man of many talents, Jonny. I appreciate you and trust you." Fuller looked around at the few customers in the restaurant. "Few would suspect that you are a Harvard graduate, a CPA, and the accountant of many of my, shall we say, diverse business enterprises."

Jonny smiled. His white teeth sparkled in the dim light. "How are things progressing with our latest enterprise?"

Fuller smiled. "He has proved more stubborn than initially expected. But it's early yet. We have a more serious problem."

Jonny leaned in closer.

"The building's cleaning lady discovered Arbuckle this morning. Your man did a job on him. No serious injuries, but he is scared. He's not talking, but it was probably about money. Arbuckle is a sleazebag. I don't blame your man. Arbuckle was a weak link in this enterprise from the beginning. Now he's a loose cannon."

"I understand. What about Nelson?"

Fuller sipped his tea. "Get a message to him. Add Arbuckle to the list. Make it a priority. Match whatever price he wants. We'll deal with him later."

Jonny "Sweet Fingers" stood. "I understand." He nodded and walked with the grace of a ballet dancer to the bar. He wrote something on a piece of paper. He whispered something to Paul at the door, exchanged his tuxedo jacket for a NY Yankee sweatshirt and cap and left.

He walked two blocks east, turned south for two blocks, then east for another block, and then south for two more blocks. Along the way, he mingled with the crowds and checked store windows to see if he were being followed. At Fifty-fourth Street, he turned west for a block and then made his way to the Citigroup Subway Entrance on Lexington Avenue and Fifty-third Street. He took the escalator down to the platform where a white man in a baggy gray suit, green sweater-vest, blue tie, and white socks was busking. He stood against the wall playing one of Bach's sonatas to a mingling crowd of waiting, mostly distracted passengers. Trains pulled in and out, and people dropped coins and dollars into his open violin case.

Jonny "Sweet Fingers" Fiore knew the violin busker well. When the man saw Jonny, he switched from Bach to the theme from *The Godfather.* Businessmen and women, tourists, and children with their parents reacted, and a large group gathered around him. They listened to the haunting violin music amid the deafening cacophony of New York subways. Some tossed money into his case as they left to catch their trains. Jonny casually went up and dropped a $50 bill wrapped around his message into the violin case. Then he caught an uptown train and returned to the restaurant.

* * * *

Cavanaugh drove home that night in silence. He didn't understand it. How could Tamika Washington have arranged for the killing of the jury foreman and the key witness against her? He reviewed her case file five times before he left. She was imprisoned for the gruesome neglect and manslaughter of a ten-month-old child. In addition to the bruising, broken bones, and severe burns, the child was covered with rashes and parasites and had a large open wound in his navel. He thought of little three-month-old Stephen. How could anyone in his or her right mind treat a child like that? When asked this same question by the police, she claimed she didn't see the bruises because of the "poor lighting" in the apartment.

Allegations of her alleged drug use and trafficking were never brought up in her trial. Could she have contacts on the outside willing to carry out her threats? He felt it was possible but not likely. Her only defense was "poor lighting" and that she was being unjustly harassed because she was "a poor Negro woman."

The image of strapping a child to a hot radiator so he wouldn't crawl away and placing duct tape over his mouth so his cries wouldn't be heard plagued him. He complained about Stephen's colic, but now he longed to get home and just hold him. Despite his crying, he was the most precious gift a man could ever have. Infants cry because they are hungry, wet, or in pain. If Stephen cried because he was in pain and holding him helped, Cavanaugh vowed he would hold him until Stephen was old enough to vote.

When he arrived home, Fran met him at the door. "How did it go with your mother?" he asked.

"It could have been better, but as your brother said, it is what it is. How about your day?"

"Similar. It could have been better." He looked around. "How's Stephen?"

She hesitated for a moment and then said, "Sleeping." He stared at her and looked around. "Yes. I know. That means he will probably be up all night."

"No, Fran, that's okay. After my day, I look forward to seeing him and holding him. Crying or not, he's the greatest gift we could have been given." There were tears in Fran's eyes when he picked her up, kissed her, and swung her around.

But then he stopped suddenly and asked, "What's that scratching noise? Do you hear it? It's coming from Jack's room."

Fran looked down. "I think you had better ask your brother yourself."

Cavanaugh looked at her. There was something she wasn't telling him. "What's going on?" he asked.

Jack Bennis opened the door to his room, and a small dog raced out and scampered toward Cavanaugh. "What the hell?"

"What do you think we should call it, Thomas?"

"How about 'Out of Here This Minute'?"

"Isn't he so cute, Tom?"

"Fran, we have an infant to take care of. We don't need a freakin' dog."

"It's a cockapoo, Thomas, a cross between a cocker spaniel and a poodle."

"Well, it can do its pooing somewhere else. It's not staying in this house."

"But, Tom, it's so cute, and look, it likes you."

"She's got you there, Thomas. You can't say that about too many people."

The little dog stood in front of Cavanaugh wagging its tail as if pleading to be petted or tickled. "Very funny," Cavanaugh said, bending down to rub its head.

"I don't know, Fran . . . ."

"I looked it up on the Internet. Cockapoos are non-shedding, good with people with allergies, good with children, friendly, intelligent, not aggressive . . . ."

Cavanaugh turned to his brother. "Where did you get this thing?"

"It's kind of a long story. I found it abandoned in Cindy Waters's house."

"The girl from the hit-and-run?"

"Yes. The dog was alone in the house. They took Cindy's mother to a nursing home in the morning. She's got Alzheimer's. Cockapoos are generally happy little dogs, but they suffer from separation anxiety if left along for long periods. It hadn't eaten. The ASPCA was going to take it away . . . ."

"So you decided to bring it home with you . . . ."

"I couldn't let them take this little thing away. I thought it would make a great companion dog for Fran and Stephen. It's already housebroken. Fran can walk it when she takes Stephen out. Besides, it will make a great watchdog."

"You've got it all figured out, haven't you?"

"Please, Tom. Stephen will love it."

The cockapoo rolled over, and Cavanaugh began scratching its belly. "I guess I have only one question . . . . What are we going to call it?"

* * * *

Book III

"Have gun will travel," reads the card of the man . . . .

—*Johnny Western*

Before they left for the trip to Bedford Hills the next morning, Cavanaugh met Goldberg, and they ran the name Aloysius Booth, the alleged hit man Latitia claimed Tamika hired to kill Judge Abbruzza. They came up with a long list of Booths, but no Aloysius Booth. They also conferred with Sebastian and Newhouser about the possibility of Cindy Waters's death being connected with Claudia Buenaventura's shooting in the Mariner's Harbor Arlington apartment complex.

It was 9:00 a.m., and Newhouser was munching on another tuna fish sub. "Do you think the two deaths are connected to the threats on the judge?" he muttered through a mouthful of tuna fish.

"How do you know about the threats on the judge?" Cavanaugh asked.

"It's all over the news. The eleven o'clock news had it on all channels. The headline on the *Post* this morning is 'Judge Fears for His Life.'"

Cavanaugh shrugged his shoulders. "I didn't get to see the news last night. My brother brought another addition home with him last night."

"Another hot Cuban chick like the last one?" Sebastian asked. "She was one hot number."

"No! This one was a dog! And before you say anything more, Sebastian, sometimes I think your gene pool needs a little chlorine to clean up your dirty thoughts."

Goldberg asked, "Back to the case, did anyone get a look at the driver of the car that ran over Ms. Waters?"

"The neighbor across the street is an ex-cop. He claims he saw the guy, but he didn't have his glasses on and couldn't give us a description of the guy or the vehicle. He also happened to have a blood alcohol level higher than the IQ of my first wife," Sebastian said. "He swore it wasn't an accident, but he couldn't give us much."

Cavanaugh recalled something his brother had said. "He saw the guy?" he asked.

"Says he did, but couldn't give us much of a description."

Cavanaugh remembered all the questions his brother badgered him with about an old army buddy. He must have had a reason for all the persistent questions. Why would Bennis be so insistent to ask his brother, a cop, to look up information for him? "Did he indicate the kind of jacket the guy wore?" he asked.

Newhouser and Sebastian checked their notes. "Yeah. It says here he had an old dirty jacket."

"He wasn't even sure of the color. Could have been green or olive or khaki. He didn't have his glasses on. The only thing he was sure of was it had a lot of black stains on it like he was a mechanic."

"Could it have been an old army field jacket?" Cavanaugh asked.

"Could be. I don't know. I wasn't there, and the witness was drunk."

Cavanaugh had that feeling again. It was small, like the first spark of a fire, but it was there. It was something. "We're heading up to Bedford Hills now to do some questioning. Do me a favor and check out a guy named Earle Nelson. He served in the army with my brother and was there when my brother went to the scene. It may be nothing, but it's worth a try. I promised him I would look Nelson up for him."

"He's not getting involved again, is he?" Goldberg asked.

"I hope not. Sometimes he can be a real pain in the ass. Between the baby crying, Fran's mood swings, his questions, and the dog, it was another rough night."

"Would you like some cheese and crackers," Sebastian asked, "to go with that whine?"

"You know, Tom," Goldberg said as he packed up his papers preparing to leave, "married life can be difficult at times. There are a lot of trials and tribulations married life brings with it. Take it from a man who has been married to the same woman for many, many years and has been blessed with many children. Sometimes I believe that married couples who live together day after day, year after year, are a miracle your Vatican has long overlooked."

Everyone in the office laughed, including Cavanaugh. "Everybody's a comedian today," he said. "I guess I deserved that. Now let's get back to finding a killer before he strikes again."

* * * *

When Kasia Kovalski, the cleaning lady, found Lloyd Arbuckle naked and tied to his chair that morning, he told her it was a prank from some of his old fraternity buddies. She didn't think it was very funny, and in her broken English, she told him to call the police. He told her it would be better for all of them if he didn't and if she forgot about the whole thing. After all, it was only a joke. Why bring the police in? They would ask a lot of questions and people could get hurt, maybe even deported. He advised her to forget about it, grabbed his clothes, went home, took a shower, brushed his teeth, gargled with mouthwash repeatedly, and sat down to think.

He paced around his apartment. Earle Nelson was crazy. He would be back. Arbuckle had no way to defend himself.

Nelson had taken his gun and his money. He had abused him. But where could he go? His cabin in the Monticello area was the only thing his ex-wife had not gotten in the divorce. She graciously let him have it. And why not? It needed a new roof, had no heat, and had little real estate value. Arbuckle initially cursed the bitch, but now that was all he had. In addition, he had a .30-06 Springfield hunting rifle with a scope hidden in the cabin. Nelson took the money in the box, but Arbuckle still had the $20,000 wired to his bank account.

Suddenly, there was a knock on the door.

"Who's there?" Arbuckle asked.

Another knock. Louder this time.

Arbuckle approached the door and looked through the peephole. It was him!

"Open up, fat boy! I know you're in there. I have a present for you."

Arbuckle turned and ran into the kitchen. He opened the window and began to squeeze through to the fire escape. He heard the door burst open. He turned. Nelson was in the apartment, and he had a gun in his hand.

"Stand still, fat boy, and I'll make it fast," he laughed.

Arbuckle plopped onto the fire escape as a bullet hit the window frame. Another shot broke the window. He threw himself forward and tumbled down the fire escape. Shots ricocheted off the iron stairs and whizzed by him. When he hit the ground, he started running down the alley toward the street. More shots whipped by him.

The street was more crowded than usual. He glanced behind him. Nelson was gone. He knew what he had to do. Arbuckle ran as fast as his fat little legs would carry him and stopped a gypsy cab at the corner. "Drive!" he told the driver as he saw Nelson emerging from the main entrance of his building. Abdul Patel did as instructed and peeled out, cutting off a woman in a Dodge Caravan, weaving around a city bus, and narrowly missing a businessman in a BMW convertible.

Ten blocks later, he stopped at a bank and got out. Arbuckle felt as if the walls were closing in on him. He would be a dead man or worse if Nelson found him. Taking Mr. X's money, however, without carrying out his assignment could lead to the same fate. He had played with fire, and now he had to get away before it consumed him.

After emptying his bank account, he took the Staten Island Ferry into Manhattan. There, he took the Number 1 subway to Forty-second Street — Times Square and walked over to the Port Authority Bus Terminal on Eighth Avenue. Mingling with the moving masses of people, he spotted wide-eyed naïve tourists as well as shameless chicken hawks and pimps waiting to lure in runaway teenage boys and girls.

He bought a one-way ticket on the Short Line Bus to Monticello. At every step of his journey, he felt as if someone were watching him. Arbuckle only began to relax when the bus left the city, and he watched the trees race by. He had over $20,000 in cash in his pocket. He breathed a sigh of relief. He would make it. Neither Nelson nor Mr. X would get him. He was Lloyd Arbuckle. He would outsmart them all. He was a survivor.

Looking out the window again, he saw his own reflection and realized he forgot to shave. His stomach growled. In his haste, he had forgotten to eat. Then he felt a series of stomach cramps and realized he had not packed any clothes for his escape. He held his head in his hands and started to cry. Reality hit him. He was in a fight for his life and the odds were against him.

* * * *

Goldberg and Cavanaugh discussed their plans on the trip to the Bedford Hills Correctional Facility. Sebastian and Newhouser were checking on Tamika Washington's telephone contacts and the whereabouts of Earle Nelson and the alleged hired assassin, Aloysius Booth. Goldberg and Cavanaugh decided they would each read and study the psychiatrist's reports and the commissary accounts for both women separately. Then they would question the women.

Goldberg's cellphone rang. It was Newhouser. They had located an address for Earle Nelson, but they couldn't check it out. Newhouser said things were pretty hectic on the island. Police were being reassigned because of reports of shots fired in the Tompkinsville section of Staten Island. A door-to-door search was going on looking for the shooter.

"Did you really mean that — what you said back there in the precinct?" Cavanaugh asked.

"What did I say?"

"You said something about it being difficult for married couples to stay together."

"It was meant as a joke, but there's a lot of truth in it too."

Cavanaugh drove in silence for a while then said, "Fran hasn't been the same since the baby . . . ."

"Give her time, Tom. It's a rough time. A woman's body undergoes a lot of changes after a pregnancy, especially a difficult one like Fran had."

"She's not the same. One minute she's happy, the next she's crying. I don't know which way to turn. It's like she's always tired. Now with her mother's dementia, she's more depressed than ever."

Goldberg smiled. "Maybe the little dog your brother brought home will help."

Cavanaugh shook his head. "It won't help my DSB."

Goldberg frowned. "What's DSB?"

"Deadly Sperm Buildup. Sometimes I think I'm going to die. It's like she's lost all interest in sex."

"I'm not getting involved in this. This is TMI — too much information. I don't want to go there!"

"But you're my best partner, my friend, probably my best friend . . . ."

"Have you read *Portnoy's Complaint*?"

"No. Why?"

"Never mind. Keep your eyes on the road, Tom. We are almost there. I'm far from an expert on these things, but Fran wanted to have the baby. She fought against the odds to have it. This is her first child. She's entitled to feel ambivalent now, but she has support in you and your brother. Give her a break. It's not easy having a baby."

"Do you think that's what happened to Tamika Washington?"

"What?"

"She had six kids from five different guys. Maybe she just snapped."

"Who knows? She tried to work the system with the baby that died, trying to get welfare benefits for it. But she grew up in a different environment. She never knew her father. She lived the life of the street. It can be hard, cruel, violent. You and I will never know what she went through or truly what drove her to do what she did. All we can do is try to make sure she doesn't kill the judge."

"What I don't understand, Morty, is how she could do what she did to a little kid. She mustn't have been in her right mind."

"I don't know, Tom. People do different things for different reasons." He stared ahead for about a mile and then said, "I don't know if prison helps. It gets people off the street, but I wonder if it really helps."

* * * *

News of the death threat on Judge Abbruzza resulted in his being provided twenty-four-hour protection and court officer escorts between his home and the courthouse. Sebastian and Newhouser went together to question the family members Tamika Washington contacted by phone from the prison. The Office of Court Administration and detectives from the Persons' Squad were doing background checks on all the other outside calls made by Ms. Washington.

Tamika had seven siblings, Shereece Campbell, Samson Williams, Roland Biggs, Askira Blackman, Violet Taylor, Raven

Smith, and Rashida Owens. But she had only made calls to three of them. Sebastian and Newhouser's first stop was Parkchester in the Bronx, where her brother Roland Biggs, a correction officer on Riker's Island, lived. He didn't want to talk to them at first, but Sebastian's implied threat that Biggs's bosses at Riker's may be interested in learning he was not cooperating in a murder investigation changed his mind, and he invited them in. He fixed some coffee from a Keurig Brewer, and they sat at a table in the foyer.

Tamika was the black sheep of the family according to Biggs. One sister, Shereece Campbell, was a secretary in the South Carolina governor's office. Another sister, Askira Blackman, went to St. John's Law School but was killed in a drive-by shooting on Amsterdam Avenue two years before. Her husband, James Blackman, was a court officer in Manhattan. Another sister, Violet Taylor, taught fifth grade at P.S. 136 in St. Albans, Queens, and her husband was a New York City sanitation inspector. She also had a sister, Raven Smith, who worked in the Motor Vehicles Bureau in Connecticut, and another, Rashida Owens, who was a Jehovah's Witness missionary in Nigeria, Africa. All eight children were born out of wedlock and had different fathers.

Biggs claimed not to have seen Tamika since her trial. Her call to him a few weeks before was to ask him to pull some strings because she had a parole hearing coming up in the future, and she was worried because of an incident she had with another inmate that landed her in the SHU for almost a year.

"What's the SHU?" Newhouser asked.

"Solitary confinement. It stands for 'Special Housing Unit.'"

"What did she do?"

"Don't know and don't care. I told her so too. We have a family to raise, and we just can't keep bailing Tamika out of trouble."

"You haven't been exactly very successful about that in the past, have you?"

Roland Biggs sipped his coffee and nodded. "No. I guess we haven't."

"We're trying to contact everyone she called from prison," Newhouser said. "Have you ever heard of an Aloysius Booth?"

Biggs scratched his head. "No. Who is he?"

"We don't exactly know," Sebastian said. "The rumor is Tamika hired him to kill the judge who sentenced her."

"That's bullshit," Biggs said. "My sister may have done a lot of bad things, but I don't think she's dumb enough to kill a judge. She's not a killer."

"Mr. Biggs, may I remind you she is in prison for delinquent abuse of a child leading to the manslaughter of a ten-month-old baby."

Roland Biggs stood. "I think that's enough, gentlemen. I got to go to work . . . ."

Both Sebastian and Newhouser rose. "One more question," Newhouser said. "Do you know where we can reach your mother? We've been unable to locate her."

"I've had enough of your bullshit. Leave my mother out of this, and get the hell out of here."

"We were hoping you would be more cooperative . . . ."

Biggs held the door open. "Listen, I don't need any of your crap at work. I've told you what I know. My mom moves around. She stayed with us a month ago. She may be staying with one of my sisters now. I don't know. She got evicted from her place in Newark for not paying rent about a year ago and has been homeless since. Like I said, she moves around a lot. I honestly don't know where she is now. Maybe one of my sisters can help."

Walking back to their car, Newhouser looked around at the high red brick buildings and the large playground areas. "You know, this place looks like a pretty damn nice place to live."

"Yeah," Sebastian said. "Once I almost dated a girl who lived here. She was a psychic."

"How did she like it?"

"I don't know." Sebastian smiled. "She left me before we met."

"How could that be?"

"It was a joke, Newhouser."

"I don't get it. It doesn't make sense."

"Forget it. Let's go to the next name on the list . . . ."

* * * *

Earle Nelson sat in a Starbucks on Richmond Avenue nursing a mocha frappuccino and taking advantage of the free Wi-Fi connection. Arbuckle had gotten away. The question was where had he gone? He had checked his office. But he wasn't there. The Polish cleaning lady in the building told him some of Arbuckle's old college friends had played a nasty trick on him. She didn't go into details. All she knew was he looked scared and went home.

He thought about killing her, but she seemed to believe Arbuckle's story. *Lawyers could be good liars*, he thought. He gave her the number of his disposable phone and asked her to call him if he came back. He told her he was looking for a good lawyer to draw up a will for his invalid mother and to do some estate planning.

He sipped his mocha frappuccino and surfed the net to find where Arbuckle might have gone. Nelson had the $5,000 in cash he had taken from Arbuckle's metal cash box and another $5,000 he received under his door, instructing him to eliminate Arbuckle ASAP with the promise of more to come with each additional hit. The problem was, where was Arbuckle?

Nelson's fingers were stiff, but they jumped across the iPad like he was playing the William Tell Overture in *presto con fuoco*. The army had taught him how to type, how to use computers, how to hunt, and how to kill. He was good at all of these, but he liked the killing best.

He looked up at the Starbuck symbol on the mirror in front of him. Starbuck, he knew, was a sailor in *Moby Dick* who loved coffee. But the logo pictured a siren or mermaid who originally seduced sailors with songs and sex before killing them. He wondered if his knowledge of mythology added to the flavor of his coffee.

Then his eyes fixated on his own reflected image. His jagged facial scar seemed to glow red across his face. "Black Jack Bennis!" he muttered aloud. A blonde with long hair and a diamond stud in her chin glanced up at him, saw the look in his eyes, and went back to texting. Nelson recalled the lieutenant who gave him the scar and cursed. He was glad he killed the righteous son-of-a-bitch in Colombia. He thought of him every day when he looked in the mirror. He visualized raining bullets down on him and watching him fall into the jungle. Who did he think he was?

But that priest at the scene of the hit-and-run . . . . There was something about him. It was like looking at a ghost from thirty years ago. It couldn't be. Bennis was dead. He killed him. But that look in the priest's eyes . . . . There was something about him that haunted Nelson.

He shook his head and resumed his Internet search. In a few minutes he had located a cabin in the Catskills area that Lloyd Arbuckle owned. It made sense. He pulled up a satellite photo of the cabin and directions to get there.

It was worth the trip. After killing Arbuckle, he would get back to the list. He looked at it again. Patrolman Kevin Reilly, Tamika Washington's arresting officer, was the next name on his list.

He turned his iPad off and smiled. This job was better than being a security guard to a group of pampered, obnoxious, overindulged "mutant teenagers." The money was better, and he got to get paid for what he loved to do-kill.

* * * *

Kathleen Bradley knocked and walked into Judge Abbruzza's chambers.

"What is it, Kathleen?"

"You got another letter, Judge. It just arrived. It's from Bedford Hills."

Judge Abbruzza put down the brief he was working on and took the letter. His hands were shaking. "Did you read the letter, Kathleen?"

"No, sir. I just opened it like I do with all your letters. I thought you might want to read this one immediately."

"Thanks, Kathleen. You can go now. I'll call you if I need you."

His secretary quietly backed out of the room and closed the door.

Abbruzza sat motionless for a moment staring at the envelope. Then he opened it and read the handwritten letter:

> Honorable Judge Abbruzza,
>
> I write you again to express my sincere concern regarding your Safety & Wellbeing Concerning the matter I've written you twice befour about of threats from Tamika Washington, This is a serious matter,
>
> Judge Abbruzza there is no way that my conscious will allow me to excuse the threats that Tamika Washington has and is making, reguarding your life and the lifes of the other people involved in her going to Jail . . . .

Judge Abbruzza wrote the names Cindy Walker and Claudia Buenaventura on his notepad. Who else might be on her list? The district attorney? Maybe her defense lawyer? How serious could she be? He went back to reading the letter.

> She (Tamika Washington) is very adament on carry out her threats . . . .
>
> She has discussed with me in detail other acts of Vengence she's carried out including a most recent

one right in Jail while she was awating court on Rikers Island.

She actually premeditated to mix up a concocktion of acid and throwing it on another inmate burning her face surverely. She recieved 200 days in SHU (segregated housing Unit.)

She also feels that you convicted her on Circumstancial evidents although she says she was involved.

"Circumstantial evidence?" Judge Abbruzza said aloud. "She admitted tying the infant to a radiator, hitting it over the head repeatedly to make it stop crying, and then putting duct tape over his mouth and leaving him in the apartment alone. His fingers were burnt to the bone . . . ."

Tamika Washington knows about guns and always carried a gun. And she's also told me that she's in all reality is a Drug transporter, of Herione, She travels out of the country to London on to Africa, several times a year. And for this reason she didn't want to give the courts her passport inableing her to recieve a lower bail than $100,000.00.

Tamika says Quote: Vengence is hers! I can not understand Your Honor when a person sits down and calcalculates to take another persons life and has paid money as a down payment to someone just in case she dosen't get out . . . to continue the act for her. Tamika and I are very close, mainly because she not only lives in my Unit but also has the cell across from me.

And of the 4 months We've talked a great deal. And she feels she can confide in me. But Your Honor I'am not one that can hold the confidence reguarding the killing of another person.

Please be careful Judge Abbruzza, and for Gods sake don't take Tamika Washington's threats lightly . . . If you could hear her you'd see reson for my great concern.

Sincerly
Latitia Jones

Judge Abbruzza sat staring at the letter until his hands stopped shaking. Then he pressed his intercom button. "Kathleen, get me through to Detective Cavanaugh . . . ."

* * * *

After presenting the necessary subpoenas and paperwork, Goldberg and Cavanaugh sat down in Assistant Warden Nancy Springer's office to read through the files on both Tamika Washington and Latitia Jones. Prison Guard Quinn brought them a message from Judge Abbruzza. They both sensed the judge's urgency. On the ride up to Bedford Hills, Goldberg questioned the legality of obtaining the psychiatrist's notes. Cavanaugh explained that the "relevance" of the files to the possible assassination attempt on Judge Abbruzza and in "the interest of justice and imminent danger" were the persuading factors in obtaining the subpoenas. Goldberg insisted the arguments sounded more like a "fishing trip" and was surprised the subpoenas were granted.

Both Tamika Washington and Latitia Jones were in a special psychiatric unit of Bedford Hills. Tamika's files indicated she dropped out of McKee Technical High School at seventeen. She was pregnant at the time and already had had a child at sixteen. The reports indicated she regarded men as objects, which could easily be replaced. The psychiatrist described her as having a mixed personality disorder. She showed no warmth or empathy toward any of her six children, five of whom were in foster care. There were strong indications that she worked for a drug dealer but no solid evidence. Witnesses at her trial stated that she used drugs and had a reputation of being promiscuous with young teenage boys. Her commissary account contained $75, hardly enough to hire a killer.

"What's the going rate for a hit?" Goldberg asked.

"Not sure, Morty. The last time I checked it was around $2,500. A judge should go for a lot more."

Tamika's counselor questioned her intellectual insight and her capacity to make good decisions. Her actions were often erratic and disorganized. She was self-centered, and Dr. Garland viewed Tamika's poor judgment a result of the hostile, prejudiced world she grew up in. The psychiatrist actually scribbled in a column of her notes, "Tamika is so cynical if she smelled flowers she would look around for a funeral." The words "paranoid," "suspicious," "hostile," "obsessed," "bitter," "biased," and "angry" were repeated in the notes they read. Tamika could be violent as witnessed in her throwing acid in the face of another inmate and in her brutal treatment of the ten-month-old child she was supposedly babysitting.

Latitia's records, however, showed a very different person. She graduated high school in Ohio and attended one year at a community college in Illinois, where she showed an interest in accounting. She just turned nineteen when she was first arrested for passing bogus checks. Since then she spent more than half her life in prisons across the country. Her arrest record was strictly for white-collar crimes. She forged checks. She tried to pass phony credit cards. She collaborated in manufacturing false credit cards. She delved into identity theft. Hers was a world of deception, trying to defraud. Each time she was caught, she cooperated fully with the authorities trying to avoid being sent into the general population of the prisons. She named names, gave up prisoners who smuggled things into the prisons, ratted on prison guards who did everything from taking pictures of the women in the showers to groping and having sex with them.

When sent into the general population, she threatened suicide and actually attempted it once. Before the Bedford Hills Correctional Facility, Latitia spent prison time in Florida, Illinois, Pittsburgh, Allenwood, and Kansas. She insisted the federal government placed a chip in her brain when she was imprisoned in Leavenworth. Her only outside calls from Bedford Hills were to a retired FBI agent who used her as his confidential informer. When Cavanaugh spoke with him, he said the information she provided him was always accurate but that he feared all the years she spent in prison had, in some way, affected her mental stability. He confirmed she never asked for favors, but she was extremely street-smart and worked the system like a skillful diamond cutter.

After studying the reports on both inmates, Cavanaugh and Goldberg were left with two questions. Was Tamika Washington, the inmate convicted of the brutal manslaughter of a baby, capable of killing the judge who sentenced her? And was Latitia Jones, the inmate who had spent more than half her life behind bars for fraud and misrepresentation, telling the truth in her accusations of Tamika's alleged threats against Judge Abbruzza?

The detectives called in Latitia Jones first. She was thin, bordering on anorexic. Her eyes jumped around the room. Her fingers tapped on the table. Her legs twitched. She wore prison-green pants and a maroon T-shirt but no cuffs or waist chain or leg irons. "Tell us about the threats you say Tamika Washington has made against Judge Abbruzza."

Her voice was squeaky, like a cross between Felix the Cat and Edith Bunker. "She said she was going to kill him."

"But why?"

"That's what I asked. I told her to relax and just do her time. What's done is done." She paused. Her eyes darted quickly around the room avoiding looking directly at either Goldberg or Cavanaugh. "She said she was going to kill him, to put a bullet in his head."

"How can she do that, Latitia? She's in prison."

"She told me she hired someone already in case she isn't granted her parole."

"How could she do that? She hasn't any money."

"Tammy told me she made a lot of money from being a mule for some drug dealer, and her moms is keeping it for her." She wiped her mouth and then added, "Her moms already paid a down payment to a dude named Aloysius Booth to do it."

Cavanaugh and Goldberg looked at each other.

"Why would she tell you this?" Cavanaugh asked.

"She trusts me. Her cell is across from mines, and we talk a lot. There ain't much else to do here."

"Is it true the government planted some kind of chip in your brain when you were in Leavenworth?"

Latitia's body tensed. She started to bite her lip. "I can't talk about that," she said. "I've been warned."

Goldberg looked at his notes. "It says here you have been in a number of different prisons over the years for basically the same thing — lying. Why should we believe you now?"

"Check my records," she screeched. "When I gave information as a CI, it was always correct. I don't lie about things like this. I've committed crimes. I don't deny it. But I can't just stand by and let someone plan to kill another human being with my knowledge. I felt I had to do something. I don't know this Judge Abbruzza, and I'm not looking for anything out of this. I just wanted to warn him so he could take some precautions."

"What's she going to do when she finds out you ratted her out?" Cavanaugh asked.

"I think she suspects already, but what's she going to do? I may not be as big as her, but I'm smarter. Besides, I couldn't live with my conscience if I didn't tell someone what she planned to do."

* * * *

Earle Nelson planned to leave early in the morning to eradicate any possible threats from Lloyd Arbuckle and then get back to completing his mission and crossing off the names on his list. But when he looked into the mirror and saw the jagged half-moon scar, the image of the priest at the scene of the first killing flashed back at him. It couldn't be Bennis. He had seen him get hit and fall. He had killed him. It couldn't be a ghost. And how could he now be a priest?

Curiosity ate at him. It was like an itch that wouldn't go away. He had followed Cindy Waters from a church in Tottenville. It was time to visit the church and satisfy his curiosity. Was the priest a ghost, or could it really be Jack Bennis, the man he shot and left for dead over thirty years ago?

Nelson fixed the broken headlight on his black Ford F-150 XLT. Soon he knew he would have to get rid of the truck, but not now. He used it in the drive-by shooting of Claudia Buenaventura. He needed it now to drive to Monticello, but first he would check out Our Lady Help of Christians and try to find that priest.

When he got to the church, Mass was going on. A scattered group of twenty to thirty parishioners, mostly bleach-blonde older women and a few gray-haired men, attended. An elderly woman with white hair, a lot of wrinkles, and an annoying smile met him at the church door and handed him a missal/hymn book.

"They're brand new," she whispered. "Father Kuffner just got them in this morning."

He grabbed the book and sat in one of the back pews. A bell sounded, and a priest started singing behind him. The parishioners joined in, and they sang "Amazing Grace." "How sweet the sound, / That saved a wretch like me . . . ."

The priest smiled as he started down the aisle acknowledging each of those present. But then he saw Nelson. Both men froze. A few seconds passed, and then the priest continued

toward the altar singing, "I once was lost but now am found, /
Was blind, but now I see . . . ."

As he began the Mass, Nelson felt as if the priest's eyes
focused in on him like a particle-beam weapon. "I confess to
Almighty God and to you, my brothers and sisters, that I have
greatly sinned in my thoughts and in my words, in what I have
done and in what I have failed to do," the tall priest said with
the congregation.

Nelson felt his blood pressure rising. It *was* Bennis. There
was no denying it. The voice, the face, the eyes. He was alive.
The son-of-a-bitch had somehow survived. Nelson threw the
missal/hymn book down with a thud and started to leave as
Bennis began, "Lord, have mercy on us . . . ."

On his way out, Nelson snatched a church bulletin in the
vestibule and checked the list of priests. There he was: Rev.
John Bennis, S.J. Nelson turned and locked eyes with Bennis
again. He mouthed, "F— you! I'll be back!" and left abruptly.

* * * *

When Nelson exited the church, Bennis came down from
the altar and walked to the rear of the church. There he picked
up the book Nelson had left and returned with it to the altar and
resumed the Mass. Initially, the small crowd wondered about
the priest's unusual action but quickly dismissed it as Father
Bennis proceeded with the Mass.

Greeting the exiting parishioners at the end of Mass, Father
Bennis smiled and called many by name. Only one parishioner,
Liam Gill, asked why he came down from the altar to get the
missal.

Bennis grinned and replied, "Yes, I guess that was a bit
unusual. Sometimes I do unexpected things. I'm glad to see
you were awake, Liam. Have a great day. God bless, and
please say hello to Margaret for me. I hope she's feeling better."

When everyone left, Bennis retrieved the missal from the altar and carefully carried it to the sanctuary, placed it in a plastic bag, and headed over to his brother's home.

Fran had left with the baby and the dog to visit her mother again. He went into his room and pulled a small Dutch Masters cigar box from under his bed. He took out a small balloon, filled it halfway up with cold water, and then lit a candle. He held the balloon over the candle's flame and watched soot accumulate on the bottom of the balloon. Then he lightly dusted the soot off the balloon and onto the missal. The smooth cover of the book soon revealed a good partial set of fingerprints. Bennis then took a piece of clear tape, placed it over the prints, and then pulled the tape away. He placed the tape on a clean white sheet of paper and faxed the prints with a note of explanation to a friend in the Central Intelligence Agency in Langley, Virginia, with whom he had served. He knew whose fingerprints they were, but he wanted to make sure. And more important, he wanted the last known address for former Sgt. Earle Nelson.

* * * *

Tamika Washington arrived at Assistant Warden Nancy Springer's office escorted by Prison Guard Quinn. Tamika's prison records indicated she weighed 225 pounds when imprisoned, but the body looking at Goldberg and Cavanaugh weighed less than 150 pounds. Her prison-green pants and maroon T-shirt looked three sizes too big for her. She stood in the doorway with no handcuffs or leg irons, glaring at both men with arms crossed and fists clenched. With her tangled web of dreadlocks, she resembled a skinny, angry black Medusa.

"Please, have a seat, Ms. Washington," Goldberg began.

"Who the hell you two, crackers? I ain't never seen you here before. Why the fuck you call me here? What you want?"

"We'd like to ask you a few questions," Goldberg said. "Please, have a seat . . . ."

"I ain't tellin' you shit!" she shouted.

Cavanaugh stood and pointed to the chair. "It's been a long day, Washington. We don't need your attitude. Let's cut straight to the chase. We hear you made some threats about the judge who sentenced you . . . ."

"This be bullshit! You ain't got no proof. I ain't said nothin'!"

"Please, have a seat . . . ."

"All you white motherfuckers be all alike. You tryin' to pin some shit on me. I ain't tellin' you shit!"

The prison guard put his hands on her shoulders and pushed her into the seat.

"Get your motherfuckin' hands off a me! I know my rights!"

"Listen, Washington, you made some threats," Cavanaugh said. "That is serious shit. We're not here for our health. If you intend to kill the judge, you're never going to get out of Bedford Hills. Tell us your side of the story."

"It be that little bitch, Sunflower. She be all sweet and nice to mines face, but she a low-life snitch." Tamika Washington slouched down in her chair, crossed her legs, and folded her arms. Her jaundice eyes glared up at him. "I ain't sayin' nothin' to you. You all tryin' to screw me. Youse think 'cause I be black you can take advantage of me!"

Cavanaugh looked at Goldberg. "Let's get out of here. If she wants to rot in jail, let her. Threatening to kill a judge is enough to add another ten years or more to her sentence. Her kids will be grandparents before she comes up for parole again."

He turned to Quinn. "Take her back to her cage. We'll file our reports. Maybe the warden will put her in the SHU for another two hundred days or so until we settle this business."

Goldberg shook his head sadly and rose with Cavanaugh.

Tamika straightened up in the chair. "Wait!" she said. "Where you goin'?"

"We're getting out of here, Washington. We don't need your shitty attitude."

She leaned forward, uncrossed her legs, and scratched her stomach. "Wait a minute. I don't want to go back to SHU. I'll go crazy in that place. I can't go back there again . . . . I can't . . . . You can't let them do that!"

"Talk to us, Washington. Tell us about the threats . . . ."

"I be talkin' smack . . . ." She started rubbing her stomach. "That be all. Sunflower believe me. She think she be so smart. I give her a line of shit, and she believe it. She an asshole, lying bitch!"

"Did you plan to kill Judge Abbruzza?"

"Hell, no! I hates the bastard, but I ain't no fool. I ain't gonna kill no one!"

"We understand you hired a killer named Aloysius Booth to kill the judge."

"There ain't no Aloysius Booth! I made the whole thing up."

"Why?"

Tamika sighed and ran her fingers through her tangled hair. Her yellow eyes glared at them. "If you ain't never been locked up, you ain't never gonna understand. There ain't nothin' to do here 'cept look at the walls and talk. That bitch, Sunflower, across the hall, she a nosy, sneaky bitch. She listen, so I tells her a whole lot of crap, and she believe it."

She started rubbing her stomach again. "I been having stomach pains, and they ain't done nothin' to fix it. They's tryin' to kill me here. I needs to get out. I don't needs to get more time."

"And why should we believe you?"

"Sunflower love to tell stories about everybodies. I loves to put her on and watch her swallow my stories. She think her shit don't stink. Everybodies know she a snitch. So I's give her a story, and she believe it. She the fool. I made the whole thing up!"

"We hear you gave your mother money to hire a killer."

"That be the story I's tell Sunflower. Where the fuck you think I get the money to pay a killer? I ain't got nothin'!"

"Did your mother hire a killer?"

"Are you out of your fuckin' mind? Where the fuck she gonna get the money? She been homeless for over a year 'cause she ain't got no money to even pay the rent!"

Cavanaugh and Goldberg questioned Tamika for another hour. She dropped some of her attitude, but the chip on her shoulder was always present. When she finally left with Prison Guard Quinn, she turned and shouted, "That cunt Sunflower be tellin' you a line of shit! You be the assholes if youse believes her!"

* * * *

Earle Nelson took his time driving to Monticello. He was in no hurry. He knew what he had to do, but seeing Jack Bennis that morning had thrown him off his game. He looked into the eyes of the man he killed over thirty years ago. He saw him get hit. He saw him fall to the ground. The group of Colombian soldiers was rapidly approaching. He saw them at the edge of the field. They fired on the helicopter as it soared into the air. Bullets whisked by him. He heard bullets ricocheting off the rotor blades and the tail boom as the copter banked away. How did Bennis survive? What was he doing now as a priest? It was his voice, his eyes, his name.

He drove at the speed limit along Route 17. It took longer than expected. But he wasn't in a hurry. He planned to get there in the dark. He turned off at Rock Hill to get something to eat. Driving down Main Street, he spotted Ken Decker's Irish Pub and parked. There was a crowd of twenty or so boisterous young people laughing as a Clancy Brothers' song played in the background. It was happy hour, and they looked like they had come straight from a tailgate party at a local game. Nelson sat at the bar and ordered a grilled shamrock wrap.

"You should try the leprechaun balls," a grizzled white-haired bartender offered as he wiped the bar with a dirty dishtowel.

"What are they?" Nelson asked.

"Deep fried jalapeno and cream cheese balls."

"What the hell. I'll go for it."

"Want frickles with that?"

"What?"

"Fried pickles. They're pretty good. All the kids like them."

"I ain't a kid. Get me a beer."

The bartender wiped his nose and pointed the dirty dishrag behind him at a row of twenty taps. "We got a lot of bottled beers too. Ale, port, larger, pilsner, you name it . . . ."

Nelson glanced at the menu of beers. "Give me that Victory HopDevil IPA on tap."

As the bartender sauntered away with his order, Nelson checked the large TV at the end of the bar. "And turn that soccer crap off and put on CNBC," he howled after him.

"Leave it alone, Vinny!" one of the tall college-aged kids shouted. "We're watching the game."

"Bullshit!" Nelson growled. "Go back to Mommy, kid. I want to check the stock market."

Three of the youths moved toward Nelson. They moved in unison acting like Tinkers, Evers, and Chance, but Nelson regarded them more like Moe, Larry, and Curly.

"Why don't you pick your ass up and go somewhere else, Grandpa?" asked the biggest one with hands on his hips.

"Where did you get that old army jacket, old man? The Salvation Army Thrift Shop?" a voice from the crowd called.

The whole bar started laughing.

Vinny, the bartender, came back with Nelson's beer. "Break it up, guys. Let the man eat in peace . . . ."

"Scarface here thinks he's a smart-ass, Vinny. We don't need his kind around Rock Hill!"

Nelson slowly sipped the India Pale Ale. It was sweet with a bitter finish and a trace of grapefruit and pine hops. He hesitated a moment as the three youths surrounded him.

"I hate to ruin a good beer," he whispered to himself and then spun around throwing the beer in the eyes of the biggest guy in the middle and smashing the glass across the face of the one on the left. The kid on the right stared for a second and then started to swing, but it was too late. Nelson came across with his backhand, hitting him in the neck. He fell gasping for breath. Nelson then kicked the biggest one in the knee cap and brought his knee directly up into his face. The one on the left shook glass from his hair and then felt himself being pulled forward into the edge of the wooden bar.

Nelson stood up and looked at the crumpled bodies on the floor in front of him. The Clancy Brothers were singing "Roddy McCorley" in the background to a silent group of college kids. One of the bodies by his feet moaned, and he kicked it fiercely in the head. The patrons in the bar were silent. Nobody moved.

"Anyone else wish to join the crowd?" Nelson asked.

The music ended. No one moved.

"Okay," he said. He turned to the bartender and said, "Thanks for the beer. Hold that shamrock wrap and leprechaun balls." He looked at the bodies at his feet. "You can give the frickles to my friends here." He gave each of the bodies a vicious kick to the head like an NFL player attempting a sixty-two-yard field goal.

He looked around at the standing crowd. "Tell your friends it's not nice to call strangers names," and then he walked calmly out of the pub, into his truck, and drove away.

* * * *

Fran, her baby, and her newly acquired dog traveled into Brooklyn to see her mother. She couldn't believe how calm the little dog was. Jack was right when he said it was trained, but it was more than "toilet trained" as he insisted or "housebroken" as his brother corrected. Within minutes, they realized it responded to "sit," "lie down," "stay," "roll over," and "paw." She brought him with her to see if it might help her mother in some way. Maybe, she thought, her mother would enjoy seeing and petting the dog like they did with service dogs in the hospital. She hoped it might help lift her mother's spirits.

Fran was more afraid of her sister Susan's reaction to the dog than her mother's. Would Susan throw her out of the house? Would she think Fran's idea was dangerous to her mother? The dog was friendly with Fran, Tom, Jack, and the baby, but how would it react to her mother? What if it bit her? Would it cause her more anxiety? Would she be afraid of it?

With little Stephen cradled in one arm and the little cockapoo on a leash in her hand, Fran held her breath and rang the bell of her mother's house. Susan answered and stood staring at Fran.

"May I come in?" Fran asked.

Susan's eyes lowered to look at the dog. It sat staring up at Susan with sad black eyes as if it were about to cry. She knelt and started to pet it. The dog's tail started wagging, and it nestled into Susan's arms. "It's so cute and gentle," Susan said. "What's its name?"

"We haven't quite decided yet. Father Jack suggested Bentley, and Tom is leaning toward Hershey. I like Mugsie. I thought you and Mom could help us decide on a name."

When they came inside, Fran let go of the leash, and the dog suddenly scampered away through the kitchen and the living room and headed straight to the family room. "Oh no!" Fran and Susan shouted together chasing after it. When they reached the family room, the dog had jumped into Elizabeth Muscatelli's lap, and she was smiling as she petted the little dog. Its tail was wagging frantically, and it was licking Elizabeth's hands. It asked no questions and made no judgments. It just wanted to be friends.

Fran and Susan looked at each other. Their mother was not threatened by the little dog. She petted it, and her anxieties and depression seemed to melt away. She was no longer staring blankly at the TV. She was actively engaging with another living being.

"Maybe we can get Mom to go for a walk with the dog," Fran said. "It will give her some exercise."

"You don't know how hard it is to get her out of bed in the morning and then get her washed and dressed. I doubt we can get her to go for a walk."

"Maybe we could try the backyard for a start. It's worth a try . . . ."

Fran moved over and took the dog's leash. "Mom, would you like to go with us to take the dog for a walk in the backyard?"

Elizabeth smiled and reached for the leash. "Come on, Bella," she said, getting slowly out of her chair. "Let's go for a little walk."

Fran looked at her sister and they both smiled. "Well, I guess we now have a name for Bella!"

Susan answered by putting her arm around her sister and hugging her. "And I guess we will be seeing more of each other — thanks to Bella! Welcome home, Fran."

* * * *

The full investigation team met in Judge Abbruzza's chambers for a debriefing. It was a standing-room-only situation. In addition to Judge Abbruzza, attending were his secretary, Kathleen Bradley; his full-time court attorney, Larry Logan, and five additional court lawyers; Senior Court Officer Wesley Walker and four assistant court officers; Court Attorney Bobby Lyons; Court Clerk Jason Key; District Attorney Leonard Ketch; Chief Assistant District Attorney Rob Ananis Jr.; Supreme Court Bureau Chief Susan Pemberton; five individuals from the Office of Court Administration; four detectives from the Persons' Squad; Police Officers Shanley, Morris, Rhatigan, and Hodges; and Detectives Cavanaugh, Goldberg, Sebastian, and Newhouser.

In evaluating the potential threat to the judge and other people involved with the trial of Tamika Washington, the discussion quickly got hot. "What about her defense attorney, Uriah Applebaum? Do we need to provide him with protection?" Assistant District Attorney Rob Ananis Jr. asked.

"Screw him!" Sebastian shouted. "He defends the scum of the earth. Let him deal with it himself."

"Inmate Washington is not scum, Detective! She is a human being," Officer Morris stated.

"Give me a break! Anyone who does what that bitch did to a ten-month-old is scum in my book. She deserves the chair!"

Cavanaugh watched the talk but remained silent. His thoughts were on his own son. They had almost lost him so many times. He recalled Dr. Parian advising Fran to have an abortion. Her pregnancy was ectopic and put both her and the unborn child at risk. But Fran refused. Some would say it was a miracle that both Fran and Stephen survived, but Cavanaugh didn't believe in miracles. He thought Dr. Badoura, the specialist they went to for a second opinion, was the reason. His brother didn't argue. He just said, "God works in mysterious ways."

Cavanaugh didn't really care. But Stephen still had a long way to go. He spent over two months in the neonatal intensive care unit of the hospital. There were so many tubes and monitors attached to him, Cavanaugh fought back tears every time he visited him. Now Stephen was home, and he got to hold him, feed him, and even change his diapers. Stephen's colic may have disturbed Cavanaugh's sleep pattern, but he was alive and the most precious gift Cavanaugh could imagine.

"She's a human being! She's not scum!" Morris insisted.

"What do you suggest, Cavanaugh? You're supposed to be the lead detective here," Senior Court Officer Wesley Walker asked.

"What?"

"Should we provide police protection for her defense attorney?"

"That's a decision beyond my pay grade, Walker. We need to inform him and ask him if he wants protection. I doubt he will. The final decision, however, will be the captain's and the D.A.'s."

He looked at the crime scene photos on the desk and wondered how anyone could treat a child that way and how anyone could defend someone who abused a child like that. He shook his head and then asked the group, "What do we have so far on the phone contacts?"

Individuals from the Office of Court Administration and detectives from the Persons' Squad reported on their background checks and interviews with the phone contacts made by Tamika Washington. They reported nothing conclusive. Sebastian and Newhouser reported on their interviews with Washington's family members.

Newhouser indicated her brother-in-law, James Blackman, Tamika's sister Ashkira's widower, was uncooperative. "He's a court officer in Manhattan, and he refused to talk to us. He told us to speak to his lawyer."

Sebastian added, "He was a real hard-on."

Shereece Campbell, the sister who worked for the South Carolina governor's office, was a secretary to the administrative assistant. She was sympathetic to Tamika's problems but claimed she had not seen her in three years and admitted her sister's manslaughter conviction was an embarrassment, which almost cost her her job. She claimed Tamika never mentioned any threats about anyone and mainly complained about her health. She never asked any questions about her children.

Violet Taylor, the fifth-grade teacher, made it a point to talk to Tamika at least once a week. She was concerned about Tamika's health and mental state. Violet said she never heard her voice any threats against anyone. Tamika's conversations were all self-centered, she said. Violet worried that Tamika was becoming paranoid as she insisted people were trying to kill her.

The friends Tamika called from prison confirmed her health concerns, but aside from that, they claimed she said she was doing well and even joked that prison was "a piece of cake."

"Did anyone get in touch with her mother?" Cavanaugh asked.

No one had. Sebastian said, "Ronald Biggs, the brother who's a correction officer on Riker's Island, claims the mother is homeless and bounces from sibling to sibling. He thought she was with one of her daughters, but they all claim they haven't seen her in months."

Cavanaugh leaned on Judge Abbruzza's desk. "We need to check all her relatives, including cousins and friends. Somebody must know where her mother is."

"How the hell do we do that?" Sebastian asked. "They all have different names and different fathers."

"It's called research, Sebastian. It's tedious and time-consuming. It's what detectives do. Goldberg will work with you."

"And what are you going to do?"

"Actually, I'm going to rule out a possible suspect. Did we get any more information on the vehicle that hit Cindy Waters?"

"From the tire threads and the broken glass at the scene, the Crime Lab thinks it's probably a Ford F-150 XLT. There was a report of a black one that was stolen in South Amboy a week ago. Could be the same one. We put an APB out on it just in case."

"Good work. What about the shooting in the Arlington Apartments? Any more information?"

"A few reluctant witnesses indicated it was a drive-by shooting. It could have been a dark truck, but no one could say definitely."

"What about bullet casings?"

"Some .357 Magnum cartridges were found at the scene, which would be consistent with the victim's wounds, but there were also a number of .22 and .32 shells found. Shooting isn't a particularly unusual occurrence at the Arlington Apartments. Ballistics is running a check as we speak."

Officer Shanley raised his hand. "There was also a shooting at a lawyer's apartment yesterday. Initial reports are a number of .357 casings were found at the scene. We've been searching for the shooter. We'll check them against the ones at the Arlington shooting."

"Somebody's loose out there killing people. We can't be sure if Tamika has already hired a killer or not. Let's find her mother. She could hold the answer. Although if she's homeless, I don't see how she would be able to pay a hired gun," Cavanaugh said. He looked around at the people in the room. "You're all doing a good job. I'm going to re-question that ex-cop who saw the hit-and-run. Officer Morris, you initially questioned him. I'd like you to come along with me. I know this isn't going to be easy, but as my mother used to say, 'If everything seems to be going well, you've probably overlooked something.'"

* * * *

William George Fuller visited the small bistro called Tranquility on Fifty-seventh Street and met with Jonny "Sweet Fingers" Fiore again. It was a short visit. He walked up to the piano player and said, "They're looking for her mother. Find her first."

* * * *

When Earle Nelson drove into Monticello, it was almost dark. His stomach continued to growl. Maybe Arbuckle would have something in his refrigerator, and he would eat after he killed him. He drove through the town and headed up a dirt road into a densely wooded area. His GPS indicated Arbuckle's cabin was down another dirt road off the one he was on. He parked his truck off the first dirt road and walked slowly up the next one. He checked his .357 IMI Desert Eagle semiautomatic. It was loaded. He had Arbuckle's .38 revolver in his pocket, but he preferred the .357. He had used it on Claudia Buenaventura, and he almost got Arbuckle with it at his apartment. This time he would make sure.

Slowly, he moved off the dirt road and weaved his way through the trees and bushes. It was dark now, and he could see a light on in the cabin ahead. It was a small dilapidated, one-room cabin. The only sound was the creaking of the trees and the rustle of leaves beneath his feet.

Through the trees, he saw Arbuckle sitting by the window. It was almost too easy. Nelson moved forward, his eyes on Arbuckle at the window.

Suddenly, he heard a snap, and a sharp pain gripped his leg. He screamed. Arbuckle jumped. He had a rifle in his hand. Nelson fired, hitting the window and shattering the glass. A bullet whizzed by him and wedged in the tree next to him. Nelson pulled himself behind the tree as another bullet narrowly missed him. He looked at his foot. It was caught in a bear trap. The bastard was ready for him.

Nelson pulled his leg closer. The trap had crushed the bone in his ankle. He put his gun down and pried the trap open. The sharp teeth of the trap dug into his leg, leaving bleeding puncture wounds around his ankle.

Then he heard Arbuckle open the door. He was coming for him. Nelson reached for his gun, but in the darkness, he couldn't locate it. He heard Arbuckle's heavy steps approaching. Nelson knew he was a sitting duck, but he couldn't move. His leg was crushed by the trap.

"You took my money, you took my gun, and you took my dignity!" Arbuckle screamed into the darkness. "Now I'm going to take your life!"

Nelson remembered. The gun! Arbuckle's gun was in his pocket. Quickly he grabbed it and fired blindly from behind the tree. He heard Arbuckle scream and something dropped. He kept firing until the .38 was empty. Then he listened. He heard only stillness.

He pulled himself up and looked for Arbuckle. But he wasn't there. In the light of the cabin, he saw Arbuckle's rifle lying in the grass where he dropped it. He felt around the tree until he found his Magnum and crawled to the rifle. Using the rifle as a crutch, he approached the cabin. When he got there, Arbuckle was gone again.

* * * *

Cavanaugh and Patrol Officer Andrea Morris knocked on Frank Stevenson's door. "What do you want?" Stevenson shouted from inside.

"Police," Cavanaugh answered. "We'd like to ask you a few questions."

"I already answered your questions. Now go away!"

Cavanaugh pounded on the door. Morris stepped back. "Open this door now, or I'll break it down!"

The door opened a couple of inches. Stevenson peered through the security door chain. "What do you want?" he slurred.

Cavanaugh kicked the door, breaking the chain and sending Stevenson sprawling backward. Morris gasped.

"Like I said, I want to ask you a few questions." He pushed the door open, motioned Morris to enter, and then closed the door.

"Detective Cavanaugh . . .," Morris began.

He put his finger to his lips and looked down at Stevenson. "They tell me you used to be a real hard-ass," he lied. "You know how this goes. We can do it the easy way or the hard way."

Stevenson looked up at the shattered door frame and then at Cavanaugh. "What do you want?"

"You saw the accident . . . ."

"It wasn't an accident," he insisted, sitting on the floor. "It was murder."

Cavanaugh reached down and pulled him up. "You're right. It was murder. Where can we sit down and talk?"

The three went to the kitchen and sat at a round Formica table. There was a half-empty bottle of Evan Williams Black Label bourbon and an empty glass on the table. "You like that stuff?" Cavanaugh asked.

"Yeah. Why?"

"I like Jim Beam Black," he said. "Do you have any?"

"Detective!" Morris started.

"Easy, Morris," Cavanaugh said. "You don't have to have any . . . ."

Stevenson looked at the petite young black policewoman with unblemished brown skin and beautiful, innocent dark-brown eyes.

"Shoot!" he said. "You're the cop who interviewed me . . . ."

"That she is, Stevenson, and we just want to clarify a couple of things."

"I told her everything I saw."

"Yeah, I know, but I want to ask you a couple of other things. You said the guy driving the vehicle wore an old greasy jacket."

"Yeah."

"You described it as olive, or tan, or gray with grease all over it."

"Yeah. I didn't have my glasses on. I told her that."

"Have you ever been in the service, Stevenson?"

"Yeah. I was a sergeant with the Ninety-eighth Infantry Division Reserves. We were called the Iroquois Division. We were headquartered in Rochester."

"I heard about you guys. I think my brother was in that unit," Cavanaugh lied again. "You were a top unit."

"Damned straight we were."

"Think back to that jacket you saw the driver wearing. Could it have been an army field jacket?"

Stevenson reached for the glass on the table and caressed it like a baby. He closed his eyes for a moment and then said, "Shit, you're right! I think it was an army field jacket!"

"I know you didn't get a good look at it, but think of the vehicle for a moment. Close your eyes and visualize it. Was it small or big?"

"Big."

"Do you think it was a car or a truck?"

"It was a truck. It had to be. It was too big."

"Good. One more question. Was the guy taller or shorter than the truck?"

Stevenson twisted the glass in his hands and frowned. Then he opened his eyes and said, "Bigger! He was a big guy, but I didn't see his face."

"That's okay, Frank. You did good. Thanks." He got up and took a $20 bill from his pocket and put it under the bottle of Evan Williams Black Label. "This is for the busted door frame, not for another bottle of booze. I heard about the gold watch the commissioner gave you. You were a good cop, and you still are. You've been a great help. Take it easy and go easy. If you ever want some help, there's a priest over at Our Lady Help of Christians named Jack Bennis you might look up. You can tell him Cavanaugh sent you."

* * * *

Earle Nelson staggered around the small cabin. The bone in his ankle was crushed. He studied it in the light of an oil lamp. It was bleeding from the teeth of the trap, but they were puncture wounds. The bone was not protruding. He knew what he had to do.

On the table he found a half-empty bottle of Johnny Walker Red, took a big swig, and then poured it over the wounds. Then he looked for something to wrap the ankle with. The room was a mess. Arbuckle was a slob. There were no first aid kits or tape. He took the pillow from the unmade bed and wrapped it around his ankle. Then he cut up pieces of the sheets and tied the pillow around the ankle. He worked quickly. The pain was intense.

Using a slat from the bed and a broken broomstick, he fashioned a splint. He used his belt, pieces of rope he found, and cut up more pieces of sheets and blankets and tied the splint around his chest, waist, upper thigh, knee, and calf. At the bottom of it, he placed the shorter part of the broomstick and lashed it to the bed board extending from under his arm and tied it to the longer part of the broomstick, which extended from his crotch. He tied his shoe to the boards and secured it to both sides of his improvised splint.

He knew manipulating the ankle was dangerous and could cause internal bleeding and nerve damage. The splint wasn't pretty, but it would have to do.

He felt his skin. It was cool and clammy. He felt fatigued, nauseous, dizzy. His breathing was rapid. Shock was setting in. "Get hold of yourself!" Nelson said aloud. He knew the routine. "Breathe." He took deep breaths and focused on the pain. He saw it trying to overwhelm him, and he embraced it. He looked out into the darkness. "Concentrate," he told himself. He had to get out of there. He saw two boxes of ammunition on the table, stuffed them into his pockets, and hobbled back down the hill toward his truck.

* * * *

On the drive back to the Tottenville Precinct, Officer Andrea Morris received a call from Detective Goldberg. The bullets found at Lloyd Arbuckle's apartment matched those that killed Claudia Buenaventura, the key witness in Tamika Washington's trial.

"Get Arbuckle's office address," Cavanaugh said. "We might as well pay him a visit."

Morris wrote down the address and asked Cavanaugh, "How come he didn't call you?"

"He knows me. I don't like cell phones."

"What? You've got to be kidding! Everybody has a cell phone."

"I don't."

"Do you text?"

"No way! You need a phone for that, don't you?"

"I don't believe you," she said. "You have to have a cell phone."

"I guess I have one. It's in the glove compartment. The captain made me get it, but I don't use it. It's for emergencies only." He blew through a red light on Hylan Boulevard and glanced at Morris. "People use these things too much. Fran, my wife, won't go out of the house without her cell phone. She's addicted to it. She's got one of those new ones that does everything but go to the bathroom for you. I'm a simple guy. I don't like talking to people unless I have something to say."

"You're a Neanderthal, Cavanaugh!"

"I prefer Renaissance man. When you see a generation of deaf people with enlarged index fingers, you'll see . . . ."

"They told me you were weird, but I didn't think this weird!"

"I prefer different." Cavanaugh smiled. "Now tell me how to get to this Lloyd Arbuckle's office."

It took them twenty minutes to get to Arbuckle's office on Bay Street. All the way, Cavanaugh complained about the traffic, the potholes, and the length of time it took to travel from one end of Staten Island to the other. When they reached Arbuckle's office, they found Kasia Kovalski, the cleaning lady, mopping the lobby floor.

"Excuse me, madam," Cavanaugh said. "We're looking for a Lloyd Arbuckle . . . ."

"You're not the only one," she replied and then held her mop like a spear in front of her. "You're not part of those 'friends' of his that played a prank on him, are you? That wasn't very funny. They should have more respect . . . ."

Cavanaugh flashed his badge. "No, madam, we're the police. We'd like to ask Mr. Arbuckle a few questions."

"Well, I'm glad you're here. I told him he should have called the police right away, but he said no. He said it was all a practical joke his college friends pulled on him."

"What did they do?" Officer Morris asked.

"When I came to work in the morning, Mr. Arbuckle was tied up in his chair — naked! He couldn't even call for help. His mouth was taped. I didn't think it was very funny, but he asked me not to call the police. He said it might be bad for all of us . . . ."

"Where can we find him?"

"He said he was going home. I haven't seen him since."

"You said we weren't the only ones looking for him. Who else was looking for him?"

"There was a man here this morning. He said he wanted Mr. Arbuckle to draw up a will or something for his mother."

"Can you tell us what this man looked like?"

"He was tall and he had short gray hair like Banacek."

"Who?" asked Officer Morris.

"He was a TV Polish American private eye played by George Peppard," Cavanaugh explained.

"Never heard of him."

"He was in the seventies. Probably before you were born."

Morris glared up at him. "Definitely before I was born!"

"Did the man look like Banacek?"

"No! No, sir! This man was big and mean-looking. He had an ugly long scar on his face."

"Do you remember what he was wearing?"

"Yes. He had one of those army field jackets you see in the movies."

"This guy is obviously not into fashion," Morris commented as she took notes.

"Were there any distinguishing marks on the jacket — like a name or an insignia?"

"In what?"

"Insignia — like maybe a patch or a logo on his sleeve . . . ."

"Yes," Kovalski said. "He had the same figure on his sleeve as he had on the card he gave me."

"He gave you his card?"

"Yes, sir. He wrote his cell phone on the back of the card and asked me to call him if Mr. Arbuckle came back, but he didn't."

"Do you still have the card?"

She fumbled inside her blouse and pulled out a business card. "Here it is," she said. "It looks like a black horse."

Cavanaugh and Morris studied the card. "It's the black knight," he said.

"Looks more like a chess piece to me," Morris commented.

"Back in the late '50s, way before you were born, there was a TV and radio show called *Paladin*. The knight was his symbol. He was a gunman, but a good gunman. His knight was silver. This one is black. Paladin's motto, however, was the same as what's written on this card, 'Have gun will travel.'"

"You lost me," Morris said.

"The number on the back is probably a burner phone, but look under the black knight — there's a web address."

"I know you don't know much about computer stuff, Cavanaugh, but that's not the same as a street address. I doubt it will help us locate him."

He nodded and turned to Kasia Kovalski. "May we keep this?"

"Sure."

"Here is my card. If either Mr. Arbuckle or the man who was looking for him comes back, call me immediately and stay away from them."

* * * *

Lloyd Arbuckle ran like a frightened wounded rabbit. He stumbled into trees, fell into briar bushes, tripped over rocks, and fell into a ravine. And he kept running. *Nelson is a maniac*, he thought. In his mind, he saw Nelson pursuing him. Why did he ever get involved in this? On he ran, not looking back.

But he was soon out of breath. His legs ached. His lungs felt like they were going to burst. He hid behind a red oak tree and slowly slithered to the ground. He was in no shape to keep running. He listened closely. The shooting stopped. He heard a stream nearby. Then he heard a low rattling noise somewhere near him. He felt something slither across his foot. It was a long timber rattlesnake. He froze. He closed his eyes and held his breath. Was he going to die in these woods?

The snake moved on, and Arbuckle lumbered up, clinging to the tree for support. He was going uphill. Beyond the ridge he knew there was a road. He had to reach the road and get help. He raised his arm to wipe moisture running into his eyes. His head stung when he touched it. He stared at his wet hand. The moisture was thick, thicker than sweat. He brought it to his lips. It was blood. He had been shot. He started to cry. But he stopped suddenly. Nelson might hear him. Maybe it was a flesh wound, he reasoned. It must be. He had to push on. If he got to the top of the hill, he could see other houses and maybe flag down a car and get help.

And so he moved on, straining with every step, hoping with every breath.

He was cut, scraped, bleeding, and exhausted when he finally reached the dirt road at the top of the hill. Below he saw the lights of the town of Monticello. There were stars in the black sky, but clouds hid the moon.

A red convertible with a group of teenagers singing and shouting to loud music came barreling over the hill. He jumped back to avoid being hit as an empty beer can flew by his head. "Damn kids!" he shouted.

A short time later, a gray Dodge Caravan appeared at the crest of the hill. "Help! Help!" he shouted waving his hands. "I've been hurt." The Caravan slowed down and then swerved around him.

"Shit!" he muttered giving the woman driving the van the finger. He started down the road toward the town and another car whizzed by him. Monticello looked so near and yet so far away. He was tired. He wanted to sit and rest, but he pushed on.

The lights of another vehicle came up the hill. He waved again at the blinding lights. "Help me! Please!" he screamed standing in the middle of the road and waving his arms. "I'm hurt! I need help . . . ."

The vehicle slowed and came to a complete stop. Arbuckle ran excitedly to it. The driver rolled down the window. Arbuckle smiled. "Thank you so much," he said.

"No problem, fat boy," the driver said.

Arbuckle looked up at Earle Nelson and the .357 Magnum leveled at his head. "No problem at all," Nelson smiled and fired directly between Arbuckle's eyes.

Arbuckle's head exploded, and he flew backward to the side of the road. Nelson looked at him for a moment and fired two more rounds into his lifeless body before driving calmly away.

* * * *

Book IV

Coincidence like ancient egg—leave unpleasant odor.

—*Charlie Chan in Murder over New York*

Goldberg picked up the news bulletin on his iPhone. "Lloyd Arbuckle, Staten Island attorney, was found shot to death on a dirt road in Monticello near his summer cabin. Robbery ruled out as Mr. Arbuckle had over $20,000 in cash on him." He called the local Monticello sheriff for more details.

"We found indications of a possible gun fight around his cabin," Sheriff Phineas Gage stated.

"What caliber, Sheriff?"

"Well, they vary. We found some .30-06 casings in the grass and .38 and .357 shells around a tree near the cabin. There was an indication someone or something may have been caught in a bear trap. There were traces of fresh blood on the trap and in the cabin."

"Did you test for blood type and prints in the cabin?"

"Listen, Detective, I'm pretty much a one-man show up here. One of my deputies ran over his foot with a lawn mower and is in the hospital. Another deputy just ran off with the town tramp. He does this every once in a while. I expect he won't be back till the end of next week. The only other guy I got to help me is the mayor's son-in-law, and he can't find his way out of a closet. When the three of them are here, it's like Groucho, Harpo, and Chico. I called the state troopers in to assist. If you want more info, get your ass up here or speak with the troopers."

"One other thing, Sheriff. You said somebody may have been caught in a bear trap. Were there any signs of that on Arbuckle or in the cabin?"

"Arbuckle had three shots in him. One between the eyes and two to the chest. It looked like he had a flesh wound to the head but nothing on his ankles. The cabin looked like it had been torn apart. Sheets and blankets were torn up, liquor was all over the place, and even the bed was broken."

Whoever the killer is, Goldberg thought, *he's hurt and he's improvising.* "Were there any other strange incidents in the area that you can think of?"

"Well, yeah. As a matter of fact, around 5:00 p.m. there was a fight in a bar down the road a piece in Rock Hill. Three college kids got beat up pretty bad."

"Any arrests?"

"Nope. They claim some old army guy started it and then just walked out."

Earle Nelson, Goldberg thought. *He's hurt and is going to need help.* "Were there any break-ins or robberies reported in the area?"

"Well, yeah, now that I think of it, there was a report a little while ago that a veterinary office over in Merriewold Park on Route 42 was broken into. Nothing much was taken except some bandages and splints. Do you think that may have something to do with the murder?"

"Don't know, Sheriff, but if you don't mind, I'd like to come up and look around."

"Be my guest, son. I could use all the help I can get."

* * * *

The address Fr. Jack Bennis received from his contact in Langley for Earle Nelson proved to be an abandoned Maritime Museum on Bay Street. Although the museum was closed,

Nelson rented an apartment directly above the museum. Bennis left his Roman collar at home and wore a less conspicuous darkblue hoodie, black sweat pants, and sneakers.

He tried the front door, but it was locked. The back door was also locked, but Bennis used an old plastic hotel card from a Miami hotel he once stayed at to open it. He walked around the downstairs. Dust covered many nautical instruments and various radar and communication devices.

A stairwell led to a second floor. The stairs creaked as he walked slowly up. It was dark and smelled of mildew. He wished he had brought a flashlight. At the top of the stairs, he stopped. A small landing led to one door. It was partially open. The low sound of a radio came from inside. He checked the door frame. There at the top of the door he felt a simple paper match. Nelson may have left the door open, but he would be able to see if anyone entered the room when he wasn't there.

Slowly, Bennis opened the door. The room was dark. The shades had been drawn. The low droning voice of a newscaster came from the radio in the corner. He waited until his eyes adjusted to the darkness. He heard the slow drip, drip, drip of a faucet. He moved cautiously into the room, hugging the wall, trying in an effort to avoid the sound of his footsteps on the creaky floor. His leg bumped against a table. He heard a cup roll and fall onto the hardwood floor. If there was anyone else in the room, they would know he was there. He ran his hand along the wall for the light switch and turned it on.

The light blinded him for a moment. Then he looked around. The room was small and dirty. Foulsmelling dishes were stacked in the sink. Old newspapers were scattered around the room. A soiled sheet and pillow lay abandoned on a faded red and blue flowered couch. A porcelain bowl filled with ashes and cigarette butts and an empty crushed pack of Lucky Strikes lay next to a pad and pencil on a table and a plate of half-eaten pizza, a rotting apple, and an empty bottle of Harpoon beer.

Aside from chipping yellowed paint and exposed sheetrock, most of the walls were bare — except for one. The wall across from the table was covered with photos. One stood out immediately. It was Judge Carlo Abbruzza coming out of his home. Bennis recognized his photo from the news. He hadn't changed much since Bennis used to tease him in grade school.

But what was Judge Abbruzza's picture doing on Nelson's wall? He moved closer. He studied the pictures carefully. There, coming out of her house on Barnard Avenue, was Cindy Waters walking her little dog. He didn't know the other people in the other photos. But Bennis was now sure — Earle Nelson had something to do with Cindy's death.

On the floor next to the couch, he found a business card. He recognized the black knight symbol immediately. It was the symbol of his old unit. It was also the symbol of Paladin, "a knight without armor in a savage land." Nelson was always a gun for hire. Did he deliberately kill Cindy Waters? But why was the judge's picture on his wall? And whose were the other photos on his wall? And why?

Suddenly, he got a strange feeling. It was as if someone were watching him. He froze and listened. The drip, drip, drip of the faucet seemed magnified. The radio noise faded into the background. He concentrated. There was someone else in the room.

* * * *

"Move and you're dead!" a voice at the door said. "Who are you and what are you doing here?"

Bennis looked for something to throw or defend himself with.

"I said don't move. Who are you?"

Bennis put his hands on his head. "I'm unarmed," he said.

"Turn around slowly. Keep your hands where I can see them."

In his mind, Bennis calculated how far it was to the door. Slowly he turned looking for something. He spotted the cup on the floor. If he kicked the cup in the direction of the voice, he might have a chance.

"Don't even think about that cup," the voice warned. "I'd have two slugs in you before it hit the ground. Now turn around."

Bennis turned and looked into the eyes of his brother.

"What the hell are you doing here, Jack?" Cavanaugh shouted.

"I was looking for Earle Nelson."

"I told you to leave this alone."

"You don't understand, Thomas. This Nelson is not a good guy. He's dangerous."

"No shit, Tracy! How many times do I have to tell you to leave police matters to the police? I almost shot you!"

Bennis looked over Cavanaugh's shoulder and saw Police Officer Morris. "Look what I found," he said, pointing to the wall. "Nelson has photos of people on the wall. One of them is Cindy Waters, and another is Judge Abbruzza."

Cavanaugh lowered his gun and walked into the room. "That's a picture of D.A. Ketch. I don't know who the others are."

Morris looked at the pictures and pointed. "The one on the left is Police Officer Reilly. I worked with Kevin in the 120 for a few months. He's a good guy. He's looking forward to retiring in a few months. The one on the right is the Uriah Applebaum, the defense attorney. The other faces look familiar, but I don't recall their names. I think one of them is the D.A."

"Look at the pad on the table, Thomas."

Cavanaugh looked. "It's blank!"

"No. Watch. I saw Charlie Chan do this in a movie." Bennis took a pencil and gently rubbed it over the paper, revealing the name Lloyd Arbuckle and his address.

"Jack, you shouldn't be here."

"Look over there. He left a box of .357 Magnum bullets. He's trouble, Thomas. We need to stop him."

"No, Jack. You don't need to stop him. You are out of this. This is a police matter. Leave it to us."

"I know this guy. I served with him. He is a cold-blooded murderer. He enjoys killing. I can help you catch him."

"You can butt out of this and you will, or I promise I will arrest you on some charge."

"I saw him this morning," Bennis said. "He came to my church to see me. He and I go back a long way. I'm the one who gave him an ugly scar on his face. He's going to come after me again, and I am going to be ready for him."

"Jack, please, just leave this alone. You are really screwing this thing up. How did you find this address anyway?"

"I still have contacts in the CIA who owe me some favors."

"Well, I think you have just about run out of favors, brother."

Bennis raised his hands. "Okay, I'll leave. But you may want to check the waste basket over by the sink. I think I spotted a paystub in there. Maybe it will tell you where he works?"

"Get out of here, Jack! Now! We've got a lot of work to do."

Walking toward the door, Bennis looked at Officer Morris and said, "And who is this beautiful, young partner of yours? She's a lot prettier than Goldberg!"

"Jack," Cavanaugh shouted, "if you don't leave now I will shoot you myself!"

* * * *

The police had little success locating Tamika Washington's mother. It was an alert MTA track inspector named Marcus Anderson who found her. He found her body nestled in a cable drop space between Fifty-first and Fifty-third Streets on the IRT Lexington Avenue Line. The cause of death appeared to be a drug overdose. In addition to a number of rats nibbling on the body, first responders found an empty hypodermic needle containing a mixture of heroin and fentanyl, a powerful painkiller usually used for cancer patients. Based on body temperature, body stiffness, and an examination of the deceased's eyes, the initial investigators estimated she had been dead for less than three hours.

* * * *

When Cavanaugh received the news of Tamika Washington's mother's death and Lloyd Arbuckle's, he asked all the people involved in the investigation to meet in Judge Abbruzza's chambers. A few hours later, Kathleen Bradley, the judge's longtime secretary; his full-time court attorney, Larry Logan; Senior Court Officer Wesley Walker; Assistant Court Officers Juan Adams, Auguste Ciparis, and William Kemmler; Court Attorney Bobby Lyons; Court Clerk Jason Key; District Attorney Leonard Ketch; Chief Assistant District Attorney Rob Ananis Jr.; Supreme Court Bureau Chief Susan Pemberton; three men and two women from the Office of Court Administration; four detectives from the Persons' Squad; Police Officers Shanley, Morris, Rhatigan, and Hodges; and Detectives Cavanaugh, Goldberg, Sebastian, and Newhouser all convened in the judge's chambers.

Cavanaugh called the meeting together. "So, ladies and gentlemen, let's look at what we have so far. A tip from a prison inmate that another inmate is planning to kill Judge Abbruzza . . . ."

"But the letter comes from a woman in for fraud who will do anything to avoid going into the general prison population," Sebastian said.

"True, but from all reports, the stories she's told in the past were factual. The information she has given in the past has always been credible."

"It's a tough call, but she may be telling the truth," Court Attorney Larry Logan commented.

"Or may not!" District Attorney Ketch stated.

"Then we have the alleged perpetrator of the threat. She's in prison for brutally abusing a child and was convicted of manslaughter. Is she capable of killing the judge who sentenced her?"

"She's shown herself to be violent even in prison, throwing homemade acid in another inmate's face!" Newhouser said.

"True, but she admits to saying stuff about the judge, but she claims it was just prison BS. Do we believe her?"

"She's capable of murder, and she does hate the judge," Senior Court Officer Walker stated.

"But how can she kill him if she's locked up?"

"Supposedly, she has money from drug dealing, and her mother has already paid a down payment to some guy named Aloysius Booth, who we can't find."

"Yeah, but if she had money, why would her mother be homeless for over a year for not paying the rent?"

"If we'd found the mother earlier, we could have asked her, but she turns up dead from a lethal heroin overdose in the hallowed tunnels of our subway system," Sebastian added.

"So where are we?" Cavanaugh asked. "Tamika has relatives who work in the legal system. They could possibly be involved, but we have no proof."

District Attorney Ketch spoke up. "That's the problem. Not enough credible evidence. Without evidence, there is no reason to continue this investigation. It's all hearsay."

"So, Counselor," Cavanaugh began, "are you willing to put that in writing just in case the judge does take a bullet?"

"There's the hit-and-run victim who was the foreman at Washington's trial and the key witness who was shot," Shanley stated.

"They could be coincidental," Ketch said.

"My brother saw a guy named Earle Nelson at the scene of the first killing, which, by the way, an ex-cop says was intentional . . . ."

"Your so-called witness, Cavanaugh, is a drunk. I read his statement. He had been drinking and didn't have his glasses on. A jury would throw that statement out in two shakes of a hopped-up belly dancer!"

"I guess you should know about that, Counselor!"

"What are you inferring by that remark, Cavanaugh?"

"The point is this Earle Nelson is a person of interest. We found a box of .357 ammo in his apartment, and we found the name of a lawyer named Lloyd Arbuckle scribbled on a notepad."

"As I recall, Cavanaugh, your brother contaminated the scene by his presence in the apartment. For all I know, he could have planted the name and the ammo."

"Well, Counselor, it turns out old Lloyd Arbuckle had a visitor who matches the description of Nelson, and then Arbuckle winds up shot to death on a dirt road in Monticello."

"So what does that have to do with the judge?"

"The slugs found in Arbuckle's apartment match those found in Claudia Buenaventura, the key witness at Washington's trial, who was shot to death the other night."

"So it looks like this Nelson guy may have killed Arbuckle and Buenaventura. Still no connection to the judge."

"The letter Judge Abbruzza received indicated the inmate was going after everyone connected with her conviction. Now we have the jury foreman and the key witness both dead. Counselor, you just may be the next on the list!"

"Is that a threat, Cavanaugh?"

"I don't make threats, Counselor. I'm just telling it like it is. He had your picture taped to his wall along with Waters, Buenaventura, the judge, and a few others. You want to lift the protection on the judge, that's your call. All I'm asking is you give us another week to check things out."

"You have forty-eight hours, Cavanaugh. If you don't find something by then, we are pulling the protection and writing this off as prison gossip."

District Attorney Ketch turned abruptly and headed for the door.

"Thanks, Counselor," Cavanaugh called after him. "In the meantime, I suggest you watch your back too!"

* * * *

The meeting continued with different opinions and suggestions bouncing around like a pinball machine. Various conspiracy theories began to grow like wildflowers.

"Why is the D.A. so set against continuing the investigation?" Court Clerk Jason Key asked. "There's obviously enough proof to continue the investigation."

"He's looking for the judge's job!" Bobby Lyons stated.

"How can you say that?" Susan Pemberton asked. "The district attorney is an honorable man."

"Susan, we all know he's one of the most ambitious, conniving people in this place!" Rob Ananis shouted. "He'd run over his mother if it meant he would get a promotion."

"That might be a poor choice of words, Counselor, in view of Cindy Waters's death," Cavanaugh suggested.

The discussion grew into heated debates and some name-calling as it grew later and later. One by one, members of the team excused themselves or quietly filtered out of the judge's chambers. It was almost midnight when Cavanaugh looked around and told Court Officers Walker, Adams, Ciparis, and Kemmler, Judge Abbruzza, his secretary, Court Attorney Lyons, and Assistant D.A. Ananis, and Supreme Court Bureau Chief Pemberton to go home and get some rest. "Are you sure, Detective?" Walker asked. "If you need anything, we are here to help."

"That's okay, Walker. We're winding up here anyway."

When they left, he looked around. Only Goldberg, Sebastian, Newhouser, and he remained.

"I thought that big black guy Walker would never leave," Sebastian said. "He looked like he was afraid he was going to miss a trick."

"He seemed pretty interested in learning what was going on. Almost too interested," Newhouser observed.

Cavanaugh stretched. "I'm tired like everyone else. I know it's late, but I wanted to speak with you alone. You are the only guys I can really trust. These people turn on each other like cats. I need you to do a few more things tonight."

"Oh shit! What now, Cavanaugh?" Sebastian moaned.

"Our best lead so far is this Earle Nelson. We found an old paystub in his apartment from the Staten Island Hilton Inn, where he apparently works part-time. I'm going over there tonight to see if I can find something on him.

"Newhouser, get word to the 120 down the block that one of their patrolman . . . ." He paused and checked his notes. "Tell them we found Patrolman Kevin Reilly's photo on a murder suspect's wall. We don't know for sure what it means, but he should be made aware of it.

"Goldberg, you take Sebastian with you and go up to Monticello and check the crime scene. Maybe there's something there that the local bumpkins missed."

"How about we go in the morning?" Sebastian suggested. "This has been a long day, and I'm tired."

"You heard the D.A. We only have forty-eight hours before he pulls the plug. The clock is ticking. Let's find something to help us catch this guy and eliminate the threat to the judge. If I'm right, a lot of lives depend on us."

* * * *

Police Officer Kevin Reilly finished his tour of duty at the 120th Precinct and headed home on the Staten Island Rapid Transit. He hated driving anymore. He used to drive the family on vacations to Virginia Beach, Cape May, the Outer Banks, Myrtle Beach, Williamsburg, and even Niagara Falls. But he was tired now. Tired of trips, of driving, of work, of almost everything. In three more months he would file his papers and maybe work part-time in his son's garage in Matawan, New

Jersey. The job of a cop wasn't what it used to be, but then again, he realized, nothing really is.

Reilly walked down to the St. George platform to catch the 12:36 a.m. train to Tottenville. He went to the first car as he usually did. At this time of night, the car was almost always empty. He sat by the window and looked around. There was only one other passenger sitting in the back of the car. Reilly closed his eyes and listened to the click, click, click of the train as it left St. George and picked up speed.

He felt the train slowing down at Tompkinsville. No one got on. He looked around. There was only that other passenger behind him. He looked homeless. The train supplied a safe, warm place to ride back and forth for a while.

Reilly closed his eyes again and drifted off as the train passed the Stapleton, Clifton, and Grasmere stations. Since his wife's death, things had changed. He was coming home to an empty, lonely house. He kept her clothes in the closet just to keep her scent alive for him. She was the good one in the family. She raised the kids, cooked the meals, did the laundry, and was his best friend. The world was a lonely, desolate place without her.

He pitched forward as the train skidded into the Old Town station. No one got on. He yawned and turned to check the homeless man. He was still there but had moved a few seats closer. It looked like his foot was bandaged. Maybe he was headed for the emergency room at the hospital.

Reilly closed his eyes again. "To sleep, perchance to dream — ay there's the rub . . . ." Why did Hamlet's line come back to him? Was it his dream or his fears? He had played Hamlet a long time ago with the Shakespeare Theatre Players. Once he thought of becoming an actor, but his father had been a cop and his grandfather and two of his uncles. Acting was a hobby. "Real men don't act," his father had pestered him. Maybe after retiring, he would join the theatre group at the church. It would give him something to do, something to fill the void.

"Excuse me, sir," a voice behind him muttered over the roar of the speeding train. Reilly smelled alcohol on the man before he turned. It was the homeless man.

He looked up. "What can I do for you?"

"Does this train go to Paradise?"

"What? You're drunk, pal. You're on the Staten Island Rapid Transit. The last stop is Tottenville."

The man looked disheveled, dirty, and in pain. There was a large scar on his face.

"Sorry, Officer Reilly," the man said. "But this is your last stop."

He pointed a .357 Magnum at the off-duty cop as Reilly reached for his own gun. But Reilly was too late.

Earle Nelson gently positioned Reilly's head against the window to look like he fell asleep and limped off the train at the next stop.

* * * *

Cavanaugh approached the Hilton Garden Inn with deep concerns and reservations. The tip about Earle Nelson came from his brother. Maybe Nelson was a bad guy, but that didn't mean he was involved in the threat to Judge Abbruzza. Maybe the D.A. was right. Maybe chasing after Earle Nelson was a diversion. It wasn't helping them get any closer to discovering whether or not the threats were valid. Maybe this hunt for Earle Nelson was a stupid waste of time. He was here because of his brother's persistent suggestions he check out Earle Nelson. Nelson's listed address had not directly connected him to the threats on the judge although the circumstantial evidence was rapidly increasing. The photos of victims in his apartment were incriminating. But was Nelson being set up? The pay stub found in his apartment listed him as working at a new nightclub called "Above" at the Hilton Garden Inn. From his brother's description of him, Cavanaugh thought Nelson might be a bouncer.

Near the building, he saw a long line of young people snaking around barriers to get in. *This is definitely a stupid waste of time*, he thought. He fought the urge to stop and check IDs. Some didn't look old enough to drive, let alone old enough to drink.

Walking straight to the front of the line, he ignored the comments from the anonymous crowd in the dark. "Hey, old man, there's a line here!" "You're on the wrong line, Pops!" "Paddy Noonan's band is playing at the Old Bermuda Inn." He smiled, remembering his mother's warning to never underestimate the power of stupid people in large groups.

Cavanaugh flashed his badge at the door and saw a big man in a tuxedo checking identification at the elevator. The man looked up and stopped the line.

"Detective Cavanaugh, how are you? What can we do for you?"

"I recognize the face," Cavanaugh said, "but from where?"

"I'm Al Teutonico. I teach social studies at Garfield Academy."

Like the man who spit into the wind, it all came back to Cavanaugh. Teutonico was a teacher who had been a suspect in the Lex Talionus killings. He stared at him. "What are you doing here?" he asked.

"Moonlighting! Teachers sometimes need to supplement their salaries. We have another baby on the way."

"Come on," a voice from the line called out. "Move it. We want to get in!"

"They're an antsy bunch," Cavanaugh said.

"Pretty much like an unruly class at times. What can I do for you, Detective?"

"I'm looking for an Earle Nelson. I've been told he works here."

"Used to. Haven't seen him in about a week."

"Do you know where I can find him?"

The line started pushing forward. Teutonico held out his hands. "Settle down, people!" He turned to Cavanaugh. "I don't know much about him to be honest. He was a little scary and kept to himself. You might try Bob Boyd, the bartender upstairs. He spoke with Nelson more than I did."

"Thanks."

Cavanaugh waited for the next elevator and squeezed in with a group of young men and women who must have believed there is no such thing as too much perfume or after-shave lotion. When the elevator stopped, he gasped for air and was propelled into a huge room with glowing lights, loud music, and a mass of people.

He weaved his way through the mingling bodies. He had never been here before, but he recognized the scene. The lovers . . . the wanna-be lovers . . . the nervous first timers . . . the desperate . . . the ambitious . . . the cocksure . . . . As the evening advanced, the noise would increase, the dreams intensify, and the illusions grow. Some would get lucky; some would just get drunk.

Behind a huge marble bar running almost the length of the room, he saw three bartenders frantically moving back and forth from customer to drink, to cash register, to cleaning glasses. There was no time for talk like in the old days. This was business, and the three men behind the counter were working their asses off.

This wasn't like the old Westerns where John Wayne would saddle casually up to the bar. Cavanaugh had to push and shove to find an opening and then wait for the bartender to acknowledge him.

"What can I do for you, buddy?" the bartender finally asked.

"I'm looking for Bob Boyd."

The bartender stared at him and smiled. "Cavanaugh, you old son of a bitch, how are you?"

It took a few seconds, but then Cavanaugh recognized him. Bob Boyd was a patrolman in the Brooklyn precinct Cavanaugh had worked in before his transfer to Staten Island.

"What are you doing here?" Cavanaugh asked.

"Moonlighting. The tips are great." Boyd grabbed an empty glass from a man with diamond studs in his ears and some kind of Asian writing tattooed on his neck.

"Another Sierra Nevada?" Boyd asked.

"If you have any left," Diamond Studs smirked.

When Boyd returned with the beer, Diamond Studs threw a $10 bill on bar and vanished into the crowd.

Cavanaugh's mouth dropped. "Ten bucks for a beer?"

"Actually, it's only $8.50. The rest is tip."

Cavanaugh shook his head. "I'm looking for a guy who's supposed to work here. His name is Earle Nelson."

"Haven't seen him in a week or so."

"What's the word on him?"

"He's big. Strong. Older. Maybe in his late forties, early fifties. Ex-army ranger. Tough. Has a temper. Pretty full of himself."

"Do you know where I can find him?"

"He used to tell me stories about great cheeseburgers at Duffy's. You might try there." Boyd wiped the Italian marble bar and looked around. "Hey, Cavanaugh, how about a beer? It's karaoke night. You might like to stick around."

A girl with pink hair, a gold nose screw, multiple ear piercings, and a tattoo of a bar code on her arm bumped against Cavanaugh, smiled, and asked for Sex on the Beach.

Cavanaugh took a deep breath. "Thanks, but no thanks, Bob. Karaoke, as far as I'm concerned, is Japanese for tone deaf, and my wild oats are now shredded wheat."

Boyd grinned.

"Anything else you might be able to tell me about Nelson?"

"Yeah. He was acting strange the last time I saw him. He said he had a job that was going to pay him big time. Wouldn't tell me what it was, but I got the feeling it wasn't good."

Cavanaugh took out his card and placed it on the bar. "Thanks. If you hear anything else, give me a call."

"Right," Boyd said, and then with both hands on the bar, he added, "Watch your back, Cavanaugh. Nelson can be dangerous."

* * * *

The murder of Police Officer Reilly made all the headlines in the morning. Patrolman Reilly's outstanding police record included awards for meritorious police duty, community service, a commendation for integrity, a medal for valor, and the police combat cross. He was three months short of retirement. Fellow officers had nothing but praise for Officer Reilly. Both the mayor and the police commissioner urged anyone with information about the killing to come forth immediately.

It was Jim Coyle, an investigative reporter for the *New York Post*, who, in a later edition, first reported on the connection of Kevin Reilly to Cindy Waters and Claudia Buenaventura. He wrote:

> Recent death threats to Criminal Judge Carlo C. Abbruzza, an unnamed source claims, are linked to the hit-and-run death of Cindy Waters, the drive-by shooting of Claudia Buenaventura, and the murder of Police Officer Kevin Reilly. All were involved in the arrest of Tamika Washington, now serving a ten-year sentence in Bedford Hills Correctional Facility for Women in upstate New York for manslaughter.
>
> Ms. Waters was the foreperson of the jury that convicted Ms. Washington; Ms. Buenaventura was the key witness at the trial; and PO Reilly was the arresting officer. Judge Abbruzza was the trial judge who sentenced Tamika Washington.
>
> At least three death threats have been received by Judge Abbruzza indicating Tamika Washington has hired a hit man to kill the judge and all those associated with her conviction. According to sources, Supreme Court Bureau Chief Susan Pemberton and

Judges Russell Terito and Joseph Mancusi have called for Judge Abbruzza to voluntarily step down. Judge Abbruzza and District Attorney Ketch were unavailable for comment.

Meanwhile, in the St. George Ferry Terminal, police teams studied surveillance discs of the station. They observed what looked like a homeless man entering the same train car as Reilly did. The man's face was hidden from the camera, but he walked with a limp, and his foot was bandaged.

"It's him!" Cavanaugh exclaimed. "Same army jacket and a bandaged foot. It's Earle Nelson!"

* * * *

When Goldberg and Sebastian arrived in Monticello, they visited the crime scene and Arbuckle's cabin. The state troopers were thorough. They confirmed what the detectives suspected. Arbuckle was killed with a .357 Magnum. Fingerprints around the cabin matched Arbuckle's and Nelson's.

Sheriff Phineas Gage showed them the $20,000 in new bills that was found stuffed in Arbuckle's pockets. "I honestly don't know what to do with this money," he said.

"Hold it for now," Goldberg advised. "I'm sure someone will come along to claim it. Was there anything else found at the scene?"

"Well, there was a crumpled piece of paper in his shirt pocket with some writing on it. Haven't had time to check it out."

"Can we see it?"

When the sheriff showed them the paper, both Goldberg and Sebastian smiled. "I guess this trip wasn't a waste of time," Sebastian admitted.

Goldberg read the words on the bloodstained paper aloud, "Cindy Waters — jury foreman, Claudia Buenaventura — witness, Kevin Reilly — arresting officer, Uriah Applebaum

— defense attorney, Rob Ananis — prosecuting attorney, Leonard Ketch — district attorney, Carlo Abbruzza — criminal judge."

* * * *

As soon as District Attorney Ketch learned about the names found in Arbuckle's pocket, his attitude changed. The mayor and the police commissioner were informed, and each person on the list was provided twenty-four-hour protection as an all-points bulletin went out for Earle Nelson.

"He shouldn't be too hard to find. He has an injured leg," Ketch said, standing between the two police officers assigned to protect him.

"He's resourceful," Cavanaugh warned. "And he seems to be always one step ahead of us."

"The whole police department is gunning for him, for god's sake! Just find the bastard!"

News reporters and TV cameras were all over the courthouse. Cavanaugh had to fight his way through them to get to see Judge Abbruzza.

"How are you holding up, Carlo?" he asked.

"It's tough, Tom. The family is upset. The kids are harassed at school . . . ."

"We'll find this guy, Carlo, don't sweat it."

"It's easy for you to say! You don't know how it feels!"

Cavanaugh remembered his mother saying one needed to know a man a long time before he could catch a glimpse of their soul. He thought back to the days and weeks of worrying about Fran and her ectopic pregnancy and then the angst of standing by as doctors and nurses worked to save little Stephen.

"I got a note this morning, Tom. It was slipped under my door. It said if I resign immediately and transfer Tamika Washington's case to another judge for review, the killings will stop."

Cavanaugh read the note. It was composed of words cut out of the paper and pasted together. "Has anyone else seen this note?"

"No."

"Who was around when you entered your office?"

"The usual. Officer Walker, my secretary Kathleen, my court clerk Jason Key, Court Attorney Larry Logan, and Officer Adams . . . ."

"Anyone else? Think, Carlo."

"I saw the D.A. when I came into the building. The custodian said hello. I think I may have seen Police Officer Morris walking down the hall, but I can't be sure. Oh, and there was a man talking to Kathleen when I passed her. I don't know who he was."

"What did he look like?"

"I'm not good at this, Tom. I really didn't notice."

"Think. This is important. Was he big or small? What did his clothes look like?"

"He was average, I think. Maybe a little heavy . . . ."

"Color?"

"What?"

"Was he white, black, yellow, brown, green?"

"He was white, and he had a baggy gray suit. That's all I can give you. Maybe Kathleen can give you more information."

"I'll ask her. The question now is what are you going to do?"

"I don't know. I don't want any more killings because of me, but I don't want to turn over the case to another judge who just might find some reason to release Tamika Washington. She brutally abused a little child!"

Cavanaugh scratched his head. "I can't give you advice, Carlo. It's your decision, but trust me, we are going to find this guy, and you and the others have been granted twenty-four-hour protection until we do. I know you're not a quitter. After all the ribbing they gave you in school, you always came back for more."

Judge Abbruzza sat behind his desk and looked at his grandfather's forty-eight-star flag in the corner. "My folks taught me a champion is always ready to go another round. They didn't like quitters." He sat quietly for a moment and then asked, "What do you plan to do?"

* * * *

Cavanaugh called in another favor. He asked Jimmy Monreale in the forensics lab to analyze the last note the judge received. Jimmy prided himself on his work and reported back he found no fingerprints, no traces of DNA, and the words on the note were cut from recent editions of the *New York Times,* the *New York Post*, the *Wall Street Journal*, and the *Staten Island Advance*.

He called Goldberg, Sebastian, Newhouser, Morris, Hodges, and Shanley together and explained his plan. "We've checked out Tamika Washington, and it doesn't add up. She may be a head-case with poor self-control, but I don't think she's capable of pulling this whole thing together."

"The papers say she paid someone to kill the judge," Newhouser said.

"As Charlie Chan once said, 'Not always wise to accept simplest solution.' The papers also said Obamacare was going to save us money. The fact is Tamika Washington doesn't have enough money to hire someone to kill all the people on this list. I think she's being set up."

"By whom?"

"That's the question. I think it has to be someone in or around the courthouse. Each of the notes was postmarked about two weeks before the judge received them. It doesn't take two weeks for a letter to come from Bedford Hills to Staten Island."

"So what's your point?"

"I think someone intercepted the letters and planned the killings to make it look like Washington was the culprit."

"But why?"

"Another good question. Check over the judge's calendar. There must be a reason why he's being set up. Judge Abbruzza has a reputation of being a fair, impartial, and just judge. Find out if there's anyone coming up for trial who may not like him as trial judge."

"What did his secretary say about the man the judge saw talking to her?" Goldberg asked.

"She said he claimed to be a reporter, and he wanted a private interview with the judge. He asked where the judge's chambers were located. Her description matched what Abbruzza said. She estimated he was about five feet ten inches tall, stocky build. He wore a gray suit, green vest, white shirt, blue-striped tie, and white socks. Women seem to notice things like white socks!"

"So what do we do now?" Sebastian asked.

"Do a background check on everyone who has access to the judge's office. 'Sometimes muddy waters, when stirred sufficiently, bring strange things to surface.'"

"Is that more of your Charlie Chan crap?" Sebastian stated.

"Affirmative, but true. Now I want to take Morris with me and go back to where Washington's mother's body was found. Her death seems quite convenient, almost too convenient."

* * * *

William George Fuller was reading *Warriors of God*, the story of the Third Crusade and the battle between Richard the Lionheart and Saladin, when he learned of the note under the judge's door. He slammed the book on his desk, knocking the Attila the Hun statue to the floor. "That wasn't part of the plan!" he shouted to his empty office.

The plan wasn't finished. There were still pieces to be played. It was like when he was a child and his mother seemed to always call him and his sister to dinner a few minutes before the end of the TV show. He wanted to see the end of the game. He needed to see it.

His plan initially was to replace Abbruzza with a judge who would be amiable and more sympathetic to Fuller's desires. But Abruzza had not resigned, and time was running out. Fuller knew who he wanted to preside over Mustafos Montega's trial. He deliberately held off on the option to kill Abbruzza but acknowledged it may now be necessary. The resulting delay in starting Montega's trial might be enough to ensure his release on the grounds that he was denied a speedy trial, but it was a gamble he didn't want to make. If Abbruzza resigned at this late stage, Fuller knew he might not have the time necessary to assure placement of the judge he wanted. If Abruzza were murdered, however, in the resulting chaos and confusion, he knew he could achieve his goal.

So far everything had been going along perfectly — until this last note. He had a conference call to make to Geneva and a meeting with the governor in the afternoon. He didn't need this complication now. Sympathy to him was a sign of weakness. Genghis Khan knew it. Attila the Hun knew it. Looking down at the book he had been reading, Fuller thought Saladin was a fool when he sent Richard the Lionheart supplies and a replacement horse when Richard's horse was killed in battle against him. Saladin admired Richard's bravery. But chivalry was dead. It was a part of the past. It had no place in war or business. Sherman was right. The object is not only to win, but to crush your enemy completely, inflicting as much pain and humiliation as possible.

He got up and walked around his office. Gradually, his anger subsided. His breathing normalized. These were the complications that made the game more interesting. He would work around this potential problem and the person who sent the note.

* * * *

Cavanaugh and Morris met MTA Track Inspector Marcus Aurelius Anderson at the Citigroup Subway Entrance on Lexington Avenue and Fifty-third Street. Together they took the escalator to the lower level. They walked past a man in shorts playing a didgeridoo to the beat of the wooden box he sat on and pounded, a woman playing eerie sounds on a musical saw, and a man playing classical music on a violin. People seemed to go about barely noticing. Occasionally, a man or woman would throw a few coins into a hat or case and move on.

"Isn't that against the law?" Morris asked.

Anderson explained, "They're pretty much a fixture here. They're just busking. Actually, they probably have a license to busk."

"What's busking?"

Cavanaugh shrugged his shoulders. "This is America, Morris. They're expressing their freedom of speech even though they're not talking. As long as they don't cause trouble, they're permitted to sing, dance, tell jokes, or do almost anything. It's still almost a free country. They may have a license, but they don't even need one. Freedom of expression! It works for everyone as long as they don't criticize the politics du jour."

They passed a poster of three cans of chili con carne with the caption, "FIRST TO THE PARTY AND THE FIRST TO LEAVE." The label on the cans was "Future Diarrhea." Cavanaugh moaned, "Sometimes I wonder where our country has sunk to."

"Oh!" Anderson laughed. "That's just an ad for the *Adult Swim* show!"

"The what?"

"The *Adult Swim* show. It's on the Cartoon Network."

"That's the one with Rick and Morty," Morris said. "Did you see the one called *Anatomy Park*?"

Anderson laughed, "That one was a pisser!"

"Okay, guys, enough of this! I don't know what the hell you are talking about, and frankly, I don't care. Where did you find the body, Anderson?"

Anderson led them along a narrow path at the end of the platform into a large empty space with tracks running into two separate tunnels. Around the bend there were steps leading up to a small enclosure.

"Is this where you found the body?"

Anderson paused and put his hand out, blocking Cavanaugh and Morris. "No," he said, "but stay back, there's a train approaching." From the far end of the tunnel, a light appeared, and the sound of the train approaching increased. It roared by, and Morris held her cap as dirt and paper flew up from the tracks. When the train passed, Anderson motioned them across the tracks. "Be careful of the third rail," he warned.

On the other side of the tracks was what looked like a small electrical room. "This is a cable drop room," he said. "I found the body in here."

Cavanaugh looked around. There was a ladder leading straight up. "Where does the ladder go?"

"To a manhole cover on Fifty-first Street."

Cavanaugh stepped out of the room, and in the dim light of the tunnel, he saw a long series of steps around the bend leading up to a door. "How about the stairs?"

"They led to an upstairs platform." Anderson checked his watch. "If you guys think you can handle this by yourself, I need to get back to work. If you take those stairs, they will lead out of here. The door opens from the inside. Just make sure it's locked when you leave."

Cavanaugh thanked him and inspected the small room. It was possible to reach the room from the subway platform, the stairs outside, or the ladder leading to the street. There was nothing else to see. He looked around briefly and then watched Anderson walk into the dark tunnel and disappear into the depths of darkness. The sounds of trains passing overhead vibrated through the walls. "Let's get the hell out of here," he said.

Morris looked at him. "Why did you ask me to come along again?"

"I wanted to ask you something — in private."

Morris' eyes snapped at him. She stepped back.

"Were you in the courthouse this morning?"

"Why do you ask?"

"Were you there or not?"

"Not that it's any of your business, but I was."

"Why?"

Morris turned away. "I don't know why you keep asking me questions. Am I not allowed to be in the courthouse?"

"Just tell me why you were there?"

She hesitated and then said, "I was there for a hearing."

Cavanaugh sighed. "Just tell me the truth, Andrea. I checked. You weren't there for any hearing. Why were you there?"

"It's none of your goddamn business, Cavanaugh. Now leave me alone!"

Cavanaugh grabbed Morris by the arms and threw her up against the tunnel wall.

"What the hell do you think you're doing?"

"I'm going to ask you one more time. You were seen at the courthouse around the same time someone slipped a note under Judge Abbruzza's door. You tell me now or answer to IAB. It's your call, Morris."

He held her tight against the tunnel wall as an express train roared by. The lights from the cars flashed across them like a series of stroboscopic flashes. The noise was deafening. When the train passed, Cavanaugh released his grip on Morris. She stared at him in the dark tunnel. "I didn't do it, Cavanaugh."

"I want to believe you, but I need to trust you. If I can't trust you, you're off the team. I report you to Internal Affairs and let them deal with you."

"If I told you, you wouldn't believe me."

"Try me."

Her hands were shaking. "It involves another person. I don't want to get them in trouble . . . ."

"You're the one in trouble now. This doesn't look much like Las Vegas, but what you tell me stays here."

* * * *

Uriah Applebaum never wanted the Tamika Washington case. At the time of her trial, he had been unofficially contacted by a Staten Island Woman of Achievement who was a "person of interest" in the murder of her husband, the owner of a successful hedge fund in Manhattan. He was convinced she was guilty but felt confident he could get her acquitted on a technicality. But in addition to being a skilled criminal defense lawyer, he was an 18B attorney, a special kind of New York lawyer who could be assigned to represent the poor. As an 18B attorney, he was one of a select few attorneys on Staten Island certified to accept murder, manslaughter, and criminally negligent homicide cases. One of the other certified 18B lawyers was in the midst of a trial involving a school teacher accused of bludgeoning his pregnant wife to death, and another was undergoing a kidney transplant in New York Presbyterian Hospital. If Applebaum refused the case, he feared he might lose his 18B credentials. If the trial was fast, he could accept the Woman of Achievement's case and make some serious money.

He spent less time preparing for Tamika Washington's case than he did flossing his teeth. It looked like an open and shut case, and the only time he spent on it was trying to get Washington to accept a plea bargain. When she refused, he went through the perfunctory moves in court, and she was convicted.

After the Washington trial, Applebaum resigned from the 18B panel, and his criminal practice changed to only representing high-paying clients, many of questionable moral integrity. When the district attorney offered him protection from the veiled threats from Tamika Washington, he turned it down.

His business now was defending criminals who had money. Why would they come to him if the police were hovering around and following him everywhere?

He knew how to work the system. Most of the prosecutors he faced were lazy or incompetent. It really didn't make any difference to him. They had city jobs and security. Most of them weren't interested in making the big money. They were content, and too often he knew that led to complacency or sloppiness. He knew the system and learned to work it like a brain surgeon. He knew how to mislead a jury, how to belittle witnesses' testimony, how take comments made in pretrial hearings out of context, how to use body language, how to make the witness lose composure. He was an actor, a charmer, a bully, a down-to-earth regular guy, a storyteller. He was slick enough to sell a car to a blind man at sticker price.

No. He didn't need protection. He had his own protection. He was connected to a number of crime bosses. No one would dare to come after him.

Sitting in his office savoring a Gurkha Black Dragon cigar while reviewing the grand jury hearing of his upcoming case involving Eddie "Two Fingers" Manigotti, Applebaum didn't see Earle Nelson on the rooftop across the street peering through the scope of a .30-16 Springfield hunting rifle aimed at the back of his head.

* * * *

Jack Bennis looked into the dark eyes of Bella on his lap and smiled. He saw how much the cockapoo brought happiness to Fran, Susan, and Elizabeth. He wondered whether Cindy Waters's mother would miss the little dog. The tragedy of Cindy's death brought at least temporary happiness to the fractured Muscatelli family. *God works in mysterious ways*, he thought.

Petting Bella under her neck, Bennis marveled at the dog's unconditional love. If only people could be more like that. His brother warned him to stay out of the hunt for Earle Nelson. There were some things he realized, in retrospect, he just couldn't let go of. Maybe he should have stayed away from Nelson's apartment. But he found the photos on the wall, Arbuckle's name on the pad, and a pay stub in the trash. He discovered enough information to establish a link between Earle Nelson and the murders of Cindy Waters, Claudia Buenaventura, Lloyd Arbuckle, and now Patrolman Kevin Reilly.

But as his brother emphasized repeatedly, the police would have found the same things a few minutes later. Now Bennis's presence in the apartment contaminated the entire scene, and as the D.A. pointed out, everything in the apartment might now be thrown out of court as inadmissible. Cavanaugh said the D.A. was thinking of charging Bennis with obstruction of justice if he continued to meddle in the case.

Holding Bella and stroking her back seemed to relax Bennis, and slowly he came to realize his brother was right. He should butt out of police business. Earle Nelson, however, was his business, and it was time he settled his business with Nelson himself.

He picked up the phone and made a long distance call to Bogotá, Colombia. It took some time, but eventually, Fr. Manuel Rivera Rodriguez answered the phone. "Hi, Manny," Bennis said over a poor connection, "it's your old lieutenant. Remember me?"

"Jack, how are you? The last I heard you were in Cuba."

"I'm okay, Manny. How about yourself?"

"We're surviving. The money you gave me helped us start a school and a health clinic. We're in the Santa Fe section of Bogotá. The people are poor, and there are a lot of problems, including poor housing, drug wars, delinquency, horrible sanitary conditions, little education. You name it, we've got it, but we are surviving, and the church is growing."

"You're doing good work, Manny."

"I hope so."

"I called you to ask for a favor, Manny."

"Anything I can do for you, Jack, just ask. We go back a long time. I will never forget how you saved my life and nursed me back to health. I try not to think of the horrors we committed before that, but dreams still come back."

"Do you remember Earle Nelson?"

"Of course. How could I forget the guy with the scar. You gave it to him when he tried to butcher that little girl. The man was a psycho. He tried to kill us both."

"Well, he's back, Manny. I saw him the other day at a hit-and-run scene. I think he deliberately ran over a young lady and that he killed at least three more people since then."

Father Rodriguez was silent.

"He came to Mass the other day to see me. He thought he killed me when they left us in the jungle. He recognized me. I know he's coming back to try to finish off what he didn't do back then."

"Jack, that was a long time ago. We both left that life to become priests and to try to make up for some of the things we did. What about your brother, the detective? Can he help?"

"He's working the case from a different angle. Apparently, Nelson was hired to kill a number of people connected to a woman's conviction for the manslaughter death of a ten-month-old child. The business between Nelson and me is personal."

"I don't like the sound of this, Jack."

"Do you remember when you helped me escape from the police in New York and drove me to Menlo Park in New Jersey to catch a train?"

"Of course. You gave me over $50,000 from Howard Stevens's money to help me start the clinic and the church down here."

"I also gave you something else . . . ."

There was silence on the other end of the phone. Then Father Rodriguez spoke, "No, Jack. You're not starting this again, are you?"

"Nelson needs to be stopped, Manny."

"Jack, this is crazy. Leave it to the police. You know what happened the last time. Don't go back there again."

"Sometimes, as you well know, the police can't help. He'll be coming for me soon, Manny. I know him. I need to be prepared." Bennis paused and then said, "You remember what I gave you to keep for me. I know you couldn't take it with you to Colombia. So my question is, where did you leave the .45 pistol I left with you?"

* * * *

Later that night, while Fran prepared dinner in the kitchen, Cavanaugh and his brother sat looking at each other in silence. Cavanaugh cradled his three-month-old son in his arms, and the little cockapoo Bella snuggled into Bennis's lap.

"Did you find Earle Nelson yet?" Bennis asked as he sipped a glass of merlot.

"No, but we will. He's hurt. It's just a matter of time." Cavanaugh paused and then added, "He's not the real problem."

"What do you mean? He probably killed Cindy Waters, the woman in Arlington, that lawyer, and the police officer. I told you he was trouble."

"Oh, I don't doubt he's the murderer. He's a hired gun. But the question I have is who hired him and why. When we catch Nelson, we still won't know who hired him."

"Knowing him, Tom, he'll never tell. But I thought that woman in prison hired him."

"That's what the papers say, but I don't buy it. She never had enough money to hire a killer like Nelson. It doesn't make sense. Her mother supposedly hired a hit man named Aloysius Booth. But Washington claims it was all prison BS. I kind of believe her."

"But why?"

"If she wanted Judge Abbruzza killed, why would she first kill the foreman of the jury, then the key witness, then the arresting officer? Why not just go after Abbruzza first?"

"Maybe she thinks they are all responsible."

"Or maybe she's being set up."

Fran entered from the kitchen with a large bowl of arugula salad drizzled with extra-virgin olive oil and balsamic vinegar with parmesan cheese. "Start on this while I get the main course."

"Aren't you going to eat with us?" Bennis asked.

"Sure. I'll be back in a minute."

"What's for dinner?" Cavanaugh asked.

"It's a surprise. Now eat your salad and behave," she ordered.

As she retreated to the kitchen, Bennis asked, "What makes you think she's being set up?"

"Timing. Her mother suddenly dies of a lethal heroin overdose when we start looking for her. The coroner indicates there was no history of drug abuse. Why now before we could question her? Then there are the letters. It doesn't take two weeks for a letter from the Bedford Hills Prison to reach Staten Island. Mail may be slow, but not two weeks slow."

"What do you think happened?"

"A lot of people had access to the judge's office and mail. Obviously, there is his secretary, Kathleen Bradley. Carlo suspects his Court Officer Wesley Walker has been spying on him because he always seems to be hanging around. Then there's Samson Williams, a janitor at the courthouse. It turns out he's a brother of Tamika Washington. Then we have D.A. Ketch and Assistant D.A. Ananis, Court Attorney Lyons, Supreme Court Bureau Chief Pemberton, and a number of other court officers and attorneys who seem to wander freely about the courthouse like a lot of ass-kissing sheep."

"So what are you going to do?"

"I don't know. Carlo has complete confidence in his secretary. She has been with him since he started practicing law. She would have no motive. The district attorney, on the other hand, is ambitious. He would love to be a judge. Then, of course, there are some of Washington's family members who may have an ax to grind. In addition to a brother who works in the courthouse, she has a very bitter brother-in-law who won't talk to us without a lawyer. And there is the assistant district attorney. He ran against Carlo in the last election and has a number of political friends in high places who would love to see him replace Carlo."

"But didn't you say Ananis's picture was on Nelson's wall and his name on the list of targets?"

"What better way to avoid suspicion than to include yourself as a possible target? Ketch's picture was there too."

Fran brought out a huge sirloin steak with baked potatoes and string beans. She laughed. "Isn't this what you Celtic boys are used to?"

"She's trying to kill us," Cavanaugh said.

"We all have to go sometimes," his brother replied raising his glass, "and I can't think of a better way than with friends, family, steak, potatoes, and wine."

"But where's the butter?" Cavanaugh asked.

Fran placed her hands on her hips. "Butter? You don't need butter with steak!"

"You did in our house! In fact, you needed butter with everything!"

"That's disgusting!"

"No. It's delicious!" Cavanaugh and Bennis said together.

The phone broke the debate suddenly. Little Stephen and Bella both jumped. Fran got it. "It's for you, Tom. It's Morty. It doesn't sound like good news!"

* * * *

Earle Nelson ditched the stolen truck in the short-term parking area at Newark Airport. He then walked over to the long-term parking area where he waited until he saw a man in his sixties park a gray Toyota Camry, unload golf clubs, and walk to the monorail. Nelson hotwired the car and used the man's E-Z pass to exit the airport. Before he left the area, however, he covered his face with a scarf to avoid surveillance cameras. Somewhere in Perth Amboy, he found a blue Honda Civic and exchanged license plates.

He drove by his apartment above the abandoned nautical museum and saw the police. He knew he couldn't go back there.

The next name on his list was Assistant District Attorney Rob Ananis. But he had another problem. Now that Arbuckle was dead, how was he going to get paid for the future hits? Arbuckle initially hired him, but someone else gave him the message to eliminate Arbuckle. He didn't know the man's name, but the military taught him to be perceptive. He knew what he looked like.

Nelson never liked following orders. Ever since kindergarten, he didn't score well in "follows directions" and "respects authority." Call it suspicion or caution, but he had chosen to follow the stranger who gave him the message to dispatch Arbuckle. He tailed the messenger who carried what looked like a violin case to the Citigroup Subway Entrance on Lexington Avenue and Fifty-third Street. Nelson watched him descend by escalator to the lower platform where he set up and started playing his violin for passing subway riders. Nelson knew the man in the baggy gray suit, green sweater-vest, blue-striped tie, and white socks was an intermediary like Arbuckle. He admired the simplicity of the operation. Someone would drop a message into his violin case and move off into the crowd. No one would see the exchange. A message could be delivered in plain sight, and no one would notice it.

He knew what he had to do. He would do what he was trained to do. He would wait. Then he would follow the man with the violin and question him. Nelson was confident he could get Mother Teresa to lie if he applied enough pressure. The violin player would be easy.

Meantime, he found a Starbucks off Broadway, ordered a red velvet frappucino, and contemplated how he was going to kill his old lieutenant, Black Jack Bennis.

* * * *

There were two patrol cars in front of Judge Abbruzza's red brick colonial house when Cavanaugh arrived. The judge was arguing with a tall muscular patrolman, while his short stocky partner stood on the side with his right hand on his holster. Two more cops were coming out of the house shaking their heads and gesturing with their hands they didn't find anything.

"I don't care who you are," the tall patrolman said, "if your alarm goes off again, we're not coming!"

"You can't be serious!" Abbruzza shouted. "I'm a criminal judge, and my life has been threatened!"

"Listen, Judge, no offense meant, but we have a job to do, and we can't keep answering your false alarms. Next time, we'll get here when we get here, but don't hold your breath."

Cavanaugh flashed his badge and asked, "What's the trouble, Officer?"

"This is the third time today we came here for nothing. We have our orders. Persistent false alarms get pushed to the bottom of the list. We're not going to break our asses answering false alarms!"

"You don't understand . . .," Abbruzza started.

Cavanaugh noted the officer's nameplate. "Thanks for coming, Officer Graham. You do what you have to. We'll work things out here."

Graham frowned. "What are you going to do?"

"The judge's life is seriously in danger. I'll contact your commanding officer . . . ."

"Wait a minute, Detective. I'm not looking for trouble here."

"I know you're not. And neither is the judge. We're going to call the alarm company and get this thing fixed. It's a new system, and obviously something malfunctioned someplace." Cavanaugh turned and walked Judge Abbruzza back to his house. Abbruzza's wife and four children stood at the large bay window watching as the patrol cars slowly pulled away.

"Okay, guys," Cavanaugh said when he entered the house. "What happened?" Ten eyes stared at him. "I know how these things work. Graham's right about persistent false alarms not getting priority, but I have a feeling we can iron this out quickly."

He looked around at the faces. "It's a new system. I know. And you're not familiar with it. So let's be honest here. What happened? Who triggered the alarms?"

Judge Abbruzza spoke first. "I was at the courthouse all day, Tom. I didn't know about the two other false alarms. I came home to this, and I guess I lost it when Graham said they weren't going to respond again."

Cavanaugh watched Carlo's wife Marybeth, and the boys, John, Michael, and Gene. Their daughter, Ella, clung to her mother and avoided Cavanaugh's eyes. "Out with it, guys. What happened?"

Cavanaugh and Abbruzza looked at the others. If guilt could be written on faces, it would be spray painted with capital letters. Marybeth looked at her three sons. John averted her eye and studied his shoes. Michael rubbed his chin and examined the ceiling. Gene folded his arms and stared back at Cavanaugh. "What's the big deal?" he said.

"I'll tell you what the big deal is," Cavanaugh began. "Someone has threatened your dad's life and his family's lives. Already, four people have been killed. You, your mother, your brothers, and your father are all in the line of fire. If you don't tell me how those alarms went off, they are going to pull the police protection on you and all of you will be sitting ducks. Or let me put it this way, you'll all be dead men walking!"

Eleven-year-old John started crying. "I came home early," he blurted out. "We had a sub, and . . . and I cut out . . . ." He hesitated. "I forgot about the alarm system. When the cops came, I ran out back, jumped the fence, and hung out at the bagel store."

"Young man," Marybeth said, "what do you think you're doing cutting classes?"

"Easy, Marybeth. You can all discuss this later. What about the other two false alarms, gentlemen?"

Fourteen-year-old Michael said, "I forgot my report for science this morning and came back to get it. I didn't even think about the alarm. I got my report and left. I didn't realize I set the alarm off. I went straight back to school and got there just as the late bell rang."

Cavanaugh stared at Gene. "That leaves one more false alarm."

"Hey, dude, don't look at me. I just got freaken home. It wasn't me."

Judge Abbruzza's face reddened. "Maybe there's a glitch in the system. I'll call the alarm company."

"No, Carlo," Marybeth said. "You don't need to. I went out to go shopping this morning after the boys left for school. I forgot my shopping list and came back home with Ella to get it. I completely forgot about the code, grabbed the list, and went back to Shop Rite. When I came home, the police were here. I was too embarrassed to tell them what I did."

"Mom!" John and Michael said together. Gene just smiled. "I told you. I didn't f-en do it!" he declared.

Cavanaugh explained he was going to speak to the commanding officer of the 120 Precinct. He asked Carlo to write a short, polite letter on official stationary to explain what happened and to make assurances it wouldn't happen again. Before he left, he pulled Gene aside, put his arm around his shoulders, and applied slight pressure to his neck. "Nobody likes a wise guy, asshole," he whispered. "Act like a man, not like a little bitch. You and your family are going through a tough, stressful time. You need to help one another." He pulled his arm back, held Gene at arms' length and looked him straight in the eyes. "Do you understand what I'm telling you?"

The smirk on Gene's face vanished. He lowered his head and replied, "Yes, sir."

* * * *

Barbara Millicent Roberts was the cleaning crew that serviced the law firm of Smith, Connelly, Applebaum, Odlivak, and Schwartz. She was born in the Philippines. Her father was a sergeant in the United States Army, and her Filipino mother had been an exotic dancer until she became pregnant with Barbara. The family came to the United States, where, after months of unemployment, her father got a job as a guard working at the Metropolitan Life Insurance Company. Her mother was pregnant then with her third child. Barbara was twelve when her mother discovered a lump on her breast, which she ignored until the cancer metastasized to her lungs, liver, and kidneys. Barbara's memories of her once-beautiful doll-faced mother were stained by the images of her terminal suffering. It became Barbara's job to take care of her sister and brother. Despite her early years as an exotic dancer, Barbara's mother tried to instill in her family strong religious ties. When her mother died, her father took to drinking heavily. He blamed God for his wife's death. When Barbara was fourteen, her father was diagnosed with cirrhosis of the liver.

His anger spilled out on his children. He treated them like they were circus animals. His word was the rule. Punishments were swift and harsh. The love the children experienced with their mother was replaced with their father's anger and abuse. It was Barbara who kept the family together — the best that she could.

When her father was diagnosed with pancreatic cancer, Barbara was sixteen and started working "off the books" in a local grocery store to help support the family. When her father died, she cleaned homes and before long was cleaning small offices buildings around Staten Island. By then her sister, Kelly, was a junior in Curtis High School's nursing program, and her brother, Kenneth, was in intermediate school. Sometimes Barbara brought her siblings along with her — both to make the work go faster and to keep an eye on them, particularly on Kenneth.

Tonight she was running behind time. Their last job at a day-care center took longer than expected. Kenny griped the whole time. "Why do I always have to clean up the puke? It's not fair. Kelly never does!"

"I do too," Kelly said. "Why do you always have to complain? I had to clean up the mess in the cafeteria. The place looked like a pig's sty."

By the time they reached the law offices of Smith, Connelly, Applebaum, Odlivak, and Schwartz, it was almost midnight. "Come on, Sis. I have school tomorrow. This is crazy. It's against child labor laws."

"You have a half day tomorrow, Kenny. We need this money. If we don't work together, they will take you away from us and put you in foster care. I only ask you to do this with me once a week. If I didn't have you here with me to help out, I'd be here all night."

"All he does is bitch!" Kelly complained. "He doesn't know what real work is. He's a spoiled little brat!"

"I am not!"

"You are too!"

"Am not!"

"Are too!"

"Stop it, you two!" Barbara said. "Let's work together and get out of here. Unless it looks like it needs it, let's skip the vacuuming tonight. Just empty the trash and clean the bathrooms. We'll split up. Kenny, you take the top floor. There's only one real office there. Kelly, you take the second floor, and I'll take the first floor and the lobby. It looks like it needs vacuuming."

The three split up. Kelly put on headphones and listened to Eminem and Rihanna singing "The Monster" as she went about the second floor. Kenny sulked into the elevator, grumbling to himself as he went to the third floor. Barbara was just about to plug in the vacuum when she heard Kenny's screams. She dropped the vacuum and raced up the stairs. Kelly took off her headphones and met her at the second stairwell. "What was that? What's happening?" she asked.

"I don't know. Stay behind me and let's find out!"

Kenny burst into the third floor stairwell as his sisters reached the landing. "Help! Let's get out of here!" He was pale and shaking.

Barbara grabbed his arms and asked, "What happened?"

Kenny looked like he was about to throw up. "Go! Get out of here! Quick!" he stammered.

"What happened, Kenny? What's the matter?"

Kenny motioned behind him. "There's blood all over the place. I think he's dead! Let's just get the hell out of here!"

"Who's dead? What are you talking about?"

"Back there!" he shouted. "I'm not going back! You can't make me! We've got to get out of here, Sis! I'm not kidding!"

Barbara looked into Kenny's eyes. She could feel his fear. Whatever he thought he saw terrified him. "Take Kenny downstairs, Kelly, and wait for me. If I'm not back in five minutes, call 911 and wait outside." Kenny and Kelly didn't wait for another invitation. They ran down the stairs as fast as they could.

The third floor contained the law office of Uriah Applebaum. Barbara walked cautiously through the reception area. Kenny, she noted, obviously had not started his cleaning there. The baskets were full. Down the hall she saw the shredding machine was overflowing. Mr. Applebaum's office door was open, and the light was on. She didn't like him. She only met him once, but he tried to hit on her. That was one of the reasons she saved this cleaning job for last. She didn't want to meet the man again and have to fight him off. She needed this job, but she didn't need to be pawed and poked by a lecherous, arrogant man who made more in one hour than she did in two weeks.

When she entered the office, she thought at first that Applebaum had fallen asleep at his desk. But then she saw the blood. It covered his desk calendar and was splattered on the floor in front of the desk.

Her first thought was get Kenny and Kelly out of the building. Her second thought was the amount of cleaning that would be required to clean up the blood. She stood motionless like a mannequin in Macy's window. She turned and walked downstairs. She told Kenny and Kelly to go straight home and not to talk to anyone. When they left, she dialed 911.

* * * *

BOOK V

Inquisitive person like bear after honey—
sometime find hornets' nest.
—*Charlie Chan at the Circus*

The tick-tock, tick-tock of the clock on the wall broke the stillness in the room. Jack Bennis looked up from the edge of his bed. The clock read 1:37 a.m. Somewhere outside, Earle Nelson was planning to kill him. He knew Nelson was not going to go away. He must have looked at the scar on his face every day for the past thirty years, thinking he killed the man who gave it to him. Now Nelson knew Bennis was alive. He would be back to finish the job. Bennis was sure of it.

He looked at the crucifix on the wall. Nelson was a bad man. Would he have to kill him before he killed more? He closed his eyes. Then he heard it.

It sounded like a soft, high-pitched moan or cry.

He opened his eyes. There in the corner sat the cockapoo, Bella, looking up at him with what looked like sad dark eyes. Visions of Nelson dissipated like exhaled breath on a cold winter morning.

Bennis tapped both of his thighs, and Bella jumped up onto his lap. Bennis smiled. It was an amazing trait dogs have, he thought. In the short time he had with Bella, he was impressed with her intelligence and affection. He saw how Bella brought smiles to Elizabeth Muscatelli and her two daughters. Bella broke down emotional barriers between Susan and Fran. Now Bella's short tail beat a rhythmic, happy tune on his legs.

170

Rubbing Bella's neck, Bennis recalled stories of Hachiko, the Japanese Akita dog who waited patiently at a Tokyo train station for ten years for his master's return, not realizing his master had died at work. Bennis wished that people would be as loyal and devoted as dogs. He smiled looking down at Bella. It's so easy to fall in love with a dog like Bella, who is kind, gentle, and understanding. Dogs can make the worst day seem bearable. They can relieve tensions and help people recover from illness and depression. They love us when we are angry, annoyed, sick, anxious, distracted, and even mean and cruel.

He thought of the shepherds in the fields and wondered if they brought their dogs to the stable where the Christ child lay in swaddling clothes. He remembered hearing that a dog was at the Buddha's side when he died. He recalled how dogs saved soldiers' lives, how they sniffed out bombs and drugs, how they rescued people. They help the blind and the disabled. They play with children and make us happy. A good dog like Bella doesn't let its owner down. They make incredible, loyal, faithful protectors, companions, and true friends who ask little of us in return. They don't judge. They can be what a true friend should be.

In a few short days, he had become attached to Bella. But so had Fran and her mother. He thought of how Cindy Waters must have loved Bella. He wondered what she called her. He realized he had rescued Bella from Cindy's home, but did he do the right thing? How much joy and comfort did Bella bring to Cindy's mother?

He picked Bella up and held her close. "You mean so much to people," he whispered. "I want to give you to Elizabeth. You brought her out of her trance. You made her smile . . . . I want to share you with Fran. Little Stephen would love to play with you . . . . I want to keep you as a friend and companion I can trust."

Bennis stroked Bella's head. "But you're not mine to keep or to share or to give. I imagine you meant a lot to Cindy's mother.

She lost her daughter. I'm sorry, little one, but I need to give you back to her. Tomorrow we find Mrs. Waters and give you back to her. I'm going to miss you. We're all going to miss you . . . ."

He cuddled Bella close to him, leaned back, closed his eyes, and tried to go to sleep. "Life is hard," he said to himself, "and then you die."

* * * *

Nelson's foot hurt. He learned in the service to embrace the pain, and he did. But it still hurt. He needed a place to stay and to recuperate. The answer was simple — the man with the violin.

Nelson left Starbucks and went to the Lexington Avenue and Fifty-third Street subway station, being careful to avoid surveillance cameras. There he waited. He watched a man in a colorful African dashiki set up a wooden box and begin playing a didgeridoo. Then a heavyset woman with long black hair started producing some weird noises on a musical saw behind him. Just as he was beginning to wonder if the man with the violin case would ever show up, Nelson spotted him walking toward the escalator.

Nelson wasted no time. He caught up with him and placed his gun in the small of his back. "Move and you're crippled. Say anything and you're dead," he said.

He whispered instructions in the man's ear, and together they left. Nelson hailed a cab on Lexington Avenue, and the man gave directions to his apartment. "You're not going to get away with this," the man said.

"Shut the fuck up," Nelson said, "or there will be a dead cab driver from Nairobi you're responsible for."

When they arrived at the man's apartment on the West Side, Nelson gave the man the money to pay the cabdriver.

The man with the violin lived in a two-bedroom apartment on the ninth floor of a building near Central Park. It had two bathrooms and a built-in sauna. Large oversized windows looked down on Central Park and a garden courtyard below. The floors were white oak like the kitchen cabinets. The living room was huge. A bookcase ran along the length of one wall. A baby grand piano rested by one window, and a marble bar separated the living room from the kitchen. This was not what Nelson expected.

He looked around. "Whose place is this?" he asked.

The man placed his violin case on the white marble bar. "You're out of your league, Nelson. My advice is quit while you still can."

"I didn't ask your advice. I want to know who pays you."

"I don't know, and I don't want to know."

"Well, you're going to tell me if I have to beat it out of you."

"You're going to kill me anyway. You might as well get it over with because I don't know."

Nelson moved closer and suddenly smashed his gun across the man's face. He fell to the floor and drops of blood stained the white floor.

"I told you I don't know. A big black guy comes by and drops a note in my case. He tells me what to do. I do it, and he comes back and pays me. I don't know who he is or where he comes from. I don't ask questions."

"Who is this guy?"

"I don't know. He looks vaguely familiar, but I don't know. He knows his music. I think he may know me from someplace, but I don't know him."

Nelson motioned with his gun. "How did you get this place?"

"He gave it to me. As long as I do as he asks, he lets me stay here."

"How does he communicate with you?"

"Like I said, he drops a note in my violin case."

"How did he first get in contact with you?"

"I was playing a gig in the village, and he came up to me afterwards and asked if I wanted to make some money. I did. And this is what I get for delivering messages."

"That's it? Does he ever contact you in other ways?"

"Usually no. Except yesterday."

"What happened yesterday?"

"He must have slipped a note under my door when I was out. It was there when I came home late last night."

"What did the note say?"

"I didn't open it. The instructions were to deliver it to a Judge Abbruzza on Staten Island."

"Did you?"

"Of course. I like this place. I do as I'm told. I had to get up early and take the ferry, but I slipped the note under the judge's door as directed."

Nelson leaned back. The pain in his foot burned. "You got any booze?"

The man motioned behind him. "Help yourself."

Nelson poured himself a tall glass of Jack Daniels. He thought for a moment and then asked, "What happens if you don't show up at the station?"

"I don't know. I go there every day. I guess maybe he'll come looking for me."

"Yeah. That's what I figured too." Nelson paused and smiled. "And you're right about that other thing too . . ."

"What other thing?"

"I am going to kill you."

* * * *

Cavanaugh stopped at a Dunkin' Donuts store before going to Uriah Applebaum's office. He was late, but he had been to too many homicide scenes to be in a hurry. The forensics team needed time to take pictures and do their thing. He picked up four black coffees for Goldberg, Sebastian, Newhouser, and himself. He had gotten to bed late and only got up once to rock little Stephen back to sleep. His hands smelled of baby powder and Desitin. He shook his head no when the girl behind the counter asked him if he wanted a senior discount. He wondered how much worse the day could get.

When he arrived at Applebaum's office, he found out. Lieutenant Parker, Captain Blackwater, and a team from the police commissioner's officer were there already.

"What's the story, Cavanaugh?" Parker asked. "I thought Applebaum was given twenty-four-hour protection."

"We offered it, sir, but he refused."

"Somebody should have been watching him," Blackwater said.

"He was adamant, sir. Insisted on his right to privacy. There was nothing we could do . . . ." He looked at the coffee in his hands. "Would any of you like a cup of coffee?"

"This isn't a social call, Cavanaugh," a tall man in a blue suit and a blond crew cut stated. "The mayor and the police commissioner are going to have a shit-fit!"

"And who exactly are you?" Cavanaugh asked.

"I'm First Grade Detective Sanchez with the Deputy Commission of Public Informations Office."

"And why exactly are you so concerned with the mayor and the police commissioner's bowel movements, Sanchez?"

"What? This isn't a laughing matter, Cavanaugh. The press is going to be all over this."

"You're with the Office of Information, Sanchez. I'll let you handle that."

"I don't like your attitude, Cavanaugh."

"And I don't like avocadoes. I guess we're even. Now if you don't mind, I've got a job to do here, gentlemen. If you have a problem, please see the district attorney. In the meantime, if it makes you feel better, write me up. I frankly don't give a shit. Now if you will excuse me, I need to find out what happened here."

"You are going to regret this, Cavanaugh," Sanchez said. "You just might find yourself walking a beat in Williamsburg . . . ."

Cavanaugh stopped and faced the others in the group. "Did you all hear what I heard? I think I just heard a threat, gentlemen. I wonder what my union rep will say about this."

Sanchez stepped back. Lieutenant Parker, Captain Blackwater, and the rest looked at him. "If you guys don't have anything else to contribute, I have work to do." Cavanaugh turned and walked away with the coffee. "By the way, the coffee's good," he said, bumping into Sanchez and splashing some of it on him. "Oops! Sorry about that!"

Newhouser, Sebastian, and Goldberg were taking notes when he gave each of them a cup of coffee. "No cream and sugar?" Sebastian said.

"Eat me!" Cavanaugh said. "Are we up to speed on everything? What do we have so far?"

"Shot came from across the street. We found a .30-60 cartridge on the roof. No fingerprints or footprints."

"Bullet hit him in the back of the head."

Cavanaugh looked out the window. "Good shot. Interesting — he left the cartridge. He's either getting lazy, or he wants us to know it's him."

"The coroner estimates the death to be between nine and eleven last night. The cleaning girl found him around midnight."

"Have you canvassed the area? Anyone see or hear anything?"

"A couple of people said they heard a sound between nine-thirty and ten-thirty but thought it was a car backfiring."

"No witnesses."

"What was the victim working on?"

"Looks like he was preparing to defend a pedophile. The guy was a sixth-grade teacher in a private all-boys school. He raped a ten-year-old boy in the school's book room."

Cavanaugh glanced over his shoulder at the brass in the corner. "Sounds like you've gotten all we can get until we hear back from forensics. Let's get out of here and go back to the rooftop where the shot was fired. I want to look around again and talk to you about a theory I need to run by all of you."

* * * *

Jack Bennis called each of the hospitals on Staten Island trying to locate Cindy Waters's mother. The Health Insurance Portability and Accountability Act or HIPPA rules hampered his search, but after unsuccessfully trying the hospitals, he hit pay dirt with one of the nursing homes. Margaret Waters was in the Von Doussa Nursing Home and Health and Rehabilitation Center, the same place his aunt Mary Jane MacIntyre was a resident.

He found his aunt in the day room playing hearts with Sal Montefiore, Mabel Franklin, and Sophia Samsonite. Ms. MacIntyre smiled and introduced her nephew to her friends. "I'd like you to meet my nephew, Fr. John Bennis. He's a Jesuit priest."

After introductions, Bennis explained why he was there. "They don't allow pets," Mabel stated.

"They wouldn't even let me keep my goldfish," Sophia said.

"Don't take our word for it," Sal said. "Ask the administration. Maybe the priest uniform will get them to change their rules."

"I doubt it will," Bennis said. "We had to threaten them to get my mother's letters."

The group grew silent. Mary Jane MacIntyre explained, "That was a bad time, Jackie. Poor Mr. McNally . . . ."

Bennis looked around the room. People at the other tables stopped talking at the name McNally.

"I don't know what actually happened here that night," Bennis said loud enough for all to hear, "but I don't believe for a second he killed himself."

"Jackie, what do you mean? You know the police said it was a suicide," she said.

"I don't know how you did it, Aunt Mary, but I know you had something to do with his death."

"Glory be to God, Jackie, how can you say that? I was in the hospital after he tried to poison me."

Bennis leaned down and kissed his aunt's forehead. "You're a MacIntyre, Aunt Mary. I know you. I don't know how many times we heard our mother repeat the old Scottish motto, 'Nemo me impune lacessit' — No one who harms me will go unpunished!"

"Let it go, Jackie. Sometimes curiosity is a poison, not only for those who drink it, but also for everyone around it."

"Aunt Mary, do you remember the Charlie Chan movie where he said, 'Detective without curiosity is like glass eye at keyhole — no good'?"

Mary Jane MacIntyre smiled. "Good old Charlie also said, 'Inquisitive person like bear after honey — sometime find hornets' nest.' But, Jackie, remember you're a priest, you're not Charlie Chan!" She patted his hand and said, "Mother Teresa offered ways for all of us to practice humility. They included minding one's own business, not trying to manage other people's affairs, and avoiding curiosity . . . ."

Bennis shook his head. "I may not be Charlie Chan, Aunt Mary, but you sure aren't Mother Teresa either."

He bent even closer and whispered in her ear, "I wasn't going to read those letters of Mom's, but I did. I read some of the things McNally did to my mother and others. If you didn't arrange for his killing, I probably would have done it myself!"

Mary Jane's eyes widened. "Jackie, you wouldn't! Lord help us, you wouldn't!"

He smiled, patted her cheek. "No more than you would, Aunt Mary." Then he winked, said goodbye to everyone, and left to find Mrs. Waters.

When he met Mrs. Waters, she initially thought he was her husband. She reached up to hug and kiss him. The nurse on duty, Susan Huckvale, took him aside and explained the disorientation Mrs. Waters exhibited was typical for many people with her form of dementia and not to be alarmed.

When he returned to her room, however, Mrs. Waters started screaming that he was the devil, and he was coming to get her.

On his way out of the nursing home, he looked for his aunt Mary to say goodbye. He found her in her room with a thin well-dressed man who looked to be in his eighties. His aunt and the man were holding hands when he knocked. Aunt Mary waved Bennis in and introduced him again as "my nephew, the Jesuit priest." The thin man pulled himself up, smiled, and firmly shook Bennis's hand.

"Jackie," Aunt Mary said, "I would like to introduce you to Tony. He used to be an orthopedic surgeon."

Tony smiled. "Now I'm just an old man."

"It's a pleasure to meet you, Doctor," Bennis said as he spotted a bouquet of red roses on his aunt's bed. "I don't remember seeing you here before. Are you a resident, or are you visiting?"

"Tony and I are going to the theatre, Jackie. He's taking me to see *Jersey Boys* in the city."

"How are you getting in there? Do you need a ride?"

"No, Jackie, no need. Tony's going to drive."

Bennis's eyes bulged. He looked at Tony. "You are going to drive into the city?"

"My office used to be off Central Park West, Father. I know my way around New York. But thanks for offering."

Aunt Mary stood, and she raised her voice slightly. "Curiosity killed the cat, Jackie, and I wouldn't want it to kill you. Tony is ninety-two, has a valid driver's license, and is a good friend. Now be on your way because we need to get to the show."

Leaving the nursing home, Bennis felt like he had been mentally pummeled. But he recognized he made some small accomplishments. He let his aunt know he knew she had something to do with the stabbing death of Augie McNally. And although the administration remained adamant about its no-pets-allowed policy, they did agree to allow Bennis to periodically bring Bella to the nursing home as a service dog to visit Mrs. Waters and other patients.

Cindy's mother, he realized, was in the advanced stages of Alzheimer's disease and didn't recognize anyone. His aunt Mary, on the other hand, at the age of ninety-three, was vibrant, healthy, and still the outspoken leader she always had been. And, he smiled — she had a boyfriend. Because Mary Jane was older than Tony, he wondered if that qualified her as a cougar. All in all, he thought as he walked to his car, the day had not been a total loss.

When he reached his car, however, apprehension and alarm slapped him across the face. The car door was slightly ajar.

Had he forgotten to close the door completely? Or had Earle Nelson been in his car?

* * * *

Jury selection for Mustafos Montega's drug dealing trial was scheduled for the following week. William George Fuller's original plan called for Judge Abbruzza to have resigned by now. But Abbruzza proved more stubborn and resolved than anticipated. Earle Nelson killed the jury foreman, the key witness, and the arresting officer. Watching the morning live TV reporting from his Manhattan penthouse, Fuller saw Nelson had also eliminated the defense attorney. Next on the original list was Assistant District Attorney Rob Ananis. He closed his eyes and concentrated. Ananis could be useful in the future. He was ambitious, and ambitious people can be reached and manipulated.

Fuller walked around the room. This was part of the game he played that he loved most. Dealing with human beings was exciting, invigorating, and challenging. By this time, he anticipated Abbruzza would have stepped down or recused himself to let another judge take over. Then Fuller would have been able to orchestrate the appointment of the judge he wanted to preside over the Montega trial and ultimately dismiss all charges against him and release him from prison.

He stopped suddenly and pounded his fists together. He would skip Ananis! Instead, he would have Nelson kill District Attorney Leonard Ketch next. Ananis and Ketch were both on his original hit list. With Ketch gone, Ananis would replace Ketch. A good plan changes as the elements dictate. He could make better use of Ananis in the future. If Abbruzza had stepped down before this, Fuller would not have had to make this decision. He smiled looking at Emerson's quote on his wall. "A foolish consistency is the hobgoblin of little minds, adored by little statesmen and philosophers and divines." Below Emerson's words were the words of Genghis Khan, "It is not sufficient that I succeed — all others must fail."

He needed to proceed quickly, however. He wanted a new judge assigned before jury selection so the trial could proceed and Montega would be acquitted and back on the streets. He wanted the Mexican cartels to recognize the power and influence William George Fuller had. Montega was a small pin in a large multibillion-dollar enterprise. Fuller wanted the Tijuanna Cartel, Los Zetas Cartel, and the Knights Templar Cartel to see how the mystery man from New York was not a force to be trifled with. Most of all, however, he wanted to impress Luis "El Caudillo" Sanchez, the leader of the Sinaloa Cartel and allegedly the most powerful and richest drug trafficker in the world.

Fuller prided himself on his system of communication with the cartel leaders. He used the encrypted technique known as "onion routing" for communicating via different computers with cartel leaders. His messages were repeatedly encoded and then transmitted through multiple different network nodes called onion routers. Each onion router would remove a layer of encryption, just like peeling an onion, to uncover coded routing instructions and then send the message to another router where the process would be repeated. Onion routing effectively prevented messages from being intercepted and concealed the origin and destination of the messages. Scrambling the messages between routers prevented unwanted intruders from eavesdropping on messages. Each router would accept the message, re-encrypt it, and then transmit it to another onion router. As effective as this method is, Fuller knew it did not guarantee complete privacy, so he was careful to transmit his onion routing messages from different public-access computers around the city.

But Fuller needed to act quickly. He needed to contact Earle Nelson about the change in plans. If Ketch's death did not stop Abbruzza, then, despite other concerns, he would have Abbruzza killed. It was business.

Fuller walked briskly to the small bistro Tranquility on Fifty-seventh Street. The speed with which Earle Nelson was killing the names on his hit list put urgency into Fuller's steps. If he didn't stop Nelson, he would kill Ananis. Right now, that did not fit into Fuller's revised plan.

Paul, the tall, handsome, white-haired maître d, smiled warmly. "Your usual table, Mr. Fuller?"

"I need to speak with Jonny."

Paul hesitated. "He's not here right now, Mr. Fuller . . . ."

"Well, get him! Now!"

Paul ran his hands through his hair. "I'm not quite sure where he is, Mr. Fuller . . . ."

"That's not the answer I want to hear, Paul. You have his cell phone number. Call him. Now!"

Paul looked down at William George Fuller. He stood motionless.

Suddenly, Fuller's right hand shot up into Paul's sternum. Paul winced at the crunching sound of the blow and fell back against the door. Pain gripped him in the chest. "I said call him, Paul. Now!"

The tall man reached into his pocket and hit his speed dial. Fuller heard Fiore's distinctive ring of Louis Valentino's

"Eat Animals, Repeat Numbers." It came from the restaurant's kitchen. "You don't know where he is?" he said and slammed his left hand into Paul's nose.

Paul slumped to the ground as Fuller strolled quickly past stunned patrons toward the ringing cellphone. Pushing the door open, Fuller gazed on Jonny "Sweet Fingers" Fiore's bare black butt. Jonny seemed oblivious to Fuller's presence while humping vigorously on the shiny chrome table to the rhythmic beat of the music on the ringing cellphone.

"Am I interrupting something?" Fuller shouted slamming the door behind him. Fiore lost his balance and tumbled off the table. His partner rolled off the other side and tried to hide beneath the table. Jonny looked up at Fuller. His muscular body was glazed in sweat. "Mr. Fuller," he panted, searching for his clothes, "I didn't expect you . . . ."

"Obviously not, Jonny!" Fuller exclaimed, standing akimbo and looking down at him. "And who is your partner this time?"

Jonny smiled. "It's okay," he said, talking to the body hiding under the table. "You can come out."

Fuller stared as from under the table, the naked body of the chef appeared. "For god's sake, man, get your clothes on and get the hell out of here! You're fired! And you, Jonny, meet me in the office right now. We have a problem."

A few minutes later, Fuller explained the problem. "I need Nelson to hold off on killing Ananis. Have your man tell him to kill Ketch next instead."

Jonny stood stark naked in front of Fuller. "That may be a problem," he began. "My contact wasn't at his station this morning."

"Well, where the hell was he?"

"I don't know. It's not like him not to show up."

"Well, find him, for god's sake! You know where he lives. Get dressed and find him. We are running out of time. I need Abbruzza to resign, recuse himself, or die before the jury is picked. If Ketch's killing doesn't get Abbruzza to quit this case, we will have to kill him. Do I make myself clear, Jonny?"

"Affirmative, Mr. Fuller. Abundantly clear."

* * * *

Cavanaugh insisted on reinspecting the roof across the street where the shot was fired that killed Uriah Applebaum. "This is really a stupid waste of time, Cavanaugh. The forensics guys were all over this place. No fingerprints, no footprints, no nothing."

"Except one empty cartridge . . . ."

"Yeah. He probably got sloppy."

"Our man doesn't get sloppy, Sebastian. If he left it, he meant for us to find it." Cavanaugh peered over the rooftop edge. It was a clear shot to Applebaum's window. "Look around for anything that doesn't belong," he said.

"You're out of your mind," Sebastian mumbled.

Cavanaugh got down on his hands and knees and retraced the path from the point where the shot was fired to the door to the roof. Goldberg and Newhouser fanned out in different directions. Sebastian stood and shook his head.

At the saddle to the door, Cavanaugh spotted something. "Somebody get me an evidence bag."

Newhouser handed him one, and Cavanaugh used tweezers to pick up a minute strand of gauze. "This is what I was looking for," he said, pointing out a slight discoloration of the thread. "If I am right, that's Nelson's blood."

"What are you talking about?" Sebastian said. "That's just some piece of junk that probably flew here on the wind."

"No. It was caught on a nail on the door saddle. Nelson was hurt up in the Catskills. His foot got caught in a trap. He's hurting and probably still bleeding. I'll bet we'll find traces of blood on the stairs."

"So he's hurt. So what?"

"You know, Sebastian, if it's true that what you don't know can't hurt you, you would be practically invulnerable. Nelson is hurt. He can't go back to his old place. The police are all over it. He needs someplace else to say. We are looking for a big guy in an army field jacket with a black knight insignia and a bandaged foot. It's not much to go on, but it does narrow the playing field a bit."

Goldberg made the call to have the forensics team come back to the roof and recheck it and the stairs. Then Cavanaugh called Goldberg, Sebastian, and Newhouser together behind some drying sheets on a clothesline on the roof. "I wanted to talk to you about something else. I don't think the Washington woman in prison is behind this. Frankly, there's no way she could pull it off. It's too complicated. Besides, with the exception of the last note, each of the letters didn't reach the judge for two weeks after they were mailed. Someone could have intercepted the mail before it got to him."

"But everything points to her . . . ."

"True. It's almost too pat. 'Not always wise to accept simplest solution.'"

"That sounds like more Charlie Chan crap," Sebastian said.

"Look at it this way: Everyone associated with her trial gets killed. But the bottom line seems to be someone wants Judge Abbruzza to step down. The note that was slipped under his door indicates the killings will stop if he resigns. Why?"

The detectives looked at one another.

"Maybe somebody wants his job," Newhouser suggested.

"It definitely could be. There are a lot of ambitious people in that courthouse. Assistant D.A. Ananis is a very ambitious person. He might do anything to be assigned as a judge, even on a temporary basis. The same goes for D.A. Ketch. He wasn't too keen on pursuing this case to begin with."

"Yeah, but both their names were on the hit list we found on Arbuckle."

"What better way to divert suspicion than to include your name as a possible victim?"

"What about that Senior Court Officer Walker? He always seems to be hanging around. Didn't the judge say he was suspicious of him? He thought he might be spying on him for some of the other judges . . . ."

"Some of the other judges really hate Abbruzza. I heard Judge Terito tried to get him removed last year."

"The papers said Supreme Court Bureau Chief Pemberton asked for Abbruzza to resign."

"Judge Mancusi is another one. I overheard him talking to that Court Attorney Bobby Lyons that Abbruzza was telling stories to the newspapers about judges falling asleep in court and texting their girlfriends," Sebastian said.

"And what about the court clerk, Jason Key, and the judge's full-time court attorney, Larry Logan? They would love to move into Abbruzza's position if he left."

"We can't, however, forget Washington's family," Goldberg stated. "They may have a motive for revenge for her conviction. Her brother's a janitor in the courthouse. He would definitely have access to the judge's chambers."

"And her brother-in-law has a hard-on for the city for the death of his wife."

Cavanaugh held up his hands. "Okay, let's slow down. There are a lot of people who could benefit if Judge Abbruzza resigned. But there may be other reasons too. We need to check everyone out and check the trials Abbruzza has coming up. The man in the gray suit may have slipped the note under the judge's door, but the question is — who is he, and who put him up to it?"

Together they made up lists to investigate everyone who could have had direct contact with the judge's mail. The list included not only the people who may have had access to Judge Abbruzza's mail, but also those who may have had a motive for wanting him removed or killed. The list included his secretary Kathleen Bradley, Court Officer Wesley Walker, Court Clerk Jason Key, Court Attorney Larry Logan, Assistant Court Officers Juan Adams, Auguste Ciparis and William Kemmler, Court Attorney Bobby Lyons, Assistant District Attorney Rob Ananis, District Attorney Leonard Ketch, Supreme Court Bureau Chief Susan Pemberton, and Judges Russell Terito and Joseph Mancusi. Then there were Tamika's brother, Samson Williams, the janitor, and Tamika's hostile brother-in-law, James Blackman, who was a Manhattan court officer. In addition, Cavanaugh pointed out that Police Officer Andrea Morris was observed in the courthouse the morning the note was found under the judge's door. Her possible ties to the case and the calendar of Judge Abbruzza's upcoming trials also needed to be explored. He acknowledged it was a lot of work but emphasized he didn't want to advertise their investigation to others. They divided the tasks among themselves and finished just as the forensics team returned to reexamine the crime scene.

As they left the rooftop, Cavanaugh reminded Goldberg, Sebastian, and Newhouser, "Dig deep, guys. It's the little details that could be vital. Little things have a way of making big things happen."

* * * *

Jonny "Sweet Fingers" Fiore knew where Phillip Curtius, the busk player, lived. He picked out the apartment, furnished it, and used it occasionally for his romantic trysts. Curtius was a consummate musician. He was a virtuoso who played concerts in Europe and South America. Success brought fame he was unaccustomed to. Fame brought parties. Parties brought strangers and sycophants. Strangers and sycophants brought alcohol and drugs. By the time he arrived in New York, his fame had fizzled as the alcohol and drugs dictated his actions. He ended up playing in small bistros in Greenwich Village and on subway stations.

"Sweet Fingers" recognized Curtius's talent and desperation and made him an offer he couldn't refuse. In return for certain "favors," which included delivering messages, Curtius was rewarded with this luxury apartment. Rent was paid by one of Mr. Fuller's multiple shell companies. The arrangement worked well for all concerned. Phillip Curtius never knew whom he was really working for, and William George Fuller's involvement was hidden under another layer of deception.

The question racing through Jonny's head as he rode the elevator to the apartment was why was Phillip not playing at his usual spot on the subway station? Could he be sick? He didn't look sick the last time he saw him. Could he have slipped back into the bottle or the needle?

It struck Jonny unusual that Curtius was away from his standard post, but there could be a number of logical explanations. He knocked on his door. Three quick knocks, three longer knocks, three quick knocks (... --- ...). It was the standard Morse code emergency signal they had worked out together. He held his key in his hand but waited. Fifteen seconds later, he heard the chain door guard opening. He waited.

The door opened, and Jonny stared into the eyes of a man he had never seen before. His eyes focused on the man's face and the long ugly jagged red scar running from his right eye to his lip.

"Good afternoon, Mr. Fiore." The man smiled. "I've been expecting you. Do come in . . . ."

It was then Jonny saw the gun pointed at his heart.

* * * *

Cavanaugh, Goldberg, Sebastian, and Newhouser dug into the lives of possible suspects who may have motive or access to Judge Abbruzza's mail.

Kathleen Bradley was married to Thomas Bradley, a New York City Police lieutenant, working out of a Manhattan precinct.

Cavanaugh knew Bradley from his old precinct in Brooklyn. He was a solid guy and a good leader. Kathleen and Tom were married for thirty-two years and lived in a modest home on the South Shore of Staten Island. Kathleen had worked for Judge Abbruzza since he started his law practice right out of Fordham University. The Bradleys had four grown children, two were police officers, one was a firefighter, and the youngest was a global macro fund manager for a hedge fund on Wall Street. Kathleen had access to the judge's mail, would open it, and place it on his desk to read. She worked an early schedule and would leave the office at 3:00 p.m. often before the judge returned from court.

Court Officer Wesley Walker was in and out of Judge Abbruzza's chambers all day. Before being assigned to Abbruzza, Walker worked closely with Judge Russell Terito. Both Judge Terito and Walker had young boys who played on the same Little League baseball team. Judge Terito was a leading force in trying to remove Abbruzza on a number of occasions. In one case, Terito aborted a preliminary hearing, expunged the transcript, and then sent the case to Abbruzza. Judge Abbruzza read all the papers and dismissed the indictment on the grounds the district attorney violated the statute for providing a speedy trial for the defendant. What Abbruzza did not realize at the time was the accused was a member of the Tombstone Gangsta gang, an offshoot of the Bloods street gang, and had been involved in a drive-by shooting that killed a six-year-old girl on Jersey Street. The news of his dismissal of the charges made all sorts of headlines in the newspapers and on television. Judge Terito led the public outcry to have Abbruzza sanctioned and removed. Abbruzza took the heat for Terito's "indiscretion." Ultimately, the Court of Appeals vindicated Abbruzza's unpopular but just decision that the D.A. had violated the speedy trial rule, and it affirmed the dismissal of the charges. Rumors in and around the courthouse were that Officer Walker reported all Abbruzza's business to

Judge Terito, who persisted in his attempts to remove Abbruzza from office.

Chief Clerk Jason Key worked for Judge Abbruzza for two years. His work habits were sloppy, disorganized, and lazy. The statistics he submitted were routinely incorrect or incomplete. He was an example of nepotism in the public sector. His uncle was Judge Mancusi. Abbruzza tried unsuccessfully to remove him a few times, but Key's connections were too strong. If it weren't for Kathleen Bradley's constant review and correction of the reports Key submitted, Abbruzza would have been perceived as inept and incompetent. As the situation developed, Abbruzza and Bradley worked around Key, while he spent most of his time perusing secretaries and arranging for noontime "matinees." He once confided in a coworker he was addicted to sex and had no scruples in hitting on one hundred women in the hope that one would accept his advances. Around the courthouse, his proclivity earned him the nickname "the Would-Be Lothario" and the rumor that even a keyhole wasn't safe when he was around.

Court Attorney Larry Logan worked in the Staten Island courthouse for seven years. He was reliable and ambitious. He was graduated at the top of his class from NYU Law School. His political affiliations were well-known. He ran unsuccessfully for councilman, state senator, and assemblyman. He was single, personable, intelligent, and handsome. He was also gay. While not actually assigned to protect Judge Abbruzza, Logan made it a point to be around Abbruzza to act as an additional body guard.

Court Attorney Bobby Lyons attended Fordham Law School with Judge Abbruzza. He scored much higher than Abbruzza on his LSAT (Law School Admission Tests) and passed his New York State Bar Exam on his first try, unlike Abbruzza, who took the exam twice. His professors in law school predicted great things for Lyons, but his rise to the top stopped at court attorney working for a judge whom he felt he surpassed in ability. Bobby Lyons's problem was horses. He was a gambler and spent most of his time trying to devise "the perfect plan" for betting on the trotters. When he won, he won big. But when he lost, he lost even bigger. He was deeply in debt to bookies and loan sharks around the city.

Assistant District Attorney Rob Ananis was the nephew of the late Brooklyn district attorney J. R. Coyle, who was shot by the serial killer who called himself Lex Talionis. Cavanaugh and Coyle's tempestuous relationship resulted in Cavanaugh's reassignment to the Tottenville Precinct. Young Rob rode the coattails of his uncle. Ananis was ambitious, calculating, and industrious. His admitted goals were high, and he already stepped on and over a number of people in his rise to assistant D.A. He was divorced from a former Staten Island beauty queen. The reason for the divorce officially was "irreconcilable differences," but he, like Key, was known to have a "roving eye."

District Attorney Leonard Ketch was a progressive Democrat elected by a wide margin. He favored legalizing drugs and partial-birth abortions and fought against gun control and charter schools. He was married to the former Peggy Stopes, whose mother became pregnant at the Woodstock Festival in 1969. His wife attended Naropa University in Boulder, Colorado, while Ananis was a Columbia Law School graduate. They had two children, Peace and Happiness, who attended a Sudbury Model free school in Brooklyn. Ketch's personal beliefs gave him the reputation of being sympathetic to drug cases. He ran against Abbruzza in the previous election for judge but was narrowly defeated. Ananis was intelligent, articulate, and forceful. His deliberate agreement with Judge Terito to remove critical evidence from the Tombstone Gangsta trial was an attempt to remove Abbruzza and move into his position as criminal judge.

Chief Supreme Court Judge Susan Pemberton was single, dedicated, and professional. She fought her way up through one glass ceiling after another. She went on record a number of times objecting to Abbruzza's actions and decisions in court. She voiced her anger to the press over statements he made indicating he was not one of the judges who slept or texted on the bench. She felt it demeaning to her staff and blamed him for "undercutting" on occasion both Judge Terito and Judge Mancusi's authority. More recently, she went on record requesting Abbruzza step down to avoid the series of murders connected with the Tamika Washington trial. Pemberton attended Princeton University, where she initially majored in psychology. Her roommate at Princeton was Yelanda Garland, the prison psychologist at the Bedford Hills Correctional Facility.

Samson Williams, the courthouse janitor and brother of Tamika Washington, graduated from McKee Vocational High School and worked at the courthouse for fifteen years. He was competent and performed his duties effectively, if not enthusiastically. He insisted he had not seen or heard from his sisters or his brother in years. Telephone records supported his claims. He had been in and out of substance abuse programs for ten years. He belonged to Alcoholics Anonymous, attended two to three meetings a week, and had been sober for five years.

James Blackman, Tamika's brother-in-law, worked in Manhattan as a court officer. On the day the message was placed under Judge Abbruzza's door, he called in sick. He refused to speak with the police, but coworkers confirmed his anger at the police for not finding his wife's killer. He cursed the fact that police were investigating a threat on a white judge but did little to investigate his wife Ashkira's death. "If she was white," he insisted, "they would have done more!"

The investigation of Assistant Court Officers Juan Adams, Auguste Ciparis, and William Kemmler eliminated them as possible suspects. Each had solid alibis, which made it impossible for them to tamper with the judge's mail.

Both Judges Terito and Mancusi had personal reasons for Abbruzza to step down, but their high profile and inaccessibility to Judge Abbruzza's chambers also precluded them from actually intercepting the letters from Bedford Hills Correctional Facility.

Police Officer Andrea Morris, however, presented another problem. A number of people saw her, and sign-in sheets and video surveillance cameras confirmed she was in the courthouse frequently during the time the letters from Latitia could have been intercepted. Moreover, there were no apparent reasons for her to be there; and to further complicate matters, she refused to disclose any reason for her presence in the courthouse.

Cavanaugh concentrated on the delay in delivering the death threats to Judge Abbruzza. The two-week delay in the initial letters indicated to him someone at the courthouse intercepted the letters. The delay in delivering the letters would give someone ample time to set up a plan to dispose of the judge and to set up Tamika Washington as the most likely instigator of the plot. After interviewing Tamika, however, Cavanaugh did not believe she was capable of funding the elaborate, deadly plan, which was being enacted.

The note under the judge's door was different from the others. It came from an unknown source, and it offered Judge Abbruzza an end to the murders if he stepped down. The man in the gray suit and green vest may have delivered the last message, but he had not sent the first messages. They had pictures of him, but the name he gave when signing in was false. Who was he, and why did someone want the judge to step down?

If you eliminate Tamika as a suspect, Cavanaugh thought, *the letters from Latitia Jones must have been intercepted by someone in the courthouse or at the prison.* He looked at the list of suspects. There were at least eight definite suspects from the courthouse who could have rerouted the letters, plus Tamika's brother and brother-in-law, and Officer Morris.

He wrote the names in his notebook:

Kathleen Bradley – Judge Abbruzza's secretary
Wesley Walker – court officer
Jason Key – Judge Abbruzza's chief clerk
Larry Logan – court attorney
Bobby Lyons – court attorney
Rob Ananis – assistant district attorney
Leonard Ketch – district attorney
Susan Pemberton – chief supreme court judge
Samson Williams – courthouse janitor and Tamika's brother
James Blackman – Tamika's brother-in-law
Andrea Morris – police officer

When everyone else went home, he studied the list and then added a twelfth name: Yelanda Garland, the prison psychiatrist at Bedford Hills. He folded the list and placed it in his pocket. He sighed. It was late. He needed to make another trip to the Bedford Hills Correctional Facility. He dreaded the trip back to the prison but smiled to himself when he recalled Charlie Chan saying, "Time only wasted when sprinkling perfume on goat farm."

* * * *

Jonny "Sweet Fingers" Fiore entered the apartment. Earl Nelson kept his gun leveled at Fiore's heart and a couple of arms' length away. Fiore scanned the room. Phillip Curtius, the busk player, was tied to a chair by the window. He was gagged and naked. His lip was bleeding. Both his eyes were swollen. The fingernails on his right hand had been pried off.

Nelson motioned to a chair next to Curtius. "Have a seat. Mr. Fiore, isn't it? Mr. Curtius, I must tell you, did not give up your name easily. Unfortunate for him. He could have made it a lot easier."

"Who are you? And what do you want?"

"I could say I'm your worst nightmare, but that is premature. Let's just say I'm the guy you hired to kill people."

"You're Earle Nelson?"

"In the flesh, Fiore."

"What do you want from me?"

"I want to know why, and I want to know who runs this operation. Who am I really working for?"

"I don't know why. I just deliver the messages."

"Why me? You don't know me. Why did you single me out?"

Fiore looked at Nelson. He was bigger than Nelson and in better shape, but Nelson could put three bullets in him before he reached him. He looked over at Curtius. Blood dripped from his fingers where his nails used to be. Nelson was trouble.

"I'm waiting, Fiore. I don't have all day." He lowered his gun and aimed it at Fiore's hand. "Maybe we should start with your fingers. Philip, over there, tells me you play the piano . . . ."

"Hold on, Nelson. There is no need for this. I'll tell you what I know. Somebody told us you were good at what you do . . . ."

"Who?"

Nelson scratched his head and then answered, "Mustafos Montega."

"He's in jail! And he's small time. I did a few jobs for him, but how did he contact you?"

"We have a lot of different sources."

Nelson backed up and was quiet for a moment. Then he asked, "There are a lot of names on this list. If your boss wanted me to kill this Judge Abbruzza, why go through all these other names?"

"You didn't seem to have a problem with that."

"No. I didn't, but why not just kill the judge to begin with?"

"You ask a lot of questions."

"I'm the one with the gun."

"My boss likes to make things complicated. He likes challenges. I don't ask questions. I think in the beginning he may not have wanted to kill Abbruzza for some reason. He thought he would step away from the trial by now. But he didn't."

"Interesting. But we have a problem, Fiore. In the course of events, I happen to have killed your bag man, the fat lawyer. Since then, I've knocked off a couple of more names from the list, but I haven't been paid. I am not running a charity here. I want to get paid."

"That list is one of the reasons I came here. The boss doesn't want you to kill the next name on the list — Assistant D.A. Rob Ananis. Instead, he wants you to get D.A. Leonard Ketch. If that doesn't get Abbruzza to step away from the trial, he wants you to kill the judge."

"I don't know if you heard me, Fiore. I want to get paid. The higher we go on the food chain, the more complicated the hits become. I need adequate compensation."

"I don't control the money."

"Well then, you need to get me to see the big man so we can talk and discuss adequate compensation."

"You've been given a lot of money already."

"True, but I'm planning to retire and settle down somewhere warm and sunny. After this, there is only one more person I plan on killing."

"I don't know if he will see you."

"He will. You are going to make that happen." He pointed to his old army jacket on the floor. "Phillip here was kind enough to give me some of his clothes. Now if you will kindly lead the way, we will take a taxi to your place where you can arrange for me to meet your boss."

"He's not going to like this," Fiore said.

"You're not going to like it if he doesn't meet me." Nelson motioned toward the door. "Be careful and don't walk too fast. I had a little accident, and I'm a little slower than usual. Remember, my gun will always be pointed at you."

Fiore started for the door and then turned to Phillip Curtius tied to the chair. "What about him?"

"Oh," Nelson said, "I almost forgot." He turned and fired a bullet straight into Curtius's head. "Now let's get going. We have an important meeting to go to."

* * * *

The ride to Bedford Hills took less time than Cavanaugh thought. He found Dr. Yelanda Garland in her office preparing to leave. She looked startled when she saw him. "Well, if it isn't Detective Cavanaugh. I thought you got everything you wanted — without my help. Are you ready for that meal I spoke about?"

"No, Dr. Garland. I have a few more questions to ask you."

"Maybe I should get my lawyer . . . ."

"If you wish. I can take you down to Staten Island, and your lawyer can meet us there. Or you can answer a few questions for me here and now. Your choice."

"You drive a hard bargain." She smiled. "Are you this hard in bed?"

Cavanaugh moved closer. "Listen, Garland, I don't know what your story is. Maybe you hate men. Maybe you like to tease to show your supposed superiority. Maybe your father raped you when you were a girl. I really don't know, and I don't care."

Garland backed away. "What are you talking about, Detective?"

"Right now you're looking like our chief suspect in the murders associated with Tamika Washington's trial. You had access to intercept Latitia Jones's letters. You knew Tamika's anger toward Judge Abbruzza. Maybe you fueled that anger. Maybe you planted the seed for Latitia to write the letters in the hopes of her gaining more privileges. Maybe Latitia asked you to mail her letters to the judge. You could have held the letters up, while you devised a plan to kill Judge Abbruzza and blame it all on Tamika . . . ."

"You're out of your mind! I never saw those letters!"

"But you knew both women."

"It's my job, Detective. I'm the prison shrink, for god's sake!"

"You're also affiliated with drug gangs."

Garland folded her arms. "What are you talking about?"

"I saw the tattoos on your hands. They're gang tats. The three dots between your forefinger and thumb represent the only three places gang members go — the hospital, prison, or the grave. They are related to what was originally a Mexican street gang known as Los Vatos Locos — the Crazy Guys. You try to cover the tats up with rings, but I saw them when we first met. I'll bet you have more. Does the warden know about your gang ties and probable drug ties? I have to hand it to you. What better way to distribute drugs in a prison than through the prison psychiatrist?"

"You're out of your mind, Cavanaugh! Get out of here this instance!"

"Listen, Garland, I don't give a shit about your gang or drug affiliations. I want to know who's out to kill Abbruzza. If it isn't you, who is it?"

"I've got no beef with Abbruzza. I don't even know him. Why would I want to kill him?"

"I don't know. He's hearing a drug case next week. Maybe that has something to do with it."

Garland moved back to her black cabinet and poured herself a drink. She turned. Her green eyes flashed at him. "You think you know everything, Cavanaugh. You don't know shit! Before I worked here, I was undercover with the FBI. Check it out! The tattoos were part of my cover. It turns out they work well here. Some of the inmates feel freer talking with me."

Cavanaugh stood like a wooden statue.

"And yes, Detective, I do have other tattoos in some pretty interesting places, but you can bet your sorry ass you'll never get to see them!"

"You know I'm going to check this out, Garland. I hope, for your sake, you're telling me the truth."

She stood before him and suddenly flung her drink in his face. "Go fuck yourself, Cavanaugh!"

"You may not believe it, but you're not the first broad to say that to me." He wiped his face, tasted the liquid on his face and said, "That's good scotch. It's a shame to waste it."

She smiled. "You're incorrigible."

Cavanaugh sat down on her couch. "If you're what you say you are. Explain your relationship with the Staten Island courthouse."

"There is none!"

"That's not what I hear."

"Well, what do you hear?"

"I hear you and Susan Pemberton know each other."

"Susan Pemberton?" Garland hesitated. "Do you mean the Susan Pemberton I roomed with at Princeton? That was a long time ago."

"Same one."

"What does she have to do with me?"

"I hear you and she were quite the item at Princeton . . . ."

"You're full of shit, Cavanaugh, and you know it. What does Susan have to do with me now anyway?"

"She's chief supreme court judge."

"Shit! I didn't know that! I haven't seen or heard from Susan since graduation. We each went our separate ways."

Cavanaugh stood and glanced around the office at pictures of Audre Lorde, Lorraine Hansberry, Ma Rainey, and Billie Jean King. He noticed a new picture of Ellen DeGeneres next to a large rubber tree plant. Looking at the newest picture, he asked, "And what does 'our separate ways' mean exactly?"

"I'm not a lesbian if that is what you are implying, Cavanaugh! Those pictures are of talented women who stood up for their individuality! They are role models for some of the women here."

"What about Susan Pemberton?"

"You'll have to ask her."

"I'm asking you! You roomed with her for four years. Is she or is she not? You must know."

Dr. Yelanda Garland moved closer and embraced him. She planted a long warm, wet kiss on his lips. He felt himself reacting immediately as her tongue entered his mouth. His groin ached as his little trouser snake responded. She drove her body into him and her hands scratched their way down to his butt, pulling him closer. His trouser snake wasn't little anymore. DSB (Deadly Sperm Buildup) moaned for release.

"Wow! Detective Cavanaugh," she said, "is that a howitzer you are carrying in your pocket?"

Cavanaugh felt his mind shutting down. This was a moment of survival. His trouser snake was growing into an anaconda and fighting to take control of his brain. He felt himself getting stupider and stupider as the growing beast in his pants sucked the blood from his brain. This anaconda wasn't listening to vows of fidelity or morality. He was a prisoner struggling for freedom. She moved her hands to his belt buckle. Cavanaugh was losing control. He knew it was now or never.

* * * *

Jack Bennis carved out the inside pages of *Lives of the Saints*. On the table next to him lay a set of pink marble Irish rosary beads his mother gave him when he left to join the army. They had been hers, and she gave them to him to keep him safe.

He was careful cutting out the pages. He wanted to dig out a crater large enough to conceal something. Little Bella sat on his lap, while he hollowed out the pages. She looked up at him as if she knew what he was doing. "Don't look at me that way, Bella. I've got to be prepared. I know he will be coming for me."

Suddenly, Bella's head shot up, and she ran toward the door. Bennis closed the book and placed the knife in his pocket.

The door opened slowly. It was Cavanaugh. Bella jumped up on him wagging her tail. Cavanaugh bent and patted the dog.

"You look tired," Bennis said. "Long day?"

"You could say that. Where is everybody?"

"It's late, Thomas. Fran and Michael are asleep. You look like you could use some sleep yourself."

Cavanaugh emptied his pockets and went to the cabinet to lock up his gun and then to the kitchen to get a beer and some pretzels. When he came back, Bennis was busy reading the notes on the suspects that Cavanaugh left on the table.

"Hey, Jack, what are you doing? Those are my notes. They're confidential. They're not for you. I don't want you involved in this case."

"Are they your suspects?"

"Maybe."

"They read like a page from Chaucer's *Parson's Tale*."

"Now what the hell is that supposed to mean?"

"They could be examples of the Seven Deadly Sins."

Cavanaugh grabbed the list from his brother. "What are you talking about?"

"I read your notes. I know I shouldn't have, but I did. You know what Charlie Chan said, 'Detective without curiosity is like glass eye at keyhole — no good.'"

"How many times do I have to tell you, Jack? You're not the detective! I am! If you remember, Charlie also said, 'Curiosity responsible for cat needing nine lives.'"

"Mom used to say it was ignorance that killed the cat and that curiosity was framed."

"It's late, and I'm tired, and I don't want to get into an argument over this. Why can't you just mind your own business?"

"Well, Thomas, in a way it is my business. The Seven Deadly Sins — pride, envy, gluttony, anger, sloth, covetousness, and lust — they are my business."

"So what?"

"Don't you see? Your suspects are blatant examples of these sins."

"It's been a real long day, Jack, and I have no idea what the hell you are talking about."

"Lust is an intense desire for sex, but it could be for money or fame too. Some people confuse love for lust. A few of your suspects seem attracted or even addicted to this sin.

"Covetousness is greed and a disproportionate desire for material things. From your notes, I see where a few of your suspects are ambitious and not afraid to step on others to get what they want.

"Gluttony can be more than eating too much. It is overindulgence and could broadly be considered selfishness and an intense desire to put a person's own interests over others. There seems to be no shortage of this in the courthouse.

"Sloth obviously could be physical laziness or not doing the things one should do. One of your suspects seems content to do little or nothing and is careless in his work.

"We know what anger is, but it often shows itself not only in revengeful acts but also even in self-destructive behavior from gambling to drinking and drugs.

"Envy is like jealousy and can be resentment of another's position or an unhealthy desire to get that position. It looks like there's an epidemic of that in your suspects . . . ."

Cavanaugh looked over his list and nodded as he reread his notes. "Interesting, but it doesn't prove anything. You would find these qualities or faults in any group of people."

"You're probably right, Thomas, but the granddaddy of the Seven Deadly Sins is Pride. This is the most important of the sins because all the others spring off it. I think whoever is orchestrating these murders is motivated by pride. Earle Nelson may be killing these people, but he's following someone else's orders. I know his pride won't allow him to stop before he tries to kill me. But I think the person behind all of these murders thinks he's better than everyone else and is trying to prove it by playing with the police. Human life doesn't mean much to him or her. It's almost like a game to him. I think whoever it is is out to show himself superior to everyone else."

"Don't worry, Jack. We're going to catch this guy."

"To be honest, I'm not worried so much about me right now as I am about you."

"Me? Why?"

"Of course, it's none of my business . . . ." Bennis tucked his book under his arm and turned toward his room. "But if I were you, Thomas, I'd take a shower and wash my shirt before I went to bed." Little Bella bounded after him. "You really do stink of perfume, and there's that lipstick on your collar . . . ."

* * * *

It was late when Nelson and Fiore arrived at the bistro Tranquility. Four tourists were finishing their meals and two sailors and a woman in a tight red dress sat at the bar. Soft Frank Sinatra music played in the background. Tall silver-haired Paul met them at the door. A flesh-colored bandage ran across the bridge of his nose.

"Is he here?" Fiore asked.

Paul shook his head. He looked at Nelson. "Who's your friend?"

"You don't want to know, big guy," Nelson answered. "Now get these clowns out of here. You're closing early tonight."

"What?"

"Do as he says, Paul. We'll be in the office."

Walking past the men and the woman at the bar, Earle Nelson recognized the scene. "Does she work for you?"

"Not officially. We let her ply her skills from time to time as long as she doesn't get too obvious."

"You get a kickback?"

Jonny nodded. "Of course."

When they got to Jonny's office, Nelson paused. A large oak desk stood at the end of the room in front of an in-the-wall aquarium with multicolored tropical fish idly swimming about.

Surrounding the fish tank was a massive bookcase. On the desk were two computer screens. On one side of the wall were floor-to-ceiling bottles of red wine separated by a large built-in cooler for white wines and champagnes. On the other side, movie posters of Anthony Quinn and Sophia Loren's 1954 movie *Attila* and Omar Sharif and Eli Wallach's 1965 movie *Genghis Khan* hung on a dark-paneled wall over a black leather sofa. Two large black leather armchairs faced the desk.

"Nice digs," Nelson commented.

"The boss picked them out. The sofa bed was my idea."

"Speaking about your boss, it's about time I met him. Call him and get him over here."

"It's not that easy."

"Which of your fingers do you want to lose first, 'Sweet Fingers'?"

"Wait! I have a number that I call. It's like a message board. He checks it occasionally."

"Text him."

"I can't. I don't know his number. I don't even know where he lives."

"Why do I not believe you?" He motioned to one of the chairs facing the desk. "Sit and call your number." He moved behind the desk and checked the monitors. "Just remember, there is a limit to my patience."

"If you kill me, you'll never reach the boss . . . ."

"If I kill you, the boss will eventually show up to see if you carried out your assignment. I will wait, and he will come."

As he started dialing, there was a knock on the door. Jonny froze. He looked at Nelson.

"Tell whoever it is to come in," Nelson said. "But be careful."

The door opened slowly. It was Paul. "I wanted to tell you everybody is out, and I just locked up. Is there anything else you want?"

"Yeah!" Nelson said. "Come in and make yourself at home. We're going to have a little party in a little while."

Paul hesitated, and then he saw the gun.

"Do as he says, Paul. This will all be over soon."

Paul moved to the vacant chair and sat. Nelson laughed. "So what's the name of the head honcho around here?" Jonny "Sweet Fingers" remained silent. Paul blurted out, "Do you mean Mr. Fuller?"

Jonny flashed displeasure in Paul's direction, and Nelson laughed again. "Paulie baby, get me a bottle of a good Merlot, will you please? It could be a long night."

* * * *

Cavanaugh followed his brother into his room. "Listen, Jack, it's not what it looks like . . . ."

"It's none of my business, Thomas. I love Fran and little Stephen Michael and wouldn't want anyone to hurt them — even my brother."

"The psychiatrist up at Bedford Hills hugged me and kissed me. I didn't do anything. I swear. She tried to seduce me, for god's sake!"

"Like I said, it's none of my business. Just don't hurt Fran!"

Cavanaugh chased his brother into his room. "You've got to believe me!" He grabbed Bennis's arm and both the book he was carrying and his little dog Bella fell to the ground. Bennis bent to pick up Bella. Cavanaugh reached for the book. "Leave it!" Bennis said.

But Cavanaugh picked up the book and opened it. Most of the pages inside the book were carved out. He stared at the book and then his brother. It was in a book like this in which Bennis concealed the .45 he used to kill mob bosses Muscatelli and Malentendo a few years before. "No, Jack, tell me you're not doing this again!"

"This is none of your business, Thomas."

"We went through this before. You can't do this again."

"I know him. Nelson is coming to get me as sure as God made little green apples. He has a score to settle with me."

"We'll protect you, Jack. You don't have to take matters into your own hands."

"It's between him and me, Thomas. He came to my church and saw me. I don't want to risk other people's lives because of a grudge he has against me." Bennis took the book away from his brother. "I happen to have a score to settle with him too."

"What happened to 'forgive us our trespasses as we forgive others'?"

"Let's just say we have unresolved issues. Sgt. Jim McCarthy died in Colombia because of him. Nelson left the three of us in the jungle. McCarthy was wounded by the rebel militia in the leg as we were escaping. Rodriguez and I were carrying him out as the helicopter arrived. With proper medical attention, he could have survived. But instead, Nelson fired at us. I was hit, and McCarthy was hit again. The chopper left us. Somehow we managed to evade the rebel troops for three weeks. During that time, I watched sepsis attack his wounds. He was in a lot of pain. It was horrible watching him suffer. All he talked about was getting home to his two-month-old daughter. He was twenty-three. He never made it. Rodriguez and I buried him in the jungle. If they had waited for us and tried to help, instead of trying to kill us all, his daughter would have a father today."

"You can't take matters into your own hands. Innocent people get hurt."

"Not this time. We know Nelson has killed at least four people already. I just want to be ready for him."

Cavanaugh looked at his brother and then reached forward and hugged him tightly. "I don't want to lose you, Jack."

Bennis pulled back. "Since when do the MacIntyre men hug each other? You are acting more Italian every day! I think it must be Francesca's influence!" He held onto his brother and gave him a bear hug. "Actually, it's not a bad custom, but remember to wash that shirt and take a shower before you go to bed!"

"I swear, Jack, I didn't do anything! I may have thought about it, but I didn't do anything."

"I believe you, Thomas, but like old Ben Franklin said, 'An ounce of prevention is worth a pound of cure.' I don't want to hear you trying to explain this to Fran in the morning."

"There's no talking to you about Nelson, is there?"

"No."

"Will you promise me you'll be careful? You're the only brother I've got."

"That's the whole point. I want to be prepared when he comes. The Black Knight, as Nelson used to call himself, is a man without honor. Nobody is safe around him. I promise I'll be careful. But you watch yourself, Thomas. The man is dangerous, very dangerous."

* * * *

Jonny Fiore didn't have to leave a message for William George Fuller. Sitting in the den of his West Side apartment, Fuller saw what was happening in the bistro's office. Closed circuit cameras hidden in the bookcase, the wine rack, the light fixture, and the door jamb gave Fuller a view of the entire room. Paul and Jonny sat in the chairs facing the desk. Earle Nelson sat behind the desk with his gun pointed directly at Jonny.

Fuller turned up the volume on his surveillance system. He smiled. He hadn't expected this but reveled in the challenge. Earle Nelson was an interesting character. He was efficient and dangerous but foolish to dare to walk into Fuller's life. Just because a chicken has wings, he thought, doesn't mean it can fly. He would be taught a lesson. But that was after he completed his mission.

Fuller dressed quickly in black sweats and running shoes. He went to his wall safe and extracted $50,000 and put it in a knapsack he flung over his shoulder. He didn't bring a gun. He didn't think he would need one for Nelson.

Jogging to Tranquility, Fuller listened on his earplugs as Nelson questioned Jonny and Paul. From time to time, he checked their body language on his phone. Paul fidgeted with his hands but said nothing. Jonny tapped his fingers on his legs and focused on Nelson's gun. Earle Nelson sat back in the desk chair and basked in the moment. "Where is this Mr. Hotshot of yours, 'Sweet Fingers'? For your sake, he better show up soon. I'm a patient man, but there is a limit."

"How many times do I have to tell you? I don't know!"

"You work for the man, and you don't know his name, where he lives, or where he works? Why don't I believe you?"

Fuller stopped at a red light on West Sixty-first Street. He checked his phone. Paul was speaking, but a tractor trailer bounded down Broadway drowning out whatever he was saying. When the truck passed, he heard Nelson's voice again. "So it's Mr. Fuller. Thank you, Paul." Fuller stood at the corner and watched Nelson stand and walk around the desk. As he started to cross Sixty-first Street, he heard the crunch of metal on bone and increased his pace.

When he was two blocks away from the restaurant, he called. It rang twice, and Nelson answered it.

"Mr. Nelson," Fuller began and moved into the shadows away from street lights. He slowed to a walk. "I understand you want to talk with me."

"Who is this?"

"This is the man whom you wanted to meet."

"Are you Fuller?"

"You can call me anything you like, but if you harm Jonny, you will regret it deeply." Fuller reached the side door of Tranquility and quietly let himself in.

"I want to meet you."

"That may not be necessary. What do you want?"

"I said I want to meet you!"

"And I said that may not be necessary. I understand you haven't been compensated for your last assignments." Fuller moved quietly in the darkness through the restaurant. On top of the piano, he placed the knapsack with the $50,000 and moved into the kitchen.

"You're damn right I want to be paid!" shouted Nelson. "I'm not knocking off people for my health. I got my foot caught in a bear trap because of you!"

"And how much compensation are you requesting?"

"I told that fat lawyer I wanted a thousand for the second hit and double for each other hit."

"And how much is that exactly?"

Fuller watched on his phone as Nelson went back to the desk and started to write on a pad. "Let's see . . . .There was the broad in Mariner's Harbor. That would be a thousand . . . ."

Fuller opened the walk-in freezer in the kitchen.

"Then there was the fat lawyer himself . . . .That would be two thousand, plus the one thousand . . . ."

At the back of the freezer, Fuller pulled a lever under a shelf, and the wall quietly opened into a small dark room.

"Then there was the cop. He'll cost you four thousand . . . ."

Fuller looked through the back of the fish tank. Nelson concentrated on the cost of his acts of malice. Paul looked like a petrified statue. He didn't move an inch. Jonny slumped in his chair. Blood ran down from a gash on the side of his head.

"So I figure you owe me seven thousand already. Now Sweet Fingers here tells me you want me to drop two more — the D.A. and the judge . . . ."

Fuller loosened the latch at the back of the bookcase. "The judge may not be necessary but probably will." He watched Nelson stand and start pacing back and forth behind Paul and Jonny.

"Are you moving around the office?"

"Yeah. Why?"

"Reception is spotty. You're fading in and out." He watched Nelson move back toward the desk. "There is a knapsack with $50,000 on the piano outside. Take it and finish the job."

"You think I'm a fool. I may have been born at night, but I wasn't born last night. I'm not falling for that trick!"

"If you don't want to go there yourself, have Jonny or Paul go and get it for you."

Fuller watched Nelson. The $50,000 was a lot more money than he expected. Nelson hesitated. Jonny was unconscious. Paul's eyes were wide, his hands shaking. "You," Nelson said, moving behind the desk in front of the bookcase, "go out and see if there's a knapsack on the piano. If there is, bring it back here. If you try something silly, your friend 'Sweet Fingers' here will die. Understand?"

Paul shook his head.

"No funny business," Nelson said. "You've got fifteen seconds to go and get back in here. Leave the door open so I can see you. I like you, Paulie. Do this right, and you are free to go."

Paul rose and left. Nelson positioned himself behind the desk with the slumped Jonny Fiore as a shield. He was directly where Fuller wanted him.

Paul quickly returned with the knapsack and placed it on the desk. Nelson leaned over and opened the bag. As he reached in to check the money, Fuller opened the bookcase.

"Watch out!" Paul shouted.

Earle Nelson whirled around and looked straight into the eyes of William George Fuller.

* * * *

Jonny "Sweet Fingers" Fiore heard Nelson's voice as if in a long tunnel. "Leave the door open so I can see you." His head ached where Nelson pistol-whipped him. He slowly opened his eyes enough to see Nelson standing before him behind the desk. Then he saw Paul dump a knapsack on the desk and step back. Nelson opened the knapsack and stared at stacks of hundred-dollar bills.

Then the bookcase seemed to move behind Nelson. Was he having a hallucination? Out of the darkness stepped William George Fuller in a black sweat suit. Jonny heard Paul shout, "Watch out!" and saw Nelson turn. Before Nelson could react, however, Fuller's foot swung up and knocked the gun out of his hand. Fuller was a blaze of action. His hands smacked Nelson across the face. Jonny heard the thud of Fuller's punch to Nelson's stomach. Nelson staggered back. Fuller grabbed him by the neck and slammed his head into the desk. Nelson groaned and shielded his head with his hands. Fuller swept his leg behind Nelson's legs, sending him crashing to the floor.

Jonny had heard of Fuller's legendary fighting skills but never saw them before. He watched Fuller pull Nelson up and stand him in front of the fish tank.

Then Jonny heard Paul's voice beside him. "Freeze, Fuller! Stay right where you are!" He glanced to the side to see Paul had Nelson's gun and was directing it at Fuller. "You think you're such a big shot, don't you, Fuller? Well, now I've got the gun. How do you like it now? You think you can go around hitting people and getting away with it? Well, you can't! You broke my nose this afternoon, you bastard, and you're going to pay for it! Sometimes you eat the bear, and sometimes the bear eats you. It's my turn now, Fuller!"

Jonny watched Paul extend his arm preparing to shoot Fuller. Instinctively, Jonny reached over and hit Paul's arm. A shot rang out. It hit the fish tank. As water and fish poured out and Nelson slid down the wall, Fuller leapt over the desk and, in a blurring series of lethal blows, pummeled Paul.

Then William George Fuller turned to Jonny and said, "Thank you. I really never liked Paul that much anyway." He looked at the limp body on the floor and added, "Get rid of his body. You can dump his body where you dumped Tamika Washington's mother's body. It will give the cops something else to worry about. Make it look like a train hit him."

Jonny nodded. His head felt like razor blades were rattling around inside.

Fuller returned to Nelson and picked him up. Nelson tried to struggle, but Fuller applied a pressure move to his wrist and whispered, "Don't make me hurt you any more, Nelson. I still have use for you. The money in the knapsack is yours, but my patience is running low. Clean yourself up and help Jonny here get rid of Paul's body. Then I want you to kill the D.A. tonight and . . . ." He hesitated and rubbed his hands together. "I tried to do this without hurting Judge Abbruzza. I honestly did. But this is all taking too much time. I don't care what I promised. If for any reason you can't get to the D.A., kill Judge Abbruzza!"

Book VI

There's no art to find the mind's construction in the face.

—*Shakespeare's Macbeth*

Fran woke up with a start. The baby wasn't crying. Something was wrong. Cavanaugh slept next to her as if in a coma. She jumped out of bed and raced to Stephen Michael's crib. He wasn't moving. Her heart skipped a beat. She reached in and felt his head. Then Stephen Michael moved. *Thank God*, she thought, *he's alive.*

But then he lifted his head and turned. She held her breath. He squirmed a little and then went back to sleep.

Why wasn't he crying? Was he sick? "Tom, Tom!" she half-whispered, shaking Cavanaugh awake.

"I don't understand it," she murmured. "Something's wrong. Wake up!"

"What are you talking about?"

"Stephen Michael is still asleep!"

Cavanaugh rubbed his eyes and swung out of bed. "I must have been having a bad dream. What's the matter with Stephen?"

"He's still asleep!"

Cavanaugh stared at Fran. "That's a good thing, isn't it?"

"Yes, but he always cries. Maybe there's something wrong with him. Maybe we should take him to the emergency room."

"And what are we going to tell them? Our baby is finally sleeping like a normal baby?"

Fran stared down at Stephen Michael. Cavanaugh joined her and put his arm around her. "He's beautiful, isn't he?"

"We're lucky, Tom."

"Yeah. Look at him, Fran. He's got the whole world ahead of him. I hope it's a good world. From where I work, I worry about that."

Fran looked up into Cavanaugh's eyes. "He'll be fine. I only hope he takes after his father."

"Thanks, Fran, but I hope he does better than that."

"This case you're working on is upsetting you, isn't it?"

"There are a lot of crazy, mixed-up people in the world. It's hard to believe someone is deliberately targeting certain innocent people for some unknown reason. We think we know who's doing the killing, but we don't know what the motivation behind the killing is. Whoever is behind all this used the letters from the prisoner to create a façade."

"But why?"

"That's the question. The last note slipped under the judge's door may be the answer. Someone wants the judge to resign or recuse himself."

"Why?"

"The only thing I can think of is the upcoming trial of Mustafos Montega. He's a small-time drug dealer, but he has ties to some Mexican drug cartels."

Fran looked down at their sleeping son. "It's hard to believe someone would deliberately kill innocent people to get a drug dealer out of jail."

Cavanaugh leaned over the crib and placed a gentle kiss on Stephen Michael's forehead. "It's even harder to believe someone could beat a child, tie it to a radiator, and duct tape its mouth so as not to hear it scream . . . ."

He looked at Fran. There were tears in his eyes. "I don't know how much longer I can do this. Having a child has changed me. Maybe because I'm older. I don't know."

"Are you planning on retiring?"

"I have the time. But no. I'm going to find the killer out there and whoever is behind the killings. Then we'll sit down and discuss it."

Fran looked from Stephen to Cavanaugh. "I just can't understand why anyone in his or her right mind would kill so many people just to get a judge to step down? It's crazy creepy!"

"Maybe we're dealing with a crazy megalomaniac."

"If you find the person who slipped the note under Judge Abbruzza's door, maybe you'll find some answers."

"That's what we're hoping. He and the murderer are our only real leads at this time. We lost track of Earle Nelson, but we know he's hurt and somewhere in the city. He can't have too many places to hide. We'll catch him. It is only a matter of time."

"What about the judge? When is this trial supposed to start?"

"Next week."

"It doesn't sound like you have much time. Do you think he'll resign?"

"I don't think so. He's a fair and honest person. Maybe he would have if that last note came in first. But now that the killings have taken place, he's not going to back away. He's got a lot of guts. In spite of all the pranks we played on him in grammar school, he still came back for more."

"But . . . ."

"He knows his life is on the line, but he told me he has an obligation to serve the position he was elected to and a responsibility to those whose lives were taken. He's not going to back down now."

"I don't like the sound of this, Tom."

Suddenly, the phone rang, piercing the stillness of the room. Both Fran and Cavanaugh checked little Stephen Michael. He was sleeping quietly. Cavanaugh raced for the phone and got it on the second ring. He smiled at Fran and moved into their newly converted living room.

Fran looked at her sleeping baby, patted his head, and followed after Cavanaugh. Her palms were wet. He stood looking at one of the stain-glass windows. "Check who owns or rents the apartment. I'll be right in."

"Who was that?"

"Lieutenant Parker. They think they found the man who slipped the note under Judge Abbruzza's door."

"Good. Now maybe he'll give you some answers."

"That's not going to be easy. He's dead. Shot between the eyes with a .357 Magnum. It looks like Earle Nelson is at it again."

The door to Fr. Jack Bennis's room opened, and Bella the cockapoo raced up to Cavanaugh, wagging what little tail it had. "Did I hear you say Earle Nelson?" Bennis asked, holding his large copy of *Lives of the Saints* in his hand.

"We can't be sure, but that's the way it looks right now. The pictures from surveillance cameras around the courthouse match the body found tied to a chair in an apartment overlooking Central Park. I've got to go in now."

"Be careful, Tom," Fran said.

Cavanaugh smiled. "I always am, Fran. I'm too ornery to die, right, Jack?"

Bennis reached down and pulled Bella back to him. He echoed Fran's advice. "Remember what I told you about Nelson, Thomas. Be very careful. He's dangerous."

* * * *

Judge Carlo Abbruzza arrived earlier than usual at the courthouse. He saw Court Officer Wesley Walker at the door to his chambers. "Good morning, Officer Walker. Can I help you?" he asked.

"No, Your Honor. I . . . ah . . . I was just looking for a pen. I thought you might have one lying around."

"Did you find one?"

"No, Your Honor, but I'll ask Judge Terito for one. It's not an emergency."

Abbruzza watched Walker scurry down the corridor like a five-year-old who was caught doing something wrong. There was no doubt in his mind that Walker was working for Terito. He would make sure Cavanaugh had this information. Walking into his chambers, however, he found Samson Williams, the courthouse janitor and brother of Tamika Washington, vacuuming behind his desk.

"Good morning, Mr. Williams. What are you doing?"

"What does it look like I'm doing? Your chambers are a mess. With all the commotion going on around here, I haven't been able to get in here to clean."

Judge Abbruzza's head ached. "It's okay now, Mr. Williams. I need a little time to myself now. Come back later when I'm in court."

Samson Williams packed up his vacuum cleaner and left mumbling to himself.

Abbruzza sat in his favorite chair and looked around the room. Someone had been in his office looking around. The briefs he left the previous night were on his desk but out of order. He checked the top drawer of his desk. It was still locked, but he saw someone tried to open the drawer with a letter opener or a screwdriver. He leaned back in his chair and held his head. It felt like it was splitting. He needed a cup of hot black coffee.

He opened his eyes at the sound of his door opening. It was Kathleen Bradley, his secretary. She held a cup of steaming coffee in her hand. "Thought you might need this," she said.

"You must have read my mind, Kathleen."

"After working with you for all these years, I tend to know your habits."

"How come you are in so early?"

"I could ask you the same question, but the truth is there's a lot of work to make up. Jason Key, your so-called chief clerk, can never be found, and the data he gives is suspect to say the least. You need to get rid of Key, Judge. He's a liability."

Abbruzza took the coffee and thanked her. "You know I've tried, Kathleen, but his political connections are too strong. We'd have a better chance if one of his paramours filed a sexual harassment suit against him, but that doesn't look like it's happening."

"Do you mind if I say something, Judge? Something's bothering me."

"Of course, Kathleen. What's the matter?"

"Those people who have been killed . . . ." She looked down and wrung her hands together. "They didn't do anything wrong. Whoever is out there killing people has you on their list. Why don't you step down and recuse yourself from trials for a few weeks. Give this business time to settle. Maybe take a vacation with the family. You're under tremendous stress. And your life is in danger."

"I appreciate your concern, Kathleen, but I can't step away now. I swore a duty to serve as judge, and I'm not letting somebody scare me away."

"But innocent people have been killed. This isn't a game. You might be next."

"You sound like my wife. But like I told her, we know the names on the list the killer is using. The police are protecting each of the potential victims. Sometimes Detective Cavanaugh has been doing some things I'm uncomfortable with, but we're going to be all right."

"With all due respect, Your Honor, I don't see any police protection here in your chambers."

Abbruzza smiled. "Unless you're the killer, I don't seem to have to worry now, do I?"

"This isn't funny, Judge. Please take care of yourself. You're a good man and the best, fairest judge we have around here. There's not one of the other judges fit to walk in your shadow."

"Hold on, Kathleen. You make it sound like I'm the Messiah. There are a lot of good people here. Maybe by my standing up for my principles, it will encourage others to do the same."

Kathleen Bradley shuddered. "You are, aside from my brother, possibly the most stubborn, incorrigible person I have ever met!"

"There you go again, Kathleen." He smiled. "You sound like my wife again. Did you both go to the same school?"

Kathleen turned abruptly. "You're impossible! I'm going to see where that police protection for you is."

"Thank you. While you're at it, could you please give Detective Cavanaugh a call and ask him to fill me in on the investigation?"

She turned and gave him an icy stare.

"I said please."

"You are exasperating!"

"Thank you, Kathleen. You make me feel at home!"

* * * *

When Fr. Jack Bennis arrived at Our Lady Help of Christians, the usual group of gray heads and bleached blondes were in the church. He had left Bella with Fran, who planned another visit to see her mother in Brooklyn. Fr. Charles Kuffner greeted him in the rectory. "There's a couple waiting to see you in the parlor."

"What do they want?"

"I don't know. They were specific. They only wanted to see you. I'll cover Mass for you."

"Thanks, but where's the pastor?"

"He said he was going to visit patients in the hospital."

"Did he pack his golf bags?"

Father Kuffner said, "Yes."

Bennis laughed. "I'm glad we have you around here. By the way, where is the sacristan, Mr. Laurie?"

"He's arranging flowers for a funeral later today."

"Okay. Where is this couple?" Bennis said, clutching his large copy of *Lives of the Saints* under his arm and heading toward the parlor. Sliding the pocket doors open, Bennis first saw a tall well-built Hispanic young man with prematurely gray hair who stood up quickly. The man looked familiar, but he didn't recognize who he was until he saw the woman sitting next to him. It was María Isabelle Rodriguez, the young nurse he helped escape from Cuba. Then he realized the tall Hispanic man was Francisco Thomás, a one-time a pitching phenomenon for the Cuban National Team, who tore the ligaments in his pitching arm when the boat he was on while escaping from Cuba crashed off Key West, Florida.

"Buenos días!" Father Bennis smiled, his heart skipping a beat as he remembered María Isabelle tending to his wounds and falling in love with him. She was the reason he had requested a leave of absence from the priesthood. He remembered her bare breast leaning over him and the soft, moist, warm taste of her kiss. Looking at her now, he thought she was more beautiful than ever. He recalled Charlie Chan's comment how it is impossible to miss someone who will always be in your heart.

"To what do I owe the privilege of your visit today?"

Both Francisco and María responded together, "We would like you to marry us."

* * * *

By the time Cavanaugh, Goldberg, Sebastian, and Newhouser arrived at the scene of Phillip Curtius's murder, the forensics team had already identified three significant sets of fingerprints from the apartment. One was Phillip Curtius's. He had a number of minor misdemeanor charges ranging from public drunkenness, trespassing, shoplifting, and urinating on subway tracks. Another set belonged to Earle Nelson. His fingerprints revealed a much more impressive rap sheet. He had been arrested numerous times in different states on charges ranging from gun possession and drug trafficking to rape and murder, but the prosecution was never able to accumulate enough evidence to file formal charges. The third set of prints, however, proved most intriguing. Although the prints were unidentified, a partial print from whoever this person was had previously been found at the scene of Tamika Washington's mother's apparent overdose.

"Coincidence like ancient egg — leave unpleasant odor," Cavanaugh said.

"More of your Charlie Chan crap?"

"One of my favorites, Sebastian, because it is so true."

Ownership of the apartment proved to be layered through so many different shell companies. They realized it would take more time than they had to determine whose apartment it really belonged to.

The detectives scoured the apartment for a clue to who this mystery man might be but came up empty. They questioned neighbors to no avail. Frankie, the doorman, a short overweight Russian with a pencil moustache, a bad case of dandruff, and a chest full of medals resembling Audie Murphy, however, was able to describe the mystery man as a tall, slender well-dressed black man who occasionally came to the apartment. He did not know his name, but he did see the man and another man fitting Earle Nelson's description get into a taxi the previous night somewhere around nine or ten o'clock.

"Great!" Sebastian moaned. "There must be over twelve thousand taxicabs in the city. How the hell are we going to find the one they got into?"

"Actually, there are over thirteen thousand taxis in the city," Cavanaugh said and then asked the doorman, "Can you describe the cab for us?"

"I didn't get the license plate, but it was one of those new cabs — the greenpainted ones."

"I never heard of green cabs," Newhouser said.

"They're Street Hail Livery vehicles called boro taxis," Goldberg explained. "They're fairly new and are allowed to pick up passengers only in certain parts of the city."

"This is good news. It narrows the field down considerably. Let's check to see who picked up Nelson and the mystery man from here last night and find out where they took them. We are closing in on this guy. I can feel it."

"You can feel it? The only thing I can feel, Cavanaugh, is a headache. What would your friend Charlie Chan say to that?"

Cavanaugh stretched and winked at Goldberg. "Time only wasted when sprinkling perfume on goat farm."

Everyone smiled except Sebastian.

* * * *

María Isabelle Rodriguez was getting married. That was what Jack Bennis told her she should do. The two of them discussed it. He was a priest. He made the decision. It was what he wanted to do. A psychologist, he knew, would have a feast examining him and delving into his past. The priesthood was the life he had chosen, he told her. She needed to get on with her life. That's what he told her to do, and she had. As he walked back to the church, however, he wondered why he felt an empty pit in his stomach like he lost his best friend.

Looking out at the small group of people at Mass from the sacristy, Bennis saw an unfamiliar face that was somehow familiar. The man stood in the back of the church as Father Kuffner gave the final blessing. The man was short and bald.

"Go, the Mass is ended," Father Kuffner said.

"Thanks be to God," the people responded.

Father Bennis kept his eyes on the stranger. Where did he know him from? As the congregation started to leave, the stranger and Bennis locked eyes. The stranger nodded, smiled, and abruptly turned to leave. That's when Bennis recognized the walk. He looked different. He wasn't wearing the cheap red toupee, he shaved his thin moustache, and a blue golf shirt and khaki trousers replaced his usual slightly wrinkled blue three-piece pin-striped suit. It was the walk that gave him away. Bennis knew the man as Oscar Cormorant, the dean of studies at Garfield Academy, who disappeared without a trace at the end of the Lex Talionis case. Cormorant was the man who never was. His resumé, his degrees, his licenses, even his social security number proved false. Who was he? And why had he come to Our Lady Help of Christians Church?

Bennis started to go after him, but a gray-haired man stopped him. "Can I speak with you, Father?" Bennis stopped short. He clutched his *Lives of the Saints* book in his left hand. "I'm in a bit of a hurry now. Can it wait?"

"Yeah, sure. Why the hell not? Some detective named Cavanaugh told me to look you up. I'll come back another time, Padre."

Bennis smelled liquor on the man's breath. "You've been drinking."

"You got a pretty good nose for a priest."

Bennis looked at the back of the church. Oscar Cormorant or whoever he was was gone. "How can I help you?"

"I don't know. The detective said you could. I'm tired of being me." The man studied Bennis carefully. "Say," he said, "you look a little like that detective!"

"Yeah," Bennis said, leading the man to an empty pew. "We get that a lot. Now tell me a little about yourself . . . ."

* * * *

Earle Nelson and "Sweet Fingers" Fiore decided to dispose of Paul's body in Tranquility's kitchen. First, they stripped Paul and hung him from a meat hook, letting his blood drain into a twenty-quart aluminum stockpot. It was a time-consuming, messy process as Paul's blood oozed out rather than flowed because his heart was no longer pumping. Ultimately, they collected roughly four quarts of blood before they disemboweled him and then sawed the body into segments. The parts were boiled and the flesh and fat peeled away and then cooked. Paul's bones were ground up into a fine dust. It took time, a lot of time, but it was private, and just before sunrise, Paul was no more.

Nelson didn't want "Sweet Fingers" Fiore hovering over his shoulder, watching his every move. He functioned best by himself. He agreed to help Fiore dispose of Paul's body, but after that, he insisted on completing his mission by himself. Too many cooks spoil the broth. He didn't like working with Fiore. He didn't trust him. But he knew Fiore was following orders from Mr. Fuller or whatever his name was. Fiore may want to kill Nelson, but he was not going to go against Fuller's explicit orders. After the hits were completed, Nelson knew his life would be expendable. It went with the job. He had all the money he needed. He could just run now. But he considered himself an honorable man like the Black Knight who would carry out his mission and then quietly escape.

To accomplish his mission, however, Nelson needed to get close to his victims. Taking Paul's wallet and keys, he hailed a cab and went to his apartment on Grant Street on the West Side. Fiore told him Paul had lived there in a rent-controlled apartment with his mother who died a few years before. Nelson smiled when he discovered Paul had not disposed of his mother's clothes and that she had been a woman of ample size. In a matter of minutes, Earle Nelson transformed himself into a lethal Mrs. Doubtfire. A flowered house dress, a pillow, a sweater, stockings, sunglasses, tattered slippers, a scarf, and a shawl to cover his gray crew gave him the disguise he needed. If necessary, he thought of stealing a shopping cart, but a large quilted patterned handbag was more than ample to carry his .357 Magnum.

From Paul's apartment, Nelson walked less than a mile to the South Street Ferry and blended in with a few tourists, students, and ordinary people going to or coming home from work. His ankle didn't hurt as much anymore. He caught the 7:00 a.m. ferry to Staten Island and sat on the outside deck. As the ferry passed the Statue of Liberty, Nelson wondered what

Jonny "Sweet Fingers" Fiore was going to do with the meat they cooked from Paul's bones. One thing he knew for sure — he did not plan on eating at Tranquility in the future.

* * * *

Cavanaugh's experience taught him how when things started rolling, they tended to pick up speed quickly. The doorman Frankie's observation about a green taxicab picking up Nelson and the tall black mystery man in the Upper West Side led Sebastian and Newhouser on the trail of the taxi. Through a process of elimination, they were able to locate one cab in the vicinity of Phillip Curtius's murder. The problem was the driver's log did not indicate picking anyone up from the West Side apartment, and he had not reported to work that morning. Sameer Afridi was a Pakistani emigrant who lived on Coney Island Avenue in Brooklyn.

"I hate driving in Brooklyn," Sebastian complained. "Why can't Goldberg go? He lives there."

"We need to find out where they went. They probably paid Sameer well not to enter the information on his log. If we're lucky, Sameer will still be alive, and we can get the address he took them to. I doubt they would have killed him because then they would have had to deal with getting rid of the taxi."

"What if he can't speak English?"

"Find him!" Cavanaugh said. "I don't care how you get him to talk."

"Okay, I get it, but why can't Goldberg go? I hate driving in Brooklyn. They are a bunch of lunatics."

"Goldberg is involved in something else. If you don't want to drive, let Newhouser drive."

"I hate the way he drives too!"

"Suck it up and get out of here," Cavanaugh said. "If Mr. Afridi gives you any problem, threaten him with deportation under the Alien and Sedition Act of 1798. You can throw in sending him to the Gitmo detention camp too. That should work."

Meanwhile, Detective Goldberg poured over the bank accounts and computer records of Lloyd Arbuckle, the lawyer murdered in the Catskills. He noticed Arbuckle's last transaction involved cashing a $20,000 check from A&R Used Tire and Junk Yard in the ironbound section of Newark for services rendered. This struck Goldberg as unusual for two reasons. The first was the address for A&R Used Tire and Junk Yard was an abandoned lot in downtown Newark. The second was the building in which Phillip Curtius, the busk player, was murdered was also owned by A&R Used Tire and Junk Yard.

"It's a shell company," Goldberg told Cavanaugh. "I'm looking into who the real estate agents were, who the rental agency is, who handled the maintenance and equipment, and who the hiring agency is. Eventually, we'll trace it back to someone. Shell companies are classic ways to avoid taxes and to launder money. Whoever is orchestrating this is brilliant. I wouldn't be surprised if when we track this down we find some holding company involved in everything from real estate, brokerage houses, mutual funds, insurance, and banking to criminal activities like gambling, prostitution, and drugs. If we follow the money, we'll find the source. It's only a matter of time."

"That's good news, Morty, but we're running out of time."

* * * *

The Alice Austin Ferry docked at St. George on Staten Island at 7:30 a.m. It was too early for the courthouses to open, so Earle Nelson walked to the parking lot and watched for a businessperson to park his or her car and rush to catch the next ferry to Manhattan. He didn't wait long before he spotted a well-fed man in his fifties wearing a blue three-piece suit cradling a black leather attaché bag under his arm like a football dash from a pearl blue Honda Accord and rush up the ramp to the ferry.

Nelson waited until the ferry pulled away and then casually walked to the Honda and "appropriated" it. He would call the courthouse a little later to check on District Attorney Leonard Ketch's location. Now he wanted to scout out another target.

* * * *

Frank Stevenson checked his watch. "I got this watch from the commissioner when I retired."

"Nice watch," Father Bennis replied. "But you didn't come here to tell me the time."

Stevenson's hands were shaking. "I ain't been in a church in years. It smells kind of funny."

"It's probably a combination of candle wax, incense, and smoke from the fire we had."

"It's kind of scary. It's so dark and cold. I feel like those statues are staring at me."

Bennis looked down at the copy of *Lives of the Saints* he held on his lap. "They're not, but if you like, we could go outside."

"Yeah. Yeah. I'd like that. This place gives me the creeps."

They sat on the steps of Our Lady Help of Christians. Bennis looked around. They were in the open. He was vulnerable. He gripped his book tighter. Earle Nelson was on his mind. Was he being paranoid again? The open car door at the nursing home was just an open door he had forgotten to close completely. Nelson wasn't there.

Stevenson coughed.

Focus, Bennis said to himself. *Compartmentalize. This man needs help.* He heard the church doors behind him lock. He glanced at Stevenson's watch. The ever-efficient sacristan Mr. Laurie locked the church doors. The funeral was another two hours away. There was no place to hide if Nelson came back.

"It's like I'm powerless," Stevenson said.

Bennis's eyes snapped at him. "What did you say?'

"It's like I'm powerless, and I hate it!"

"What do you mean?"

"I saw that girl that got run over. The school teacher. I heard the thud when he hit her, and I saw him get back in his car and deliberately run over her. I wanted to do something, but I didn't. It was like I was powerless."

"Why did you feel that way?"

Stevenson played with his watch. He said, "I was drunk. I've been pretty much drunk for a long time. It's like I can't stop. It was early in the morning, and I was drunk."

"You've been drinking this morning too."

"Yeah. Yeah. It's like a compulsion. I get up in the morning and go for the bottle right away. It didn't used to be this way. I could have a few drinks with the guys after work, and that would be it. Sure, I sometimes drank too much and made a fool of myself, but I could handle it."

"So what makes it different now?"

"Seeing that guy run over that teacher made me look at things. When the cops questioned me, I didn't have any answers. I only had excuses. I couldn't find my glasses. I couldn't get to my gun . . . ."

He clasped his hands, rubbed them together, and then ran them through his hair. "The detective I told you about . . . I don't know. Maybe it was something he said. After he left, I started thinking. I realized my life is out of control. I let the booze control my life. I ruined two marriages because of it. Now I'm ruining the life I had left with it. I don't go out of the house anymore. My best friend is an Indian liquor store owner, and I've never even seen his face. I have the booze delivered."

"So what are you telling me?"

"I want to get my life back."

"And how do you plan to do that?"

"How the hell do I know? That's why I came to you!"

Bennis smiled. "Well, it sounds like you've come to the first step. You realize your drinking has taken over your life. You've come to see for yourself you have a problem. It's like an allergy, and it takes over."

"Yeah. Yeah. That's what it's like. An allergy. But a compulsion too. Sometimes the craving is so strong I feel I can't breathe unless I have a drink."

"So now you see how your drinking has caused you a lot of problems."

"I've been drinking all my life, Padre. My father would drink a case of beer a night, and it didn't seem to bother him. He went to work the next day."

"You're not your father. We're talking about you. Do you see how your drinking has become bigger than you? How it has taken over your life? How, despite how you used to deal with it, you can't control it anymore?"

Stevenson rubbed his eyes. "Yeah. Yeah. I guess I do. But I don't know why."

"We human beings are sometimes strange creatures. Sometimes it takes years for us to realize things about ourselves. I imagine many people have told you to stop drinking over the years, but you never thought you had a problem. Why would you? Your father drank all his life. How about your mother?"

"Yeah. Yeah. She drank too, but she used to sneak her drinking. When my father would accuse her of drinking, she would deny it, but I found bottles of booze she hid all over the house. She even had one hidden in the toilet tank."

"You grew up with drinking. You never saw anything wrong with it. Why would you? Your parents drank, your friends drank, your coworkers drank. But gradually, the alcohol took hold of you. It affected you physically, emotionally, financially, socially, and spiritually."

Stevenson nodded. "You can say that again!"

"It's like you've been in a dark tunnel. People may tell you there's a light at the end of the tunnel, but until you see it for yourself, you don't believe it."

Stevenson nodded.

"Once you admit you have a problem, you're on your way out of the problem. You now accept the fact you have a problem with alcohol. Facing this is difficult, but admitting it to others as you have to me makes the realization stronger."

"So what do I do now?"

"Well, the next step usually is to realize if you are powerless to control your demons, you need help. It's like you got stabbed in the back, and you can't reach the wound to stop the bleeding. You need someone to help. That's where you are now. You need to see there is a power greater than us that can help us come back. I believe that power ultimately is God, but you could see it as a therapist, a friend, a group, or even meditation. The important thing is you know you have a problem, and experience has taught you that you are powerless in handling this problem by yourself. The problem rests in your actions, your attitude, and your behavior. Now it's time to fill those feelings you have of loss, emptiness, depression, and anger. You need help. That's what you're here for, and what I'm here for!"

A pearl blue Honda Accord beeped its horn, and a woman in a flowered dress and a scarf waved at them. Bennis waved back, and the car proceeded down Amboy Road.

* * * *

Earle Nelson drove to a convenience store in Great Kills and called District Attorney Leonard Ketch's office. After a series of computer messages, he finally spoke to a human being. "This is Special Agent Robert Diamant of the Federal Drug and Alcohol Division. I need to speak with District Attorney Ketch about an upcoming trial."

A nervous young female voice responded, "I'm sorry, Special Agent Diamant, but District Attorney Ketch is not available. May I take a message?"

"I need to speak with him, young lady. Where can I locate him?"

"May I transfer your call to Assistant District Attorney Ananis's office?"

"You sound like a conscientious worker, Miss . . . . I'm sorry. I didn't get your name."

There was a moment of silence, and then she answered, "My name is Marsha McDonald, Special Agent Diamant. I hope you understand I'm just following orders . . . ."

"Of course, I do, Marsha. Is that what your friends call you?"

Marsha giggled. "No. Actually, they call me Bunny. It's a long story."

Nelson smiled. He had reached a Chatty Cathy. "I'm sure it is, Bunny, but my orders are to speak directly with D.A. Ketch. My orders come directly from the White House."

"Oh my gosh! I don't know where he is, Special Agent Diamant."

"You can call me Bob, Bunny. I'd really appreciate your help on this one."

"All I know is he's out of town. He and his wife have gone on a vacation. Actually, they're out of the country. I think they may have gone to Bermuda or Jamaica or Mexico. If you leave your number, I will have him call you back. He will be checking in later today."

"Thanks, Bunny, but I'm in the field all day. Maybe I can stop by later, and if you're not doing anything, we can go out for a cup of coffee or maybe even a drink."

Nelson could feel Chatty Cathy blushing on the other end of the line. He guessed he was probably twice her age, but she didn't know that, and besides, he never planned to meet her anyway.

"Gosh," she said. "I'd like that. I go to lunch from noon to one."

"Unless an emergency crops up, count on me coming by."

"I'll look forward to it."

"Oh," Nelson added, "I almost forgot. Bunny, is Judge Abbruzza in today?"

"Yes. I saw him earlier. He is at a murder trial this morning. Can I leave a message for him?"

"No, Bunny, that won't be necessary. But thank you. I'll drop by and see him a little later."

* * * *

Fran's visit to her mother and sister, for the most part, went better than she expected. It was good to talk with her sister and catch up on events. Her younger brother, Bobby, was doing well in college. He was studying psychology, and both Fran and Susan laughed at how he could make a living studying their family.

Susan loved little Stephen Michael. She held him, played with him, and asked permission to feed and change him. Fran savored reuniting with her sister.

Elizabeth Muscatelli, however, ignored Stephen Michael. Fran thought seeing and playing with her son would be good for her mother, but Elizabeth chose to play with Bella, the cockapoo. Both sisters marveled how a little dog was able to get their mother out of her seemingly catatonic state.

After lunch, Fran, Susan, and Elizabeth went for a little walk around the block. Susan pushed Stephen Michael in his carriage. Within minutes, he was sound asleep. Fran watched her mother with Bella. The smile on her mother's face brought tears to Fran's eyes.

Fran looked around. The sky was blue. Birds chirped in the trees. Flowers were in bloom. Her mother and her sister were smiling. Stephen Michael was asleep.

It was a perfect day until the black squirrel ran across the path.

* * * *

Sebastian and Newhouser tracked down Sameer Afridi to an apartment off Coney Island Avenue. "I hate Brooklyn," Sebastian said as they walked up the three flights to Afridi's apartment.

"I used to live here," Newhouser said. "It's not a bad place."

Aromas of lamb, turmeric, coriander, cumin, saffron, cauliflower, pepper, and cabbage mingled in the stairwell. They stopped on the third floor landing and caught their breath. "I'm out of shape," Newhouser admitted.

"Maybe it's all those tuna fish subs you eat!"

Newhouser knocked on apartment 3F. A thin olive-skinned man with black hair and a handlebar moustache that connected to his sideburns answered the door. He stood before them in a white tank top, boxer shorts, and bare feet. Sebastian and Newhouser flashed their badges. "Police," Newhouser announced. "We'd like to ask you a few questions."

"Are you Sameer Afridi?" Sebastian asked.

"I no speak English."

"Shall I find someone to translate? There must be someone in this building who speaks English."

"No need, Newhouser. If this camel jockey drives a cab in New York, he speaks enough to give us the info we need. If not, we bring him to the precinct and book him as an accessory to a crime. Who knows? We may find out the guy's illegal, and they'll send him back to his hut and his favorite sheep."

"No!" Afridi exclaimed. "I didn't do nothing!"

"Good," Sebastian said, pushing the door open and walking into the apartment. "Man, this place smells like shit! Don't you ever clean this place?"

Two little heads peered out of the kitchen. Behind them, a young woman with black hair held a hand on each of their shoulders.

"Your wife and kids?" Newhouser asked.

"My sister and my kids."

"Where's your wife?" Sebastian asked, checking out a large cloth spread on the floor.

"At work."

"Where?"

"Coney Island Hospital."

"What's she do?"

"She's a nurse's aide." He hesitated. "She was a pediatric doctor when we lived in Pakistan."

Sebastian laughed. "Maybe you should go back to Pakistan. What did you do there? Were you the surgeon general?"

"No. I was a colonel in the air force."

Newhouser asked, "Why did you tell us you couldn't speak English when we knocked on your door?"

"In my country, we are afraid of the police." He looked directly at Sebastian. "They can be mean. We don't trust them."

"Well, you're in our country now, and hopefully it's your country too. We just want to ask you about a fare you picked up last night on the West Side between nine and ten o'clock. Two men. You didn't enter it on your log sheet. Why?"

"The man with the scar, he paid me $100 and told me not to enter it, or he would kill me."

"Where did you take them?"

Sameer Afridi shook his head and walked toward his children. "I don't want any trouble. That man was bad. He had a gun . . . ."

"Where did you take them?"

Afridi rubbed his eyes. He checked his children. "I don't want any trouble."

"We'll protect you and your family. Where did you take them?"

"A small bistro called Tranquility. It's on Fifty-seventh Street in Manhattan."

* * * *

The first call came from Newhouser. They had found the destination Earle Nelson and the tall mystery black man had gone to, and they were headed directly there. Cavanaugh relayed the information to Goldberg, who immediately started checking ownership records for Tranquility. Within minutes, Goldberg announced, "Guess who leases the property for Tranquility?"

"You're kidding me!"

"Nope. A&R Used Tire and Junk Yard in the ironbound section of Newark."

"Keep digging. Check the vendors, employment records, equipment suppliers, tax records. Check where they get their food, their napkins, their toilet paper. We're getting closer."

Cavanaugh called Judge Abbruzza. Kathleen Bradley answered the phone. "Hi, Kathleen, this is Tom Cavanaugh. Can I speak with Carlo?"

"I'm sorry, Detective Cavanaugh, but Judge Abbruzza is in court. How can I help you?"

"We're probably going to need a search warrant for a bistro in Manhattan called Tranquility. Can you get a message to the judge? It's important."

"Sure, Detective. I'll deliver the message."

"Thanks, Kathleen."

Cavanaugh looked over at Goldberg whose fingers were racing across the keyboard searching computer records for Tranquility. The phone rang again. Goldberg didn't flinch. It was as if he were in another dimension.

The voice on the other end of the telephone identified himself as Dr. Robert Liston of the Bedford Hills Correctional Facility. "Warden Hartman asked me to call you. Inmate Tamika Washington has died."

"What? How did it happen?"

Dr. Liston spoke in a detached, robotic manner. "She died in the hospital unit early this morning."

"What happened to her?"

"Preliminary reports are she died of pancreatic cancer."

Cavanaugh recalled Tamika complaining of stomach pains. "When we visited her, she said she was sick. She had lost a lot of weight. She claimed the prison was trying to kill her."

"Absurd. I don't expect you to understand, but pancreatic cancer is difficult to diagnose and in its advanced stages difficult to treat. The warden wanted me to inform you as her death might have something to do with an investigation you are conducting."

"You're right. I don't understand how you could ignore the symptoms she claimed to have."

"I delivered the message, Detective Cavanaugh. Tamika Washington is dead."

"I'm going to need a copy of her autopsy report."

"You will have to go through proper channels for that. Goodbye."

Cavanaugh heard the click on the other end of the phone. "I don't believe it!" he shouted.

Goldberg looked up. "Believe what?"

"Tamika Washington is dead."

"That changes things."

"How so?"

"If she actually hired a killer, there's no way to call him back now. If she didn't, then whoever did no longer has her as his scapegoat. This puts the judge's life even in more danger."

Cavanaugh nodded. "I called Judge Abbruzza to ask for a search warrant for that restaurant, but he's in court. I think we are going to need it fast. Maybe I'll call one of the other judges and request it."

"I don't know about that, Tom. They're all possible suspects in being the link between the letters and the murders. Plus, I'm not sure they would even be able to issue a warrant outside their Staten Island district or that you'd be able to get it to Sebastian and Newhouser in time."

"We've got to do something fast. They are headed to the restaurant now. They need to get in there and search the place." He hesitated and then went to his address book. "Remember Lieutenant Bradley? He's assigned to Manhattan now. Maybe he knows a judge who will issue a warrant without a written affidavit."

Cavanaugh dialed Bradley's office. "Lieutenant Bradley, this is Tom Cavanaugh. I need a search warrant ASAP. Do you have a sympathetic judge in Manhattan who could accept a sworn testimony over the phone?"

"What the hell have you gotten yourself into now, Cavanaugh?"

"This is important, Lieutenant. We're tracking down a killer. The guy's killed at least five people already. His next victim may very well be Judge Carlo Abbruzza."

"I read about the threats to his life. I hear good things about Judge Abbruzza."

"Can you help us?"

"Sure. I've got a cousin, Jim McCarthy, who's a supreme court judge, and I think he knows Judge Abbruzza from a softball team they used to play on. Jim's always been able to help in an emergency and routinely signs search warrants and eavesdropping warrants for us in sensitive cases. Plus, he's a 'safe judge.' No one will ever know what warrants he signed. What's the deal?"

"We need a search warrant for a small bistro called Tranquility on Fifty-seventh Street . . . ."

"You're kidding me! I know the place. It's small and quiet, but the food is good. I've eaten there a couple of times. They have a great piano player."

"We think the guy we're looking for may be hanging out there. Can you help us?"

"Sure thing. I'll call my cousin and explain the exigency and have him fax me the search warrant. He's family. He'll help. Then I'll have one of my men meet your guys at the restaurant. Anything else I can do?"

"Thanks, Lieutenant. You're the best. Maybe you'd better send a couple of uniforms over with the warrant. My detectives may need a little help."

Cavanaugh sat back and breathed a sigh of relief. Goldberg returned to the computer. They were going to get Earle Nelson. It was only a matter of time. He stared at the phone. He hated being idle. He wanted to check out Tranquility himself.

Then the phone rang again. When he picked it up, he heard Fran crying hysterically. People were shouting in the background. "What happened, Fran? Are you all right? What's happening?"

Fran's voice broke up. "The car hit him, Tom!"

"What happened, Fran? What car? Is he all right?"

"He was run over, Tom. I don't know if he's going to make it!"

Cavanaugh felt his heart hammering against his chest. He took a deep breath. He pictured Stephen Michael as he had last seen him. This couldn't be happening.

"He ran in front of the car. I couldn't stop him," Fran sobbed.

"He ran in front of the car? Who ran in front of the car?"

"Bella! She's hurt bad. I don't know what to do!"

"The dog? Is Stephen okay?"

"Yes, but Bella is hurt bad and in a lot of pain."

* * * *

Earle Nelson drove around the Staten Island courthouse several times and then parked. Police surrounded the courthouse like fleas on a dead horse. This was not a suicide mission. Nelson sat in the stolen car and planned Judge Abbruzza's assassination.

His disguise as a woman could get him into the courthouse, but the metal detectors would pick up the .357 Magnum concealed in his handbag. Exiting the courthouse would be another problem.

If he couldn't get at him in court, he would have to get at him another way. His military training taught him no one was invulnerable. The infamous Seven Ps he learned in the army swung into his mind: prior proper planning prevents piss-poor performance. He checked his notes. Judge Abbruzza lived on Oakland Avenue.

Gradually, a plan began to form. He drove to Judge Carlo Abbruzza's home. It was located on a quiet one-way tree-lined street with a mixture of old Colonial, Tudor, and Victorian homes. Unlike the cookie-cutter homes in newer sections of Staten Island that were attached or crammed into small lots and looked almost identical, each of the homes on Oakland Avenue was distinct and gave the feeling of a Norman Rockwell small-town scene.

One police car sat idle in front of the judge's home. A heavyset police sergeant sat in it reading the *New York Post* as if it were the *Book of Revelation.* Nelson expected Abbruzza would be escorted home by one or two additional patrol cars. He checked his watch. He had time, but he needed to do some shopping. It was part of prior proper planning.

The street was on a steep incline. Judge Abbruzza's house was roughly in the middle. A white picket fence enclosed his lot, and a huge picture window revealing a room lined with book shelves looked out on the street. There was a large porch with two white rocking chairs and a matching porch swing. A beige cocker spaniel slept by the main entrance.

The scene turned Nelson's stomach. It looked too perfect. This was the kind of thing you saw in the movies. He half-expected to see Gregory Peck sitting in one of the rocking chairs talking to Scout and her brother. Nelson's own father left him and his mother on his fifth birthday, but not before he broke two of Nelson's ribs and left his mother bleeding and unconscious. From there it was a series of nondescript hovels, a dirty hotel room in El Paso, Texas, a trailer park rental in Snead's Ferry, North Carolina, an alley in New Orleans, Louisiana. Together with frequent moves there were the frequent men. They came in and out in all sizes, shapes, colors, and attitudes. Some tipped him to get lost, some ignored him, some abused him. He left whatever place they were temporarily calling home when he was fifteen and lived a day-to-day struggle on the streets of different cities until he joined the army.

The army gave him a home, meals, and clothes and taught him how to survive and how to kill. Somehow he enjoyed the killing part more than the others. Was it because of the traumas of his youth? Was his impulse to kill sublimation for the abuse he had endured as a child? Sometimes he wondered whether his joy in killing was a pathological problem. In the end, Nelson concluded he didn't care. It gave him power knowing he controlled the life and death of another human being.

He looked at the judge's house again and imagined how it would look after Abbruzza came home. Nelson smiled. This was going to be fun for him. But first he had some shopping to do. Thanks to his military training, he knew exactly what he needed. In a few hours, this quiet neighborhood would never be the same.

* * * *

The dog wasn't his. Technically, it was Cavanaugh's brother's dog, but he had grown to love her. "Calm down, Fran, and tell me what happened."

Fran's mother was walking Bella when a squirrel ran across the path. The dog started to chase the squirrel, and Elizabeth Muscatelli lost hold of the leash. Bella chased the suicidal squirrel into the road as an SUV came down the street. It crushed the squirrel and sent Bella flying twenty feet into the air.

"How's the baby?"

"He's fine, but Bella is in pain."

"How's your mother?"

"She took a good fall. She fell flat on her face. She's complaining of rib pain and one of her fingers is starting to swell up."

"Call 911."

"I did, Tom. Do you think I am an idiot? An ambulance is coming down the block now."

"Good. Have them take your mother to the emergency room. She needs to be checked out."

"What about Bella?"

"Find out where the nearest veterinary office is and take her there. You have one of those fancy phones that will give you the information. Tell Susan to go with your mother to the hospital, and you take Bella and Stephen to the vet. I'm in the middle of a case right now and can't come there. Give me a call when you find out how things are."

"What about Jack?"

"What do you mean?"

"Bella's his dog. Shouldn't he know?"

"Yeah, Fran, you're right. I'll give him the message. Make sure you let me know how they both are, and I'll tell Jack."

Cavanaugh hung up and looked over at Goldberg. "You okay?" Goldberg asked.

"Yeah. The dog got hit by a car. Fran's upset. Her mother fell trying to hold the dog back."

"Is she all right?"

"I think so. She may have hurt her ribs, but I think she's okay."

"It's your brother's dog isn't it?"

"Yeah, but we've all fallen in love with her. I didn't know you could feel this way about a dog."

"Dogs have a special talent. They give unconditional love and don't ask for much in return. It's like they don't know evil. They seem to have more integrity, fidelity, and trustworthiness than a lot of humans have. They give us the feeling of love just like a baby. It's like they pick up the energy of the people around them. The longer I work at this job, the more I find myself loving and appreciating dogs. Freud had it right. He said dogs love their friends and bite their enemies, unlike people who are incapable of pure love and always have to mix love and hate."

"I never thought of it that way, Morty. What kind of dog do you have?"

"Oh, we don't have one. They're too much work, and we have small children. With all our children in a small apartment, it gets a bit tight, and there's not much room for a dog!"

The phone rang again. Cavanaugh grabbed it. He listened for a while and then said, "Thanks. I'll leave now and meet you there."

"What now? I recognize that look of yours. Is everything all right?" Goldberg asked.

"That was Sebastian. He's at the bistro Tranquility."

"Did the search warrant get there for them?"

"Yeah. Lieutenant Bradley came through. Two of his men met them there. But there was another problem."

Goldberg frowned.

"The fire engines beat them both there. Someone torched the place."

* * * *

Earle Nelson's plan to kill Carlo Abbruzza was simple. Create a diversion, shoot the judge, and escape. He knew what he needed to make a few improvised explosive devices. The army had taught him how to make an IED, and he was good at it.

First, he made a trip to a local hardware store to pick up a hammer and a five-gallon gasoline container. Then he stopped at a garden store for some stump remover for the potassium nitrate he would need and some ammonia fertilizer for its sulfur content. For some additional sodium nitrate, he purchased a quantity of cold packs from a pharmacy where he also bought a bag of charcoal and five cans of coffee. At a small convenience store, he picked up five disposable phones. He checked his watch. He was running out of time. As he pumped gas into the gasoline container, he knew if he had more time, he could have created a more destructive IED, but he was only looking for a diversion.

He parked in a deserted area in Mariners Harbor near the old Proctor & Gamble buildings, emptied the coffee from the cans, pulverized the charcoal, and mixed it with the sodium nitrate and the sulfur to make homemade gunpowder. He then poured gasoline into the cans, floated a piece of cardboard with the gunpowder over the gasoline, connected the disposable phones, and sealed the containers.

He checked his watch again. He still had work to do. He drove to Judge Abbruzza's block and parked his car at the top of the hill. Keeping an eye on the police sergeant who now was asleep, he carried the four IEDs in a large paper shopping bag and walked down the block on one side, placing one can under the gas tank of a blue Jeep Cherokee two houses above Abbruzza's house and another under a silver Nissan Versa five houses below his house. Then he crossed the street and worked his way back, stopping to pretend to tie his shoe as he placed an IED under a blue Dodge Caravan three houses from the judge's house and another under a red Toyota Corolla three houses above the house.

He returned to his car and waited. He was used to waiting. Once he had waited ten hours in one position to get a good shot at his target. He checked his watch. The phones were preset for speed dialing. It would soon be over. He never wondered what Judge Carlo Abbruzza had done to merit assassination. That wasn't his job. He was hired to kill the judge, and that was what he would do.

About a half-hour before he expected the judge to return, Nelson poured the remaining gasoline into two empty two-liter bottles of soda and poured them across the road and over the hoods of a black Mercedes-Benz and a silver BMW convertible a few cars below his. He hoped the gasoline would not totally evaporate before the judge returned, but that could not be helped. This was just to create an added diversion and a possible fire wall behind, which he would escape. The fact that both cars were expensive added to his pleasure. There was something about rich people and opulence that he hated. He would set off the two IEDs below Abbruzza's house first, creating the distraction. He would start walking toward his house when he saw the police escort turn the corner. When

Abbruzza exited his car, Nelson would set off one explosion. As they turned to look at the explosion, he would set off the next one, which was closer to the judge's house. Then he would pump three shots into Abbruzza and turn as if to escape the explosions. On his way back to his car, he would set off the last two explosions, which would create a wall of fire between him and the police. He would casually pull away and head for his next target — Fr. Jack Bennis.

* * * *

When Cavanaugh arrived at Tranquility in Manhattan, the former restaurant was still smoldering. Sebastian, Newhouser, Lieutenant Bradley, and a number of police officers stood outside. "What's the story?" Cavanaugh asked.

"Looks like arson," Bradley said. "The fire marshal said it started in the kitchen. He thinks gasoline was scattered all over the place. Apparently, they didn't have time to even make it look like an accident."

"Anyone hurt?'

"No bodies found, but the lab guys haven't been able to get in there to check things out."

Cavanaugh turned to Bradley, Newhouser, and Sebastian. "Who did you tell about the search warrant?"

They each said nobody. "The only person I told," Bradley said, "was my cousin who faxed over the warrant immediately."

Sebastian's phone rang. "It's for you, Cavanaugh! Why the hell don't you get your own phone?"

It was Goldberg. "I think I may have found something. A few weeks ago a grand piano was delivered to Tranquility. It was sent special delivery from Hamburg, Germany."

"What's so special about that?"

"It's a genuine limited edition Steinway piano made in Germany in 1867."

"So what's so special about an old piano?"

"This one won three awards at the 1867 Exposition Universelle in Paris, including the Grand Medal of Honor. Supposedly, Rachmaninoff and Elton John played on it. An expensive rare piano like this belongs in the Rockefeller Estate, Carnegie Hall, or the White House, not a small bistro in Manhattan."

"Cut to the chase, Morty. What's the bottom line?"

"The piano was special ordered from Hamburg by William George Fuller."

"Who's he?"

"He's one of the richest guys in America. He maintains a low profile, but rumor has it he'd give Bill Gates and Warren Buffet a run for their money."

Cavanaugh looked at the black smoke still billowing out of Tranquility.

"I did a little checking on Fuller," Goldberg continued. "He's a bachelor, has places all over the world, and is involved in everything from hotels and casinos to holding companies, real estate, and hedge funds."

"Is he connected to the Tranquility restaurant?"

"I can't be sure just yet. There are so many layers involved. It looks like one of his companies supplies their liquor, though."

Cavanaugh thanked him and flipped the phone back to Sebastian.

"Hey, watch it," Sebastian said. "These things are expensive!"

Cavanaugh stared silently at the firefighters climbing through the charred remains of the bistro. The fire was deliberate. Someone didn't want them investigating Tranquility. But why? How did whoever it was know they were planning to search the restaurant? He turned and looked at Sebastian, Newhouser, and Bradley. The only ones who knew about the search warrant were Goldberg, himself, Lieutenant Bradley, and Bradley's cousin the judge. Someone had to tip them off that the police were coming. The fire was a rush job.

"Lieutenant Bradley, you said you ate here before. Do you remember a piano in there?"

"As a matter of fact, I do. It's kind of funny really. I don't know much about music aside from the Beatles, Springfield, and Billy Joel, but there was a tall piano player there who was great. I wouldn't know one piano from the next, but my brother-in-law pointed out it was an original something or other."

"A Hamburg Steinway?"

"Could be. I really don't remember."

An idea began to form in Cavanaugh's mind. He vaguely recalled his brother's comments about the Seven Deadly Sins. Like a compact fluorescent lamp light bulb, the idea became a hunch, and it began to get brighter. He snatched Sebastian's phone back and dialed Goldberg. "Morty, do me a favor. I've got a strange idea. I want you to check one more thing . . . ."

* * * *

William George Fuller paced around his office. Nelson had proved effective but more of a problem than he anticipated. He looked at his bruised knuckles. He had taken his frustrations out on Paul. It was Paul's own fault. He thought he was bigger than he really was. Nobody could get away with lying to him. Who did he think he was threatening to shoot him? He had to be eliminated. He rubbed his hands together and nodded. He was glad he did what he did.

The private line on his desk buzzed. He recognized "Sweet Fingers" Fiore's voice immediately. "It is done, Mr. Fuller."

Fuller hated destroying Tranquility, but it was necessary. The police were approaching with a search warrant. They might find fingerprints, DNA, receipts, bone fragments, traces of blood. There was no time for an antiseptic cleanup. Fire would consume the evidence.

"Good. What about Nelson?"

"I followed him to Paul's apartment. I almost lost him when he left. He changed into Paul's mother's clothes and walked to the ferry."

"He's adaptive and smart. Did he spot you?"

"No. I stayed back pretty far and barely made it to the ferry myself. I saw him hot-wire a car in the Staten Island Ferry parking lot."

"How are you going to track him?"

"Before we left Tranquility, I gave him a disposable phone to give me a call when the job was done. There's a tracking device on the phone. He's been busy driving to a number of different locations. Right now he is parked at the top of the subject's block. Looks like he's waiting."

"Good. Give me a call when the mission has been completed. I want to confirm our accomplishment with our friends south of the border." Fuller paused for a moment and picked up the statue of Genghis Khan. He ran his fingers over it. "Then finish the job as we discussed," he added.

"I understand."

* * * *

Fran carried Bella in her arms into the first veterinarian she could find. She realized she couldn't handle Bella and Stephen at the same time and gladly accepted her sister's offer to take Stephen until she returned. Susan promised to call Fran about their mother's condition as soon as she heard.

The waiting room in the veterinary office was noisy and crowded. An assortment of dogs awaited treatment, including a golden retriever, a doleful-looking black bulldog that reminded her of Winston Churchill, a collie that brought back memories of Lassie, and a growling pit bull that recalled stories of Michael Vick. There were an Abyssinian cat and a Siamese cat staring regally at the barking dogs. One stout man with glasses sat like a pirate with a gold and blue macaw perched on his shoulder.

The chaos and noise in the waiting room reminded Fran of the bar scene in the first *Star Wars*.

The receptionist, a small woman with an English accent who looked like a librarian, took her information, saw that Bella was bleeding and in pain, and escorted them to an examining room where a tall blonde who looked young enough to be Fran's daughter came in a few minutes later. She announced her name as she washed her hands and put on blue rubber gloves that matched her lab coat.

"I'm Dr. Kelly," she said. "What happened to Bella here?"

Fran explained as Dr. Kelly gently examined Bella. She carried Bella out of the examining room and returned a short while later with X-rays. "Bella sustained serious fractures of her left rear leg. Both her tibia and metatarsal bones are broken. She's going to need surgery immediately. The leg may be able to be fixed, but there is a chance it may need to be amputated."

Fran didn't hesitate. "Do what you have to do to save Bella, Doctor."

"I'm afraid that was the good news, Mrs. Cavanaugh. The bad news is we don't operate here, and the best animal hospital that can handle an emergency like this is located in New Jersey. It is critical you get Bella there as soon as possible. We stopped the external bleeding and put her leg in a temporary cast, but if you wait too long, we could lose her from internal bleeding."

Dr. Kelly added, "I don't know how to put this tactfully, Mrs. Cavanaugh, but the surgery will be expensive. We gave Bella some Demerol, but she is in a lot of pain. If you can't afford the surgery, we can euthanize your dog here."

"The last thing I'm thinking about now is cost, Doctor! Bella's part of our family, and families stick together."

* * * *

Earle Nelson sat in his car at the top of Oakland Avenue and waited. He was used to waiting. His rearview mirror gave him a view down the block. Judge Abbruzza would be coming home soon. The homemade explosive devices were all placed and ready to go. They were a diversion. There would be a series of loud noises, smoke, and hopefully some fire. If the grease and oil under the cars and the gasoline in the coffee cans ignited, there would be fire. If a gas tank or two exploded, that would be a bonus.

The dress he was wearing began to itch. He couldn't wait to get this over with and change clothes. He smelled of mothballs and old age. He took the phone "Sweet Fingers" had given him and called Our Lady Help of Christians and asked to speak with Fr. Jack Bennis.

"Who may I say is calling?"

"Mr. Palladin, an old friend. We go back a long way."

"I'm sorry, Mr. Palladin, but Father Bennis is not in right now. His dog was hit by a car. We don't expect him back today."

"When do you expect him back?"

"Let me check . . . . He's scheduled to say the six-thirty Mass tomorrow morning. Would you like to speak with Father Kuffner?"

"No."

"Would you like to leave a message?"

"No. I'll see him tomorrow."

Proper prior planning, that's what it's all about, Nelson said to himself. *I want him to know I'm coming for him.* He was savoring the image of putting a bullet in Black Jack Bennis's head when a patrol car rounded the corner followed by a silver Ford Taurus sedan and another patrol car. "Show time!" Nelson said springing out of his car and beginning to walk toward the cars.

As the first patrol car pulled up to Judge Abbruzza's house, and all the cars stopped, Nelson speed dialed coffee can number 1. An explosion shattered the silence of the block and smoke billowed from a car down the block behind the police car.

Abbruzza got out of his car and turned to look. The next explosion came closer and across the street. Nelson was close enough now to see the look of shock on the judge's face. Abbruzza and Nelson looked at each other, and as Nelson triggered the next two IEDs with his left hand, he fired three shots directly into Abbruzza's chest. The judge crumbled to the ground. Police rushed to him oblivious that he had been shot as Nelson turned and disappeared behind a wall of growing fire. He calmly got back into his car and pulled away, leaving behind smoke, flames, car alarms going off, and Judge Carlo Abbruzza lying motionless in front of his house.

* * * *

William George Fuller was not accustomed to waiting. It was the part of the "game" he disliked. Things were out of his hands now. The die had been rolled. He enjoyed the "game." Now he awaited the decision.

A police scanner in the corner of his office squawked that someone had been shot on Oakland Avenue. It was Abbruzza's street, but was he the victim? Ambulances and fire engines were dispatched to the scene.

He checked his watch. Where were "Sweet Fingers" and Nelson? A breaking news bulletin came across the radio. Unconfirmed reports were that a man was shot in front of Judge Abbruzza's house. Firefighters were struggling to extinguish a series of car fires on the block.

His special phone rang. Fuller tripped on his oriental rug rushing to get to the phone. He needed to know. Scrambling to his feet, he briefly reviewed the elaborate plan he concocted. It would have been easier to kill the judge immediately, but that would have spoiled the excitement and the thrill of the "game." And he had made a promise not to kill Abbruzza. It wasn't Fuller's fault that Abbruzza was so stubborn! It was a good plan. And sometimes promises need to be broken.

"Jonny, is it accomplished?"

"Señor Fuller, this is not Jonny. Have you taken care of the situation as promised?"

Fuller recognized the voice of Luis "El Caudillo" Sanchez, the leader of the biggest drug cartel in the world. The arrangement he made with Sanchez was an unavoidable one. It was a promise that best not be broken. An unexpected, unfamiliar emotion hit him. His heart beat against his chest. His hand started shaking. "I'm listening to the police reports now. It appears the judge has been shot in front of his own house . . . ."

"Appears is not definite. Can you assure me Abbruzza will not preside over the Mustafos Montega trial?"

"I assure you. The matter has been taken care of. You have my word."

"Bien." The line went suddenly dead.

Sweat began to roll down Fuller's forehead. He just told Luis Sanchez that Carlo Abbruzza was dead. But he didn't know for sure. What if the person shot was Nelson or a police officer? He wiped his forehead and collapsed into his desk chair. Mustafos Montega was a small-time drug dealer who happened to be the first cousin of Luis "El Caudillo" Sanchez, the leader of the Sinaloa Cartel. Family and loyalty were critically important to "El Caudillo." The statue of Attila the Hun stared at Fuller. What would Attila have done? He rubbed his hands together. They were wet.

The phone rang again. His hand shook as he answered it. "Mr. Fuller," Jonny Fiore said, "the mission has been accomplished."

"Are you sure?"

"Nelson just called me. He put three .357 Magnum shots directly into his chest. Nelson doesn't miss. Abbruzza is dead."

Fuller closed his eyes and exhaled.

Fiore continued, "He apparently set off a whole series of incendiary devices as a diversion. The whole block is aflame now."

"Excellent. Now you know what needs to be done."

"Yes, sir. He's in a Starbucks on Forest Avenue having what he doesn't know is his last meal."

"Great! Get it done as soon as possible. I'm going to relay the message to our friends south of the border. You've done well, Jonny. Be careful, but don't let Nelson get away!"

"Trust me. I won't. I owe him!"

* * * *

Jack Bennis met Fran at the Fazio Carterelli Veterinary Hospital in New Jersey. It was clean, well-lit, and fresh smelling. Pictures of various healthy dogs, cats, birds, and even monkeys adorned the walls. The staff was polite and efficient. They took Bella into surgery immediately. A young brunette veterinary receptionist named Scarlet with sparkly eyes and a glowing smile reviewed the procedures that were about to occur and went over the costs individually.

Bennis held Fran, who occasionally slipped into a series of quiet sobs.

"It's not your fault," he insisted. "Bella's my responsibility, and I'll take care of her. You have Stephen to take care of." He sent her home, while he waited till the surgery was over.

Five other people sat around the waiting room with him. A father with his six-year-old son waited anxiously for news of their Labrador retriever who was shot by someone in a passing car. An elderly woman with a blue checkered housecoat sat in the corner trying to read a magazine about natural cures while awaiting news of her cat's mysterious tumors. A heavyset balding man with glasses sat with a young blonde who could have been his daughter or his trophy wife awaiting news about their poodle's gastrointestinal problems. They offered one another sympathy and empathy. Joined by grief, hope, and love, he listened and watched as they shared their stories.

Bennis looked around the room at different people worried about their different pets. And here he was — waiting for news of a dead girl's cockapoo. A lot had happened in the last few days. He could have been thinking about the fate of Bella. He could have been thinking about the threats to his former schoolmate Carlo Abbruzza or about Elizabeth Muscatelli's condition. He could have been thinking about the threat to his own life from Earle Nelson. But his thoughts were somewhere else.

He checked his hands. His palms were sweating. His headache returned. She was getting married. The image of María Isabelle reaching out to him during his nightmares returned. He could see her leaning over him. He could almost smell her. He remembered her gentle hands tracing the wounds on his back.

A dog barked somewhere in the distance and a bird squawked, but he only heard María Isabelle's voice whispering, "I love you, Father Bennis."

He had told her to get on with her life. And she had.

Her fiancé looked like a nice enough guy. Like María Isabelle, he was Cuban. He had been an outstanding pitcher in the Cuban baseball league. In his family's escape from Cuba, his pitching arm was injured when their boat crashed off the Florida Keys. María met Thomás at the nursing home where she worked.

Father Bennis told her to get on with her life. And she had. Then why did he feel this way, like a tiger was crawling around inside of him? Was he jealous? Did he still have feelings for her? Why had she asked him to marry them?

The pounding in his head continued. Only a few months ago, she wanted to be with him, and now she found another man who wanted to be with her.

Talking with the two of them, he felt like a traitor. María and he had shared so much. She had been there for him, and he had been there for her. He knew secrets about her past life that Thomás may not know. How would he react to discovering she once was a prostitute? Should Bennis tell how only a few months ago she told him she loved him and wanted him to leave the priesthood?

He pressed his hands against his temples. Should he tell Thomás that he was in love with his wife-to-be? Was he really in love with her?

"Father Bennis?" a voice seemed to echo from a long dark tunnel. "Father Bennis?"

He looked up to see a young attractive woman in green surgical scrubs before him. For a moment he didn't know where he was.

"Father Bennis, I'm Dr. Luccarelli. I wanted to tell you Bella is going to be fine. One of her hind legs was broken, but we were able to save it. There was some internal bleeding, however, and we'd like to keep her here for a few days to monitor her progress."

Bennis stared up at her in silence.

"Are you okay, Father?"

He shook his head and smiled. "Yes," he said. "I was just thinking of something else. Actually, you remind me of someone . . . . Will Bella be okay?"

"It was a bad break, and we needed to place screws in her leg. It will take time, but she should be jumping around in a few months if not sooner. We'd like to keep her here for a few days if you agree."

"Sure, Doctor. Thank you. I appreciate your help."

"You look worried, Father. You got her here in time. Is there anything I can do to alleviate your fears?"

"No. I wish you could. I apologize. My mind was somewhere else. You have done what you could for Bella, and I truly appreciate it. It's just that I have a few other matters I have to take care of myself."

* * * *

Earle Nelson walked into the Forest Avenue Starbucks once again. This time, however, he was dressed as a woman. A young Asian girl behind the counter smiled at him. He thought of how many Asians he had killed over the years. There were so many. The beauty in Bangkok instantly came to mind. And the young teenager in Thailand. She simply asked too many questions.

He placed his order for another mocha frappuccino and looked around. There they were — middle class Americans paying exorbitant prices for coffee. The college kids busied themselves texting and using the free Wi-Fi for internet connections. The salespeople were getting charged up for another round of trying to ply their wares to unforgiving, ungrateful clients who were only interested in the bottom line. Self-absorbed as most of them were, they didn't respond to the fire engines and police cars whizzing by outside.

He moved to the end of the line and waited for his order. And then Nelson spotted him in the parking lot walking nonchalantly to the front door. Jonny "Sweet Fingers" Fiore stood out like a raisin in the snow. The Yankees jacket and baseball cap could do little to conceal his height and color. Despite Nelson's disguise, Jonny had followed him. But how? Immediately, Nelson realized it was the phone. How stupid and careless could he be?

He understood the how and knew the why. Nelson was a loose end, and Mr. Fuller or whatever his name was didn't like loose ends.

"One mocha frappuccino," another Asian girl announced.

Nelson reached into his purse and moved toward the restrooms and the emergency exit.

As Jonny entered the store, Nelson shouted in his best alto voice, "Watch out! He's got a gun!" Fiore froze in the doorway. He was the only black man in the restaurant. He reached for his gun looking for Nelson. Patrons dove for cover, computers crashed on the floor, staff dropped behind the counter. Nelson fired first. Three shots squarely hit "Sweet Fingers" in his chest, and he fell back like a giant sequoia. Blood flew in the air. Women screamed. Earle Nelson snatched his mocha frappuccino and calmly slipped out the emergency exit.

* * * *

Cavanaugh drove like a suicidal stuntman with siren blaring and lights flashing. Newhouser manned the microphone, warning drivers and pedestrians to get out of the way. "I should have been there," Cavanaugh repeated over and over again as Newhouser held on like a child on a roller coaster.

Sebastian stayed at the fire scene, and Goldberg was already on the way to the hospital where they had taken Judge Abbruzza. "Dial Goldberg and give me your phone," Cavanaugh said.

"You can't drive and talk," Newhouser said. "It's against the law."

"Fuck the law! Call Goldberg and then give me your damn phone!"

"You're crazy!"

"Man the loudspeaker, hang on, and give me your goddamn phone!"

Reluctantly, Newhouser dialed Goldberg's cell phone and handed his phone to Cavanaugh. "You should get your own phone!"

They darted in and out from one lane to another. Cars swerved to avoid them. They jumped the curb getting onto the FDR Highway and nearly sideswiped a taxi. They nearly rear-ended a Volkswagen with a "Make Love, Not War — See driver" bumper sticker.

"You're going to kill us!" Newhouser shouted.

Goldberg answered his phone on the first ring. "Tom," he said, "I think I may have found what you were looking for . . . ."

"Skip it for the moment, Morty. The judge has been shot. I need to know how he is. They took him to the hospital. Get over there now, and if he's alive, hold off the press. Tell them he's dead."

"What? Are you out of your mind? What about his family? I can't do that!"

"If he's dead, it's academic. If he's alive, his killer needs to think he succeeded. It's important. Tell the family and get them to go along with it."

"Tom, you're crazy! They're not going to go along with you. You're talking about a wife and four children."

"If I'm right, they'll be there with him. You can tell them it's my idea to keep Marybeth and the rest of them safe."

"The reports are he got shot three times in the chest. He's probably dead."

"They took him to the hospital, didn't they? They didn't take him to the morgue. Now, Morty, trust me. I know what I'm doing. Get them to spred the rumor that he is dead. The press will lick it up like a hungry dog. If he is dead, no problem. Well, maybe that's not the best way to put it, but you get the idea."

"You're crazy!"

Cavanaugh cut off a tractor trailer and spun into another lane. "I've heard that before. Now get your ass over there. Have the cops there spread the rumor. They'll lend authenticity as unnamed sources. They'll love it! Everyone knows a juicy rumor is better than a barrel of facts."

Cavanaugh weaved in and out of cars barreling through the Brooklyn Battery Tunnel.

"I think I may have found the leak you were looking for . . . ."

"No time for that now, Morty," he said, swerving into the construction lane on the Gowanus Expressway and knocking orange rubber cones in all directions. "I'm heading toward the Verrazano Bridge, and I have to pay attention to the road. Some of those Staten Island drivers think they own the damn road! I'll meet you at the hospital. *Ciao!*"

Cavanaugh flipped the phone back to Newhouser.

"Be careful, will you? These things are expensive. Why the hell don't you get one yourself?"

Cavanaugh floored the gas pedal. "Just between the two of us, Newhouser, I have one. It's in the glove compartment."

"Then why the hell don't you use it?"

The speedometer crept toward ninety miles per hour. "Don't tell anyone this, Newhouser. If you do, I'll get you one way or another. I swear. You know I'm crazy." He hesitated. They hit a bump and flew into the air. "My mother used to say, 'Just because a chicken has wings doesn't mean it can fly.'"

"What's that supposed to mean?"

"I don't know how to use the damn thing!"

"You definitely are a head case, Cavanaugh."

"Thanks."

* * * *

Father Bennis left the veterinary hospital as if in a trance. He walked out of the parking lot and down Smith Street. Large maple trees lined the block and old, well-kept Victorian homes were set back from the street. He walked on, not looking at the houses. After a few long blocks, the well-kept homes began to disappear, replaced by smaller homes in need of repair. Ten minutes later, he reached the business part of the town. He stopped and looked around. Some of the stores were closed, possibly abandoned. Signs in windows indicated an increased Spanish population as well as a strong Polish community. A small grocery store advertised chorizo, paella, kielbasa, and potato-cheese pierogi. The times, he thought, were definitely changing. Down Main Street, he saw a Burger King, a McDonald's, a Hooters, and two pharmacies.

Down the alley of Hooters he saw a shoeless disheveled man with a dirty white beard, a tattered army field jacket, and an empty bottle of Two Buck Chuck lying against the side of the building. "Hey, Padre," the stranger shouted, "can you spare a few bucks for a hungry man?"

Bennis reached down and pulled the man to his feet. "How about I get you a good meal?"

"No need. I can get it myself. How about you advance me a few bucks for the meal?"

Bennis looked around. "What's a good place to eat around here? I'm kind of hungry myself."

The man motioned down the block. "There's a diner down the next block. They serve pretty good apple pie."

"How about you show me the way? I'm kind of lost around here."

Reluctantly at first, the man led the priest to the diner. Along the way they talked. The man told him he had been on the street for three or four years. After he lost his job in the recession, he took to the streets. He liked living on the streets better than in shelters. The few times he sought refuge in a shelter had been disasters. He was robbed and beaten and abused. He found it a demeaning and humiliating experience. On the street, he was his own boss.

They ate together in the diner. He said his name was Stanislav. He devoured the steak and eggs Bennis ordered for him like he hadn't eaten in weeks. Bennis drank black coffee and watched in wonder as Stanislav stuffed one spoonful of mashed potatoes after another into his mouth. The two men exchanged military experiences and laughed at the oxymoron "military intelligence."

Stanislav licked his plate when finished and then looked at Bennis. "Would it be too much to ask for a piece of that apple pie I told you about?"

Bennis laughed, and they both ate some apple pie with vanilla ice cream. As they finished eating, Bennis asked, "Is there a church nearby?"

Stanislav smiled. "St. Raphael's is a couple of blocks away. They have a great food kitchen."

"Can you take me there now?"

Bennis paid the bill and looked back to see Stanislav putting the leftover bread and butter in his jacket.

At the church, Bennis spoke to the pastor, an elderly priest who lived alone in the large rectory and administered this church and school as well as the Spanish church on the other side of town. Bennis asked if he could use someone to help with maintenance. Monsignor Anthony San Filippo admitted he did need a handyman, but the parish was poor, and he couldn't afford to pay anyone. Bennis, Stanislav, and the pastor worked out a deal where, in return for helping with the food pantry and repairs to the church and adjacent school, Stan could live in one of the vacant bedrooms in the rectory.

When he was about to leave, Stanislav turned to Bennis. "How can I thank you enough? I promise I won't let you down. Is there anything I can do for you?"

"Yes. Say a prayer for me and, for god's sake, take a bath. You definitely need one!"

Bennis looked at Stan and saw he was crying. "I didn't mean to insult you. I'm sorry . . . ."

"No. That's not it. I know I stink. It's just that for the past two years no one has even touched me. You are the first person who dared to come near me. Even when I went to the soup kitchens, no one would touch me. It's like I had some contagious disease or something. You are the first person who treated me like a human being, not an animal or a cockroach. You're a good man, Jack, and a good priest. I'm glad there really are people like you in the world. Thanks."

After saying some prayers in the church, Bennis left and headed back to his car in the veterinary hospital's parking lot. Along the way, he held the rosary beads his mother gave him that day he left to enlist, and he prayed. The rosary's Connemara pink marble flickered in the headlights of oncoming cars. She had a difficult life, and he had not always lived up to her expectations. He always wanted to make her proud of him. He cringed to think what she would say about the people he killed. Tonight, he realized, more than ever before, however, he made the right decision becoming a priest. He only wished she could have seen her prayers and sacrifices worked. He looked to the starlit sky above and thought — maybe she did.

Driving back on the Garden State Parkway, he turned on the car radio and heard the country group Alabama singing, "There are angels among us sent down to us from somewhere up above." He thought about Stanislav, St. Raphael's, Monsignor San Filippo, and his mother. His headache was gone, and his confidence was back. He smiled and imagined he had, indeed, been touched by angels.

* * * *

Cavanaugh drove straight to Judge Abbruzza's office.

"Where are we going?" Newhouser asked. "I thought we were headed to the hospital."

"No need for that. Goldberg can handle that scene. He's good at stuff like that. We're going to find the leak, the person responsible for holding back the letters from the prison and for informing someone else about what was going on."

"But we've been all over this. There are so many suspects who had access to his chambers and who had possible motives. How do we know who passed the information on?"

"Trust me. If Carlo did what I told him, he'll be fine."

"You're nuts! He was shot three times in the chest."

As they pulled up to the courthouse, Cavanaugh told Newhouser to call Goldberg again and tell him to call him back in six minutes. Newhouser shook his head but did as instructed.

Inside the courthouse, Cavanaugh headed straight to Judge Abbruzza's chambers. Outside the office, Senior Court Officer Wesley Walker, Court Clerk Jason Key, the judge's full-time Court Attorney Larry Logan, and Assistant D.A. Rob Ananis huddled around Kathleen Bradley's desk. Off to the side, Supreme Court Bureau Chief Susan Pemberton and Police Officer Andrea Morris stood side by side listening to the discussion. Down the corridor, Samson Williams, the janitor, leaned against the marble wall with a broom in his hand quietly observing.

Hearing Cavanaugh and Newhouser approaching, the group turned. "Any news of the judge's condition?" Assistant D.A. Ananis asked. Susan Pemberton, Andrea Morris, and Samson Williams moved closer.

"I'm expecting a call from my partner at the hospital," Cavanaugh began. "I'm glad you are all here. One of you has been conspiring to get the judge to step down from the Mustafos Montega trial next week . . . ."

A murmur went through the group as they looked at one another. "That's insane, Detective," Bureau Chief Pemberton stated. "Why would any of us want Judge Abbruzza not to preside over the trial of a small-time drug dealer?"

"I can think of seven reasons — pride, greed, anger, envy, sloth, gluttony, lust . . . ."

Court Officer Walker laughed. "That's the most ridiculous thing I've ever heard!"

"Is it really, Walker? Then maybe you can tell me why you've been spying on the judge and reporting everything back to Judge Terito, who has been one of the leading forces trying to remove Abbruzza from the bench. Some people will do anything to get ahead!"

Chief Clerk Jason Key laughed. "He's got you there, Walker!"

"Mr. Key, you've been working for Judge Abbruzza for two years. Your work habits have been consistently sloppy and disorganized. He's accused you of being lazy time and time again and tried to have you removed, but your uncle is Judge Mancusi, and he has connections. So you have been able to philander around while avoiding work like it was a contagious disease."

Police Officer Morris inched closer to the wall, while Samson Wilson advanced closer, still clutching his broom like a weapon.

"So what's your point, Cavanaugh?" Assistant D.A. Ananis asked. "So we're not all saints . . . ."

"No, but each of you had access to the judge's chambers. Each of you could have intercepted the letters from Latitia

Jones and forwarded the information on to someone else who orchestrated the deaths of innocent people involved in the trial and conviction of Tamika Washington . . . ."

Suddenly, Newhouser's cell phone rang. He answered and gave the phone to Cavanaugh. "It's for you. It's from the hospital."

A palpable silence engulfed the group. Cavanaugh took the phone. "It's me," he said. "What's the news?"

Everyone stared at Cavanaugh. He nodded frequently and bit his lower lip. "Can you give me the details?"

The group looked at one another but said nothing. After a few minutes, Cavanaugh handed the phone back to Newhouser and addressed the group. "You can check it on your smart phones, Judge Abbruzza is dead . . . ."

Kathleen Bradley started to sob. Susan Pemberton and Andrea Morris moved to comfort her.

"I guess things didn't turn out as you planned, did they Kathleen?"

She looked up. Her eyes were swollen. "What are you talking about, Detective?"

"I have to tell you right off the bat, Kathleen, you have the right to remain silent. Anything you say or do may be used against you in a court of law. You have the right to consult an attorney, or if you can't afford one, one will be appointed for you . . . ."

"What the hell is going on, Cavanaugh?" the judge's full-time court attorney Larry Logan asked. "Kathleen is the judge's strongest supporter. She's worked with the judge since he got out of law school. She would never hurt Judge Abbruzza!"

Cavanaugh ignored Logan and approached Kathleen Bradley. "You're under arrest for complicity to commit murder and for being an accessory to murder."

"This is preposterous!" Supreme Court Bureau Chief Susan Pemberton stated. "Kathleen would not hurt anyone."

Cavanaugh looked down at Kathleen Bradley. "You're the one who delayed those letters. You didn't think it would end up with the deaths of so many people, but it did. You could have stopped it, but you didn't. Why?"

Assistant D.A. Ananis spoke up, "Don't say anything, Kathleen!"

"Shut up, Counselor! Mrs. Bradley knows what she did. You didn't think he would kill those people, did you, Kathleen?"

"No! He told me he just wanted the judge off the Montega trial. I thought the death threats from that prisoner would be enough to get him to step down. But he didn't. He promised me he wouldn't hurt the judge . . . ."

"But then the murders started . . . ."

"Then it was too late. They happened so fast. I couldn't stop him. He promised he wouldn't kill the judge . . . ."

"You slipped that last note under the judge's door, didn't you?"

"No. I went to Phillip Curtius's apartment and slipped it under his door. He delivered the message."

"You were trying to save the judge's life. If he walked away from the trial, he would live. But the jury foreperson, the chief witness in the trial, the defense lawyer, and the arresting officer were all killed in this elaborate plan to get Carlo to step away."

"But he was so stubborn! I tried to warn him. I pleaded with him to walk away from the trial, but he wouldn't. He wouldn't listen!"

Chief Clerk Jason Key said, "I don't understand. Kathleen is the nicest person around here. Why would she do this? It doesn't make sense."

"Where is he now, Kathleen?" Cavanaugh asked.

"I don't know. He has places all over the world. He promised he wouldn't hurt the judge. How could he do this? He promised . . . ."

"Great abilities can produce great vices as well as virtues. A very old Chinese wise man once said, 'Madness is the twin brother of genius because each lives in a world created by his own ego. One is sometimes mistaken for other.'"

"He's not crazy! He's a genius. He hired our son to work on one of his hedge funds. He may be eccentric and overly ambitious, but he's not crazy!"

"But he is your twin brother, and you have been the one steady force in his life. I'm sure you bailed him out a number of times when you were young, but this time he went overboard. You can't help him anymore."

Cavanaugh looked down at Kathleen Bradley. She was sobbing quietly. Her husband was a good friend and a good cop. He hated to arrest her. She was the antithesis of her twin brother, William George Fuller. He was one of the richest men in the world, while she was a middle class working mom. To get where he was, Fuller had stepped on and crushed others. Until she got involved with this scheme of her brother's, she had never intentionally hurt anyone.

Kathleen buried her head in her hands and continued to sob. "If he'd only have listened . . . . I tried to get him to listen, but he was so stubborn. Why did he kill Judge Abbruzza? He promised me he wouldn't hurt him."

Cavanaugh reached down and placed handcuffs gently on her wrists. "How did you know?" she asked.

"Goldberg checked a few things. He's good at details. Ownership of the apartment Phillip Curtius was murdered in, the lease for the building Tranquility was in, the special order of that limited edition grand piano in Tranquility . . . . The piano turned out to be extremely rare and was flown directly in from Hamburg, Germany. Somewhere down the line, buried under multiple holding companies, your brother's name kept coming up. Then Goldberg checked what limited information we could find on William George Fuller. And guess what we found? He has a twin sister named Kathleen. She married a Thomas Bradley and has been working for Carlo Abbruzza since he started his law practice. Only a few people knew of our request for a search warrant for Tranquility Restaurant — Goldberg, your husband, his cousin, me, and you. It was simply a matter of connecting the dots.

"The more Goldberg checked the more we discovered your brother is involved in a lot of things. Rumor is he is a big time gambler, and he enjoys the excitement of the game. My guess is this was all a big game for him. The fact that he wanted Carlo off the Montega trial makes me think he's involved someway with drug trafficking. You made a tragic mistake getting involved with him, Kathleen. When a player can't see the man who's dealing the cards, it's much wiser to stay out of game."

"But he's my brother. I'd do anything to help him . . . . He promised he wouldn't hurt the judge . . . . I didn't think anyone would get hurt . . . ."

"It's like Charlie Chan said, 'The biggest mistakes in history are made by people who didn't think.' The bottom line, Kathleen, is your twin brother's a killer, an egocentric megalomaniac who lied to you and is responsible for the deaths of a lot of people. And you helped him."

"He promised he wouldn't hurt the judge. He promised . . . ."

Officer Walker, Clerk Key, Attorney Logan, Assistant D.A. Ananis, Bureau Chief Pemberton, PO Morris, and Janitor Williams stood motionless like frozen ice statues watching Cavanaugh and Newhouser arrest Kathleen Bradley. Down the corridor, footsteps rang out as a man came running toward them. Cavanaugh reached for his gun. It was Court Attorney Bobby Lyons, and he was shouting, "It just came over the wire! CNN is reporting Judge Abbruzza is dead! Abbruzza's dead! Somebody shot him in front of his house!"

Lyons stopped short when he saw the look on everyone's face. "What's going on?" he asked.

No one answered.

Newhouser looked at Cavanaugh. "But you said . . . ."

"Never mind what I said. For everything there is a season — a time to live and a time to die, a time to be truthful and a time to lie. Let's get our prisoner out of here before the press descends on us like a pack of hungry wolves. We are not going to be able to hold them off for that long."

As they left the courthouse, Cavanaugh locked eyes with Andrea Morris and Susan Pemberton. He winked and nodded. They each breathed a sigh of relief. *If that was what they wanted,* he thought, *their secret relationship is safe with me.*

* * * *

William George Fuller heard the news on CNN. "Judge Carlo Abbruzza was shot and killed in front of his Staten Island home this evening . . . ." Earle Nelson succeeded. Fuller smiled. His plan was working perfectly. The cartel would be pleased. He sat in his chair and dialed "Sweet Fingers" Fiore. The last piece in the puzzle was Nelson. Was Nelson dispatched? But Fiore did not pick up. Something was wrong.

He tried again and again. A raspy male voice picked up. It wasn't Fiore's. "Who is this?" Fuller asked.

"Who are you trying to get?"

In the background, Fuller heard sirens and shouting. "I'm trying to reach Mr. Fiore. Who are you?"

"I'm Police Officer Rhatigan. What's your relationship with Mr. Fiore?"

Something had happened. This wasn't good.

"My name . . . my name is Reetz, Richard Reetz. I wanted to talk to Mr. Fiore about an insurance policy. I'll call back later."

"Wait . . .," Rhatigan said, but Fuller had already hung up.

His plan was falling apart like a house of cards. He needed to get away. His private plane was at Teterboro Airport. It was less than twelve miles away. He grabbed his passport and left. It was a matter of time now, and he needed to get away. A quick call from his limo, and his G150 would be ready to go. Abbruzza was dead. The cartels would be pleased. Luis "El Caudillo" Sanchez would know he could be trusted. Fiore was an unfortunate casualty of war. He could be replaced.

Driving through the Lincoln Tunnel, Fuller thought briefly about his sister. Kathleen was naive. She always had been. He tolerated it but found his twin sister's attitude frustrating and annoying. She was the "do-gooder" in the family. She wouldn't understand this was just business. Attila and Genghis Khan would, but not Kathleen. She lacked the ruthlessness necessary to succeed. He promised her not to hurt Abbruzza, but promises are just words that only a fool truly believes. He learned early that in business and politics, promises are broken on an hourly basis. No promise was going to stop him from achieving his goal. She had given him what he wanted. She wasn't his concern. His only concern now was escape.

* * * *

Detective Goldberg cautiously walked down the hospital corridor. Police presence was everywhere — at the elevators, the stairwells, and in the halls. Two large patrolmen who could have been linebackers for the New York Giants stood guard in front of a closed door across from the nurses' station.

Every visitor's ID was checked and rechecked. Nurses, aides, and doctors went in and out of various rooms, but the room guarded by the police remained closed and silent. Goldberg nodded at the two behemoths in blue, knocked, and walked in. Beside the lone bed in the room, Marybeth Abbruzza and three of her children gathered. Little Ella sobbed quietly hugging her mother's legs. In the corner of the room, her older brother Eugene sulked in a blue leather recliner. A muted television over the bed showed scenes in front of the hospital.

"This is ridiculous," Gene said. "How long do we have to be imprisoned here?"

"It won't be long now," Goldberg answered. "We've identified the person who collaborated with the individual who orchestrated the murders. That person is being booked as we speak. We have an APB out for the mastermind behind the plot," Goldberg announced.

"Have you caught the woman who shot my husband?"

"Actually, Mrs. Abbruzza, it wasn't a woman. The man's name is Earle Nelson. He's the person responsible for killing Cindy Waters, Claudia Buenaventura, Police Officer Reilly, Uriah Applebaum, and a few others. We think he was also the perpetrator of a killing a few hours ago at a Starbucks closeby."

"Have you caught him?"

"Not exactly, but we know who he is, and we've closed off all exits from Staten Island. It is only a matter of time."

"Whose brilliant idea was it to keep us held up in this antiseptic shit hole?"

"I'm warning you, Eugene. Clean up your mouth. I don't care how old you are. I'll wash your mouth out with soap. We definitely don't need your attitude at a time like this."

Goldberg looked at Eugene Abbruzza. "To answer your question, Detective Cavanaugh asked me to keep you here. It's for your own protection."

"But you caught the leak, and you know who's responsible for this. Why not let us go?"

"There's an old Mayan proverb, Eugene, that says just because the water is calm doesn't mean there are no crocodiles in the water. Earle Nelson is still out there."

"But I still don't understand why anyone would want to kill my husband."

"Your husband has a great reputation for being a fair and honest judge. It looks right now like someone did not want him presiding over the trial of a small-time drug dealer named Mustafos Montega. Why exactly? We are not sure."

"If you ask me," Eugene commented, "this Cavanaugh guy is a nitwit."

"Nobody's asking you," a voice from the bed said. "Cavanaugh saved my life today by insisting I wear a bulletproof vest to and from the courthouse. It definitely was uncomfortable, but it saved my life."

Judge Abbruzza sat up in the bed and rubbed his chest. He opened his hospital gown and showed three huge welts on his chest. "I wouldn't be here right now if it wasn't for Cavanaugh."

Abbruzza turned to Goldberg. "So, Detective, who did the leak turn out to be? Was that prisoner responsible in any way?"

"No, sir. Tamika Washington died earlier today of pancreatic cancer. She had nothing to do with the killings. Someone intercepted the letters and tried to scare you into resigning from the Montega trial by using her prison threats. Neither Latitia Jones nor Tamika Washington had anything to do with the threats or the murders."

Carlo Abbruzza swung his legs over the edge of the bed. He rubbed his chest. Ella moved to her father's side. "Then who did, Detective?"

Goldberg rubbed his hands together. "I'd rather Detective Cavanaugh told you directly himself."

"Well, Cavanaugh is not here. I'm asking you. Who leaked the information about the threats?"

Goldberg inhaled deeply, licked his lips, and stared at the judge for a long moment. "I'm afraid, Your Honor, it was your secretary, Kathleen Bradley . . . ."

Silence fell over the group.

Then a voice from the corner quietly commented, "There's no art to find the mind's construction in the face . . . ."

"Eugene?" Marybeth said.

"It's from *Macbeth*, Mom."

"I know that, but . . . ."

"Come on, Mom. I'm not just a pretty face . . . ."

"Hey, Dad!" Michael called out, pointing to the television. "Check at the TV. They're saying you're dead!"

All eyes turned to the television as they read the captions at the bottom of the screen. Ella started to cry again.

Carlo Abbruzza stood up. "What's going on, Detective Goldberg? I don't think I'm dead!"

"We wanted the people involved in the killings to think they succeeded. It's worked thus far. Kathleen Bradley confessed. She was trying to save you from her brother. She made him promise not to hurt you. Her plan, unfortunately, failed, and he started killing anyone involved with Tamika Washington's conviction — from the jury foreperson and the key witness to the arresting officer and her defense attorney."

"Who is this brother of hers, and why would he want to kill me?"

"His name is William George Fuller, and he is a multibillionaire. We think he may have ties to drug cartels. We are trying to locate him, but the truth is we don't know where he is right now. His private jet took off from Teterboro Airport about twenty minutes ago. He has homes and assets all over the world. He knows we're looking for him. My guess is he is headed to a country that has no extradition like Mali, Croatia, Dubai, or Morocco. There's really no way of telling where he is headed."

"Then I think it is time for us to go home, Detective. I have a trial to prepare for. Boys, please get my clothes."

"What are you going to tell the press, Dad?" John asked.

"I think I'll paraphrase Mark Twain's famous line and tell them the reports of my death were slightly exaggerated and somewhat premature."

* * * *

William George Fuller was high over the Atlantic Ocean when the previously reported news of Judge Abbruzza's death was corrected. Steve Impellizieri, a crime reporter for ABC *Eyewitness News*, was the first to break the news. An EMS volunteer in the Old Bridge Township of New Jersey, Impellizieri infiltrated the hospital and managed to get a picture of the judge and his family leaving the hospital. A few well-placed twenties to a couple of his confidential police informers, and he learned Judge Abbruzza was hit in the chest with a tight grouping from a .357 Magnum, but his bulletproof vest worked, and he only sustained severe bruising.

Subsequent reports indicated Abbruzza planned to return to work and preside over the trial of Mustafos Montega.

Fuller never heard the reports, however, as he altered his designated flight plan to Miami, Florida, and headed to a secret landing field in the eastern section of Honduras. Olancho, Honduras, was a dangerous place and a main transit route for South American cocaine. Dense forests filled the area within which cartel leader Luis "El Caudillo" Sanchez maintained a beautiful fortress, a small army, and an airfield. Here, Fuller would bask in his victory and confer with Sanchez about mutually advantageous avenues of growth and profit.

He sat back in the cockpit, placed his plane on automatic pilot, and poured himself a tall glass of Drambuie on the rocks. He smiled to himself. The police were fools. His sister was a fool. He would miss Jonny "Sweet Fingers" Fiore and wondered what happened to him. Whatever happened, however, he felt Fiore must have let his guard down. In Fuller's eyes, there was no excuse for that. To succeed, Fuller believed one must be able to plan carefully, think quickly, and adapt to changing situations. This philosophy led to his success in business, but it was in the area of crime that Fuller experienced an adrenalin rush missing from his regular life. Cruising through the clouds, he felt a freedom and a sense of excitement that bordered on erotic.

He, William George Fuller, was King! Attila and Genghis Khan would be proud of him! He chuckled to himself thinking of meeting face-to-face with Luis "El Caudillo" Sanchez. "Louie," he shouted over the roar of his G150, "I believe this is the beginning of a beautiful friendship!"

* * * *

Cavanaugh, Fran, and Bennis ate pepperoni pizza at home that night. In part, it was a celebratory party. Carlo Abbruzza was alive and safe. The mystery of who planned the killings was solved. Kathleen Bradley confessed to being an accomplice, albeit an unwilling one, to a series of murders designed by her twin brother, William George Fuller. Earle Nelson was the triggerman, but he was still at large. Instead of champagne, however, they sipped Becks beer with their pizza.

"Fuller never arrived in Miami as his flight plan indicated," Cavanaugh announced. "Radar picked his plane up headed toward Central America."

Jack Bennis reached for another piece of pizza. "Do you think they will take him into custody wherever he is headed and ship him back here?"

"I doubt it, Jack. The man's got tons of money. He can buy off practically everyone."

"He couldn't buy off Judge Abbruzza, though," Fran commented.

"No. Carlo sure was stubborn. I think if he knew Fuller intended to kill people to get him to step away, however, he might have."

"I think he would have too, Thomas. Carlo is a good man. I just wish his secretary told him what was happening."

"Apparently, according to her, she didn't know. She forwarded the information of the letter threats to her brother, and he took it from there. I think it was all a game to him. Human life was expendable as long as he achieved his goal."

Bennis rested his beer on top of his copy of *Lives of the Saints*. "I've been thinking, Thomas. Do you have enough evidence to convict Fuller in a court of law? Wouldn't it come down to her word against his? Do you have any real, solid proof he masterminded this whole thing?"

Cavanaugh rubbed his eyes. His brother was right. The case against Fuller was based on circumstantial evidence. The fact he purchased a piano for the Tranquility bistro was hardly enough proof to convict him of murder. Almost everyone associated with the murders was dead. The manager of

Tranquility, Jonny Fiore, was killed earlier that day at Starbucks. Lloyd Arbuckle, the lawyer who supposedly hired Earle Nelson, was dead. Phillip Curtius, the busk player who slipped the last note under the judge's chamber door, was dead. The only one remaining who could tie Fuller to the murders was Earle Nelson himself.

"He's got enough money to hire the best lawyers possible. He's smart, Thomas. He didn't get where he is by luck. The only direct link to him that I can see might be Earle Nelson. But even if you catch Nelson, he won't talk."

"This is insane," Fran said. "We know he did it! The judge's secretary held up the letters because Fuller asked her to . . . ."

"It's her word against his . . . . He could claim it was one of your other suspects. Maybe that young woman police officer. What was she doing at the courthouse?'"

"It wasn't Officer Morris. Believe me. She was there to see her lover who happens to be a woman. I don't want to drag her into this. When we get Nelson, he'll give up Fuller in a heartbeat to save his own neck!"

"Thomas, you don't know Nelson like I do. You could torture him, water board him, pull his fingernails off one by one, and he still wouldn't talk. He's got a distorted set of principles. He's good at what he does because he doesn't talk!"

"I feel sorry for Fuller's sister," Fran said. "She's left holding the bag, but she didn't plan any of the killings. She was trying to help her brother. When she gave him the information in the letters, she made him promise he wouldn't hurt the judge. She never realized he would kill those people."

"But he did, and they're dead. She holds some responsibility. I'm hoping we can get the charges against her reduced. She has a lot of good friends in the legal field."

"How does Carlo feel about her?" Bennis asked.

Cavanaugh hesitated. "I think it would be safe to say he's devastated. He trusted her completely. He never thought she would betray him."

The conversation shifted from topic to topic like a tentative table tennis match at a senior center. Stephen Michael's colic seemed to have ended, and he was sleeping. The hospital treated Elizabeth Muscatelli for a broken finger and bruised ribs but kept her for dementia testing and diagnosis. Bella, the cockapoo, survived surgery, but would remain in the animal hospital for a few more days.

As they finished the pizza, Bennis got up for another beer and announced, "I think I know how you can catch Nelson . . . ."

Book VII

The best-laid schemes o' mice an' men / Gang aft agley.

—*Robert Burns*

"You can't be serious, Jack!"

"Of course, I am. It makes complete sense. Nelson wants to kill me."

"This is ridiculous! I'm not going to let you be a target for this psychopath!"

"Listen to me, Thomas. I told you about my history with Nelson. He came to the church and told me he was coming back. All you have to do is place some plainclothes cops around the church, and you can get him when he comes back."

"It's not that easy, Jack. They're not going to give you twenty-four-hour protection based on your theory that he will try to kill you."

Bennis placed his hands on his copy of *Lives of the Saints*. "I'm not asking for twenty-four-hour protection. I told you from the beginning Nelson was the killer, but you didn't believe me. I even went to his apartment and found the proof that he was the one . . . ."

"And you contaminated the evidence so we couldn't use it!"

"Balderdash! Didn't I lead you to the informant when I told you about the Seven Deadly Sins?"

"Wait a minute! How do you figure that?"

"It's obvious. Kathleen Bradley was, on some level, in love with Carlo. That's why she made her brother promise not to hurt him. That's why she had that guy place the note under Carlo's door."

Cavanaugh got up and went to the refrigerator for another beer. "I think you're stretching the facts a bit there, Big Brother!"

Bennis smiled. "Maybe a little, but I know Nelson is going to come after me. Every day he looks in the mirror and sees that scar, it reminds him of me. I gave it to him. He won't settle till he tries to kill me."

"Of course," Bennis added, tapping on his book, "I'm not going to let that happen."

Cavanaugh shook his head. "We have cops looking for him now. He won't get off the island. We're checking the bridges and ferry. It won't be long now before we get him."

"He's smart, Thomas, and vicious. He eluded you before. I know him."

"I'll try to get you protection, but I don't think they'll buy it. Remember they almost charged you for contaminating evidence in his apartment!"

"I'm not asking for protection. I can take care of myself. I'm just suggesting that if you want to catch him, you keep an eye on me."

Cavanaugh took a long slug of his beer. "I might be able to get a few guys to cover you for a few days. When do you think he'll come after you?"

Bennis looked at Fran. "Soon. That's why I've decided to move back to the church. I don't want him coming here. It's too dangerous for you, Fran, and Stephen."

"Where are you going to sleep?" Fran asked. "They are still repairing the fire damage to the rectory."

"I'll sleep in the church. I can't think of a better place. All I'll need is a pillow and a blanket."

"You're crazy, Jack!"

Bennis laughed. "For a while there, I thought I was. But I've come to believe I'm in the right place. I think I was always meant to be a priest. I met someone on my way home from the animal hospital, and I realized I'm doing the work God wants me to do. Whatever happens, happens for a reason. If that means I have to be a target, so be it!"

"I'm not going to let him hurt you!"

"Thanks, Thomas. I really hope he doesn't!"

* * * *

Cavanaugh convinced Lieutenant Parker and Captain Blackwater to assign a patrol car to Our Lady Help of Christians. He even managed to get Sebastian and Newhouser to spend a few of their off-hours checking in on his brother.

A week went by, and there was no sign of Earle Nelson. Traffic delays on the Verrazano Bridge, the Goethals Bridge, the Outerbridge Crossing, and even the Bayonne Bridge caused massive delays and frustrated drivers. It was not long before the mayor, the borough president, and various politicians responded to complaints from their irate constituents, and the screening of cars and trucks leaving Staten Island ended. Earle Nelson, it was argued, had managed to elude the police roadblocks and escaped.

Eventually, the patrol car assigned to Our Lady Help of Christians was relocated, and Fr. Jack Bennis resumed his daily duties without police surveillance. He picked up his dog, Bella, from the hospital and she became his sole protector.

A month later, the police in Olancho, Honduras, informed the United States ambassador to Honduras that the mutilated body of an American citizen was found in the northeast city of Dulce de Nombre de Culmi. It showed signs of brutal torture. All of its fingers and toes were broken. Burn marks all over the body indicated a slow, deliberate torture. Its shoulders were dislocated and its knees broken. Identification papers and a US passport left on the body indicated the murdered victim was the multibillionaire William George Fuller. Authorities in Juticalpa, the capital of Olancho District, believed Fuller was viciously tortured and killed by members of the Sinaloa Cartel on orders of Luis "El Caudillo" Sanchez in retaliation for Fuller's not fulfilling a promise to kill Judge Carlo Abbruzza and secure the release of his first cousin Mustafos Montega. The police chief who spoke directly with Cavanaugh told him, "We have a saying in Olancho. 'Entre si quiere, salga si puede.' Enter if you want, exit if you can. This is a dangerous place, Detective. Your rich American learned that the hard way."

"My mother used to say," Cavanaugh told the police chief, "'What goes around, comes around.' Señor Fuller got what he deserved."

Another month passed, and repairs to Our Lady Help of Christians' rectory were completed. Cavanaugh and Fran spent many hours conferring about his possible retirement from the New York City Police Department, and they both went to see a police union pension consultant.

A multistate search for Earle Nelson proved futile. It was as if he vanished into thin air.

On the third Tuesday in June, Father Bennis said the 6:30 a.m. Mass. Bella seemed a bit uneasy that morning and stayed with Mr. Laurie in the sacristy during the Mass. There was a lot to do that day. Father Bennis and Father Kuffner tried to convince Monsignor Rosito into having a church carnival to raise money for SMART Boards and books for the school. Rosito resisted but finally agreed when the bishop pointed out the feasibility of the idea. The carnival's working crew was coming that afternoon to set up rides and booths. Rosito demanded Bennis and Kuffner be there to supervise the placement of equipment and activities. He himself would not be there as he said he had an important meeting with potential benefactors at the Richmond County Golf Club that afternoon.

Bennis woke up that morning thinking about Cindy Waters and her tragic death. He couldn't shake the memory of her body lying in the street as he began the Mass. Carrying his ever-present copy of Lives of the Saints with him to the pulpit to give his homily, he spoke about Cindy and how her life was cut short. He reminded everyone of the violence, destruction, murder, and war we see all around us. "In times like these," he said, "we may ask like the Psalmist in the Old Testament did, 'Why, Lord, do you stand far off? Why do you hide yourself in times of trouble?' There are so many innocent, good people like Cindy, who seem to be caught up in the random acts of malice. It is natural to question. But as I myself found out recently, the Lord is always there. In my case, he came in the form of a hungry, shoeless, homeless veteran begging from an alley by a Hooters in New Jersey. We just need to look for him. As he said, 'Seek and you shall find. Knock and the door will be opened to you.' I know from personal experience, there is a darkness in all of us. But there is also a spark of light, which, if nurtured, will penetrate the darkness."

Referring to the gospel of St. Matthew, he reminded the small congregation that, like Cindy, we do not know where or when we will be called from this world. We need to be prepared. If we knew when the thief was coming to our house, we would be prepared. "Whether we like it or not, that's the way it is," he said. "The important thing is that we live each day to the fullest and try to love our neighbor even if we don't like him. The world would be a much better place if we all tried to do this . . . ."

Suddenly, a tall nun in a black habit stood up in the third row. Bennis saw her black veil partially covering her white coif. And he saw the partially hidden long jagged half-moon scar leading from her right eye to her lower lip as she pulled a .357 Magnum from her pocket.

A voice cried out, "Watch out! She's got a gun!"

Bennis reached for his *Lives of the Saints* book. Three shots echoed in the church. The nun fell back, knocking over the short white-haired woman with a dowager hump next to her. The nun's coif slid to the side, and blood began to ooze from two bullet holes in her starched white wimple.

Frank Stevenson, who was celebrating his third month of sobriety, held his .38 over the nun and announced, "Holy shit! It's not a nun! It's a man!"

Screams filled the small church. Mr. Laurie opened the sacristy door, and Bella raced out. On the carpet behind the pulpit lay Fr. Jack Bennis. His eyes were closed, and blood seeped through the gold cross on his green chasuble.

As Bella licked Bennis's face and whimpered softly, Laurie dialed 911 and looked down at the open book of *Lives of the Saints*. There within the carved out pages was a set of pink Connemara marble Irish rosary beads that once belonged to Margaret Cavanaugh, Jack Bennis's mother.

The End

REST IN PEACE

James Ward
David Slattery
Kenneth McClory
Bernard Flynn

CPSIA information can be obtained at www.ICGtesting.com
Printed in the USA
BVOW03s1838200515

401223BV00002B/81/P